WONDERSC△PE

HXPERION

JENNIFER BELL

**WALKER
BOOKS**

First published 2020 by Walker Books Ltd
87 Vauxhall Walk, London SE11 5HJ

6 8 10 9 7 5

Text © 2020 Jennifer Bell
Cover illustrations © 2020 Paddy Donnelly

The right of Jennifer Bell to be identified as author of this work has been asserted by her in accordance with the Copyright, Designs and Patents Act 1988

This book has been typeset in Utopia and Futura

Printed and bound by CPI Group (UK) Ltd, Croydon CR0 4YY

British Library Cataloguing in Publication Data:
a catalogue record for this book is available from the British Library

ISBN 978-1-4063-9172-5

www.walker.co.uk

MIX
Paper from
responsible sources
FSC® C020471

For the heroes
of tomorrow.

1

It was early morning and Arthur was already running late for school when the gnomes exploded.

Racing past his neighbours' houses, he'd just cornered a road on Peacepoint Estate when he came to the old cottage at Number Twenty-Seven. Without warning, there was a loud *bang!* and a barrage of brightly coloured missiles came whizzing out of the front garden in all directions.

"What the—?!" Shielding himself with his school blazer, Arthur ducked behind Twenty-Seven's garden fence and peeked through a gap to try to see what was going on.

And there it was. For some bizarre reason, the owner's large collection of grinning, ruddy-cheeked garden gnomes – whether sitting on toadstools, pushing wheelbarrows or fishing from ponds – was spontaneously exploding, one by one. Arthur could only guess they were part of some malfunctioning pest-deterrent system, but before he had a chance to investigate, pressure built inside his ears and with an almighty ground-trembling *BOOM!*, all the windows in the building shattered, and the front door shot off its hinges and spun across the lawn.

There wasn't time to run. A shock wave with the force of a swinging punch bag walloped Arthur in the chest, knocking all the air from his lungs. He flew backwards and tumbled into the street, wincing as the contents of his rucksack jabbed him in the ribs. "Oomph! Ow!"

He landed on his side with his cheek pressed against a cold metal drain cover and the taste of blood filling his mouth. "Erg..." Pain shot through his jaw. Slowly, he moved his hand up and gave it a rub. At least his limbs were all working.

Despite a worrying ringing in his ears, he got to his feet. Most of his neighbours' driveways were empty so he assumed they'd gone to work. He wiped his grazed hands clean on the bottom of his shirt and took a closer look at Number Twenty-Seven. The cottage had the same red-brick walls and mossy roof tiles as all the others on the estate, but was separated by an overgrown hedge on one side and a dingy alleyway on the other.

Strange. The building showed no signs of fire damage or smoke. Arthur tried to remember if he'd covered the topic of shock waves in his physics lessons last term. Science was his favourite subject at school, so he normally paid attention.

"Hello?" called a well-spoken voice, making Arthur jump. "Did you see that?"

A tall girl with braided turquoise hair stood waving at Arthur from the alleyway at the side of the house. Her school uniform was accessorized with a cross-body leather handbag and lace-trimmed socks that poked above the edges of her brogues. Arthur recognized her instantly, although he didn't know what she was doing there. Cecily Madaki didn't live on Peacepoint Estate; none of the popular kids did.

"Are you all right?" she asked, striding towards him. "What just happened?"

"Err…" Arthur shuffled his feet against the pavement; he'd never spoken to Cecily before and talking to new people always made him feel nervous. He watched as she turned the corner of the fence, her pleated grey skirt swishing around her knees. All he really knew about her was that her parents were celebrity hairdressers, which was probably why she changed her hairstyle all the time – last week she'd had a candyfloss pink Afro Mohawk.

"I asked, are you all right?" she repeated, coming to a stop next to him. "You fell over."

"You saw that?"

"No, but it says *sanitary* backwards on the side of your face, in the same writing as it does down there." She signalled to the drain cover at the edge of the road.

Great. He hastily rubbed his cheek.

"You don't look hurt," she decided, surveying his uniform. "Are you sure you're OK?"

Arthur straightened his shoulders to make his second-hand blazer appear better fitted. He was average height for his age but scrawnier than most of the boys in his class, which didn't help when he had to wear clothes that were already too big. Just once he wished he could start the school year with a new uniform like everyone else, and not feel so self-conscious. "I'm fine." He glanced back at the house. "I'm not sure what happened. Some sort of explosion?"

"That much is *obvious*," commented a third voice.

A petite girl in oil-splattered school trousers and combat boots emerged from behind a couple of wheelie bins. Her long jet-black hair was worn in a high ponytail, with a chunky fringe covering one half of her face. "Number Twenty-Seven is abandoned," she told them bluntly, brushing dirt off her knees. "The blast was probably triggered by a burst water pipe."

"Abandoned?" Arthur had seen the girl sitting alone at the back of his geography class a few times, but didn't know who she was. "Where did you hear that?"

"Nowhere. My garden backs onto Number Twenty-Seven's." She walked over to the gate and surveyed the gnome remains. Her wide hazel eyes were outlined with kohl, giving her an intense gaze. "There are never any lights on inside and the garden looks like a jungle. It's been like that ever since we moved in last summer, but I don't know how long the place was empty before that."

Arthur assessed the cottage again. The lawn was over-

grown with weeds and the doorstep was black with grime. Now he thought about it, he'd never actually seen *anyone* inside...

"It's Ren, isn't it?" Cecily asked, scrutinizing the girl's face. "Ren Williams? I showed you around school last term; it was your first day."

Ren folded her arms, looking unimpressed. "That's right. You're Cecily."

Ren Williams, the new girl...

Arthur did know who she was after all. He'd heard two rumours about Ren: one, that she'd been expelled from her last school for riding a motorbike through the canteen; and two, that she'd recently had her knuckles tattooed for her thirteenth birthday. He covertly glanced at her hands to see if it was true. Her nails were bitten short and coated in chipped black varnish. Sure enough, there were four dark brown symbols – a heart, club, spade and diamond – staining her skin.

"And you are?" Ren asked, glaring at Arthur.

He grinned nervously. "Arthur Gillespie. I'm in your geography class." It was just his luck to get stuck talking to two of the most intimidating students at school. Normally, he did his best to avoid everyone and keep himself to himself. That way there were fewer questions about his uniform and less chance he'd make a fool of himself.

"Well," Cecily said, zipping open her bag, "seeing as no one else is here yet, I suppose one of us should ring the police." She withdrew a phone with a manga-decorated case and tapped at the screen. As she lifted it to her ear, a sad howl drifted over from somewhere inside Number Twenty-Seven.

Arthur tensed. It sounded like the cry of a dog. "Have you seen any animals near the house?" he asked Ren.

"There was a little white dog running around the garden this morning," she admitted, her brows drawing together. "I assumed it was another neighbour's pet. Do you think it's been hurt in the blast?"

Cecily lowered her phone. "The operator's putting me…" Her voice tailed off as she heard the howling. "There's something trapped inside! Quick, we have to help it." Without hesitation, she opened the garden gate and began navigating a path through the gnome debris towards the house.

"Wait!" Arthur hurried after her. "You can't go inside; it's too dangerous. What if another explosion goes off?"

"That's why we need to be quick."

"Yes, but—" Arthur's neck stiffened as the dog wailed again, more feebly. The sound tugged on his heart; he couldn't ignore it. He glanced back at Ren, her arms crossed. "Are you coming?"

Muttering irritably under her breath, she marched after them.

As they made their way over the grass, Cecily talked loudly into her phone. Her voice was so full of confidence she reminded Arthur of their head teacher. "Yes, we're fine…

No, OK… We're not sure about that… Right, thank you." She put her phone away. "The police have our location. They're en route."

Arthur wondered if she'd been advised to stay a safe distance from the building. Probably. He looked around to see if any of his neighbours had ventured outside, and spotted an elderly man talking with a heavily pregnant woman in a dressing gown. Both were pointing at Number Twenty-Seven, but neither came any closer.

"So how far is your house from here?" Cecily questioned, hurdling the remains of the front door.

Copying her steps, Arthur tried not to focus on any decapitated gnome bodies. "Just at the end of the next road. The estate isn't that big." He shot her a sidelong glance, wondering again what she was doing there. "I haven't seen you around Peacepoint before. I thought you lived on the other side of town."

She sighed. "I do, but my aunt lives here. I have to stay with her when my parents go away on business." She hurried the last few paces to the house and stepped through the hole where the front door had been. Arthur and Ren followed.

Number Twenty-Seven's hallway looked like it had last been decorated in the 1970s. Patterned orange-and-yellow paper lined the walls and a cobwebbed bamboo ceiling fan rattled overhead. The air smelled musty and stale, as if the windows hadn't been opened for decades.

"Hello?" Cecily called loudly. "Can anyone hear me?"

Other than the dog's whimpering, there was no response.

Arthur's footsteps crackled over the broken glass as he shuffled around a fallen coat stand. You couldn't see much of the shaggy avocado-green carpet as the floor was coated in dust. "Looks like you were right," he told Ren. "No one's lived here for ages."

She threw him a scowl and shoved her hands into her trouser pockets.

They passed the doorway to the front room, turned a corner and came to a set of dusty hardwood stairs that led up to the first floor. The dog's pitiful whining sounded louder than ever and Arthur began to worry whether they'd have the skills to help it. If the animal was seriously hurt, it would need a vet.

"The poor thing's in distress," Cecily said, as they started to climb. "We'd better hurry."

The stairs creaked loudly, reminding Arthur that the explosion had probably weakened the structure of the building. He pictured the roof caving in on them, and fought a strong desire to flee.

When they got to the top of the stairs, the dog was nowhere to be seen. Three doors led off from the landing. Two of them matched the ones downstairs in the hallway, but the third, which stood ajar, looked completely different. It was made of pale, gnarled driftwood and encrusted with barnacle shells, like it had been cut from the hull of an ancient ship.

But that wasn't the strangest thing about it.

Arthur felt the tiniest hairs on the back of his neck stand on end as he gazed upon the swirling sapphire-blue smoke around the slightly open door. Some sort of energy was radiating out from it; he could feel it reverberating inside his chest.

"What is *that*?" Ren asked, her voice cracking just enough to betray her nerves.

Before anyone could answer, a weak bark sounded behind the door and Cecily's brow wrinkled with concern. "The dog's in there. It needs our help." Angling herself away, she hooked her fingers around the edge of the door and pulled.

Arthur's skin prickled as a draught of cool, salty air brushed past them. The room beyond was dark. A stubby, unlit candle and a pile of old brandy-leather notebooks sat on a desk a few metres inside. Books lay scattered across the dusty floor and the hulking shapes of furniture loomed in the surrounding shadows. Wind whistled from some-where – a vent, perhaps.

"Over there!" Cecily pointed to where a tiny, whimper-ing bundle of white fur was trying to wriggle free from under a toppled bookcase. "It'll take all of us to lift that," she said, rushing over.

Ren glared at Arthur as if this was all his fault. "Keep the door open," she grumbled, plodding after Cecily.

The blue whirlwind glittered ominously as Arthur

stepped through it. He had an instant feeling of brain freeze – that strange headache you get after eating ice cream too quickly – but it immediately faded. He scoured the floor for the heaviest-looking book he could find and carefully placed it in the threshold of the door, so it wouldn't blow closed.

"Arthur, you take that side," Cecily ordered, gripping the top of the bookcase. "We lift on three."

He hurried into position and bent his knees. Ren took a place opposite.

"OK," Cecily said. "One, two ..."

Arthur clenched his jaw.

"... three!"

They all heaved. A few remaining books slid off the shelves and thudded to the floorboards as the bookcase tilted. Cecily arched her back in order to peer underneath and assess how they were doing. "Just a little higher..."

Without warning, the dog yelped and shot between Arthur's legs. It was all Arthur could do to not let go and drop the bookcase on everyone's toes. As the three of them rested it back down gently, the little dog raced over to the driftwood door and turned to face them. It had pointed ears, a stubby tail and scraggly white fur that grew in two arches over its dark eyes, giving it a permanently inquisitive expression.

Cecily crouched and extended her hand. "Don't be afraid. We're not going to hurt you."

The dog growled uncertainly, like it was saying, *I'm not so sure.* Slowly, it padded over and sniffed her fingers with the end of its black nose.

"Can you see any injuries?" Arthur asked. He noticed a red collar hanging around the dog's neck, but it wasn't limping and there were no obvious wounds. Perhaps it wouldn't need a vet after all. Maybe they could just hand the animal over to the police and make it to school before first period...

"I don't think so," Cecily replied. "It must still be a youngster; it's really small." She waited till the dog seemed relaxed before lifting it into her arms.

Arthur searched its collar for a tag and found a thumb-sized obsidian prism dangling beside an engraved metal disc. *"Cloud. West Highland Terrier. Male,"* Arthur read from the disc. Below the writing was a strange symbol made of three shapes: an equilateral triangle filled with a hexagon and a small plus-sign. The prism, Arthur noticed, had a hexagonal base etched with the initials: *HW.*

"So the Fuzzball is a *he*," Ren concluded, scratching the dog between the ears. It was the friendliest thing Arthur had seen her do so far. "Nice to meet you, Cloud."

Cloud yapped and turned his head between their three faces, wagging his tail.

"Come on," Cecily said with a satisfied smile. "We'd better go. The police will get here soon."

Cool, sweet relief washed over Arthur as they turned

to leave. All things considered, he felt oddly pleased with himself. Not only had they safely rescued Cloud, but if you didn't count him face-planting on the pavement, he hadn't made a total fool of himself in front of Ren or Cecily.

Too late, he realized the air was thrumming. He shot a look over at the driftwood door and saw that the book he'd placed in the door frame was gone and the blue smoke was whirling faster.

In the space of a heartbeat, the candle on the desk flickered into life and the door swung shut. There was a loud *click*.

And then the entire doorway disappeared.

2

Cecily placed Cloud down on the desk, gaping at the burning candle. "W-what just happened?" she stuttered.

Arthur rushed to where the driftwood door had been seconds earlier and ran his hands over what was now a wood-panelled wall. It was difficult to believe his eyes. "I don't get it. The door can't have just evaporated into thin air." He gritted his teeth and cursed himself for using a book to hold it open and not something heavier, like a piece of furniture. Ren and Cecily would probably blame it on him.

"There's no sign of any hidden mechanism in the floor to suggest it was some kind of trick," Ren said, kneeling by Arthur's feet. Her long ponytail swung as she stood up and glared at him. "I don't know where it's gone, but if we want to get out of here, we need to find another exit."

Ren sounded equal parts worried and annoyed, which made Arthur more anxious. He tried to ignore the sinking feeling in his stomach as he scanned the shadows at the edge of the room. *Surely that couldn't have been the only way in or out...* He spotted a small wooden bed and dressing table hidden between more bookcases, but no other doors. For a second, he thought he could hear hornpipe music playing from somewhere – the kind sailors traditionally danced to. "Can you hear that?" he asked the others.

Cecily scrunched her nose disapprovingly. Clearly, hornpipe didn't feature on her daily playlist. "This place obviously isn't as abandoned as we thought. I'd better ring the police again." She retrieved her mobile from her bag and then went very still. "That's weird. My phone won't turn on. Can you two test yours?"

Ren slipped her phone out of her pocket. "Mine's not working either."

With a growing sense of unease, Arthur slung his rucksack off his shoulder and glanced at his old second-hand Samsung. The screen was blank and when he held down the power button, it had no effect. "Something must have happened to disable them all," he realized nervously. "What's going on?"

There was a dull thud as Cloud jumped off the desk and scampered to the other side of the room, where a heavy canvas drape hung against the wall. Taking hold of it in his jaw, Cloud wiggled his bottom and tugged. The cloth slumped to the floor, exposing an iron door with a silver key glinting in the lock.

"Good *boy*!" Cecily cheered. She dashed over and tried the handle, but the door wouldn't budge. "I think the lock's broken," she said, twisting the key round and round. She rammed her shoulder against it, trying to force it open.

All of a sudden, the floor swayed.

"Whoa!" Arthur spread his arms, trying to balance. Ren skidded into the side of the desk.

"What's happening?" Cecily cried, gripping the door frame. Her eyes darted around the walls as objects creaked and rattled in the darkness.

It felt like the whole room was on a see-saw. Arthur wondered if there had been an explosion in another part of the house, but then he hadn't heard anything. Reaching for something to steady himself, his fingertips found a small cabinet. Through the glass doors he spied bottles of ink, a jar of quills and several lanterns. "Here, grab one of these." He passed one lantern to Ren and slid another across the desk for Cecily. "We've got to see what's going on."

Taking it in turns, they lit their lanterns using the candle on the desk, and then held them above their heads. The remaining shadows were swept away to reveal an uneven wedge-shaped room with timber-framed windows hidden by more canvas drapes. Old-fashioned scientific instruments including hourglasses, brass weighing scales and leather-cased microscopes were stored on the shelves.

Cecily scanned their surroundings with a look of horror. "What *is* this place? And why does it stink of fish?" She banged a fist against the door. "Hello? Can anybody hear me? We're trapped!"

Arthur sniffed, catching an unpleasant briny odour, but that wasn't what troubled him most. He focused on the canvas drapes. Given the layout of the house, those were *inside* walls – they shouldn't have windows.

He crossed the floor in a few wobbly steps and threw back the curtains. Beyond the glass, a glowing orange sky stretched all the way to the horizon where a red sun was crowning. He couldn't process at first what the dark streaks flashing across the landscape were, and then it hit him like an exploding gnome to the face: they were *waves*.

"I don't understand," he spluttered. "That's the *ocean* outside."

"What?" Cecily joined him at the window, pressing her face up against the glass. "No way. That can't be real." She twisted the window handle and pushed the pane open. The roar of the crashing waves and the cries of gulls blew in, along with a spray of cold droplets, which settled on Arthur's cheeks.

It was real, all right.

"Look," she whispered. "We're *sailing*."

To their left extended the side of a huge wooden ship, over thirty metres long. The hull was punctured with gun ports and topped by heavy rope netting, which hung down over the edges of the deck. Suspended at the ship's bow was the gold figurehead of a triangle-hexagon-cross symbol – the same one Arthur had seen on Cloud's collar. "We're in a cabin at the stern of a ship," he realized. He read the vessel's name, painted in ornate black letters on the hull. "It's called the *Principia*."

Ren's lantern clattered as she staggered back from another window, further along. "But … we *can't* be. A minute ago we were in a house on Peacepoint Estate. How is this even possible?"

Arthur shook his head, struggling to find answers. Earlier that morning, the sun had risen as he was waking up, and yet here it was, dawning again. He stumbled over to the desk, pulled a chair out from underneath and fell into it.

Questions circled in his mind, making him dizzy. He wondered if the three of them had been exposed to some sort of chemical that had given them all hallucinations, but that wouldn't explain why they were all experiencing the exact same thing at the same time.

"Do you think we somehow … travelled from Number Twenty-Seven to the *Principia* when we walked through that weird door?" Cecily guessed, biting her lip.

Thinking of the spinning ring of smoke, Arthur was reminded of one of his favourite computer games – *Portal 2* – in which characters used teleportation to negotiate various obstacles. "I suppose the door could have been a *portal* connecting the two places," he offered. "But portals don't exist. At least, not in reality." He briefly speculated whether none of this was real and they were all, in fact, trapped in some sort of VR simulation.

But then, he could still feel the ocean's spray on his skin and taste its salty tang in the air, and as far as he knew, even the most advanced virtual reality headsets couldn't do that. And anyway, *how* would they have stepped into a VR simulation at Number Twenty-Seven? The whole thing was crazy.

Before they could discuss things further, the *Principia* changed direction, tossing everyone to starboard. Cloud issued a panicked bark as he slipped across the floorboards, surfing on several books. A handful of scientific instruments slid from the shelves and clanged to the floor. Arthur just about managed to catch the pile of brandy-leather notebooks in one hand before they toppled off the desk.

"Someone must be steering this ship," Ren decided. "If we can find a way to get their attention, they might be able to help us. I could try squeezing through one of those windows and climb up to the deck?"

Arthur raised his eyebrows. Ren might have ridden a motorbike through her school canteen, but scaling the side of a ship on the open seas was a different matter. He clambered back to the window and examined the *Principia*'s hull. Varnished and speckled with sea spray, it looked extremely slippery; and there were no footholds that he could see. "It's too dangerous," he told her. "We'll have to find another way."

As he pulled the window shut, Ren narrowed her gaze

on the iron door. "All right, then, Cecily, do you have any hairgrips?"

"Err..." Cecily rummaged through her bag as Ren made her way to the door. "I've got a few. Why?"

"One of my mums does locksport as a hobby," Ren explained, crouching to inspect the keyhole. She pulled a multi-tool key ring out of her back pocket – the kind that included a bottle opener, screwdriver and laser pointer in one device – and began fiddling. "It's where you compete in races to defeat locks as fast as possible. She's taught me enough for me to try picking this one, depending on how broken it is."

Arthur had never heard of locksport before but it sounded interesting; he made a mental note to look it up on YouTube when he next got the chance.

"That's odd," Ren murmured. She pushed her ear against the door and slowly turned the silver key, then cleaned the key plate with the tip of her finger. "This lock isn't broken, it's in disguise. It's a combination lock. The numbers zero to nine are etched around the keyhole. If you turn the key in the right sequence, the door should open."

"Then we just need to find the correct combination," Arthur concluded, trying to stay calm and think logically. This would all be over soon. They just needed to break out, find whoever was in charge and ask for help in order to return to Number Twenty-Seven. They couldn't be *that* far away. "Can you crack it?"

"I can try," Ren said. "In the meantime, you two might want to look around for something with some numbers written on it. It's a long shot but whoever set the combination could be one of those people who write their password down in case they forget."

While Ren persevered with the lock – which involved a great deal of hushing them to be quiet – Arthur and Cecily searched the shelves, drawers and cabinet cupboards, hunting for notes or scraps of paper. Cloud sniffed around the floor, wagging his tail whenever he found random food crumbs.

After checking through the books on the shelves, which were all bizarrely blank, Arthur turned his attention to the half a dozen notebooks on the desk. Gathering them up one by one, he noticed that the spines were numbered from one to six, and the same neat brown handwriting flowed across every page. He opened the first notebook to the middle and, with an unexpected degree of effort, managed to read a small section of strangely worded English:

…it may be knowne how motion is swifter or slower. In each degree of time wherein a thing moves there will be motion or else in all those degrees put together…

The author seemed to be writing about physics, but Arthur was too giddy from the shock of everything to follow what they were saying. He tipped the book upside down and gave it a shake in case there was anything tucked inside. Nothing fell out, but he did spot that one of the pages in the notebook had been folded over. When he searched through the other volumes, he discovered that a single page in each one had either been bent in half, or had a corner turned down.

"This guy seems important," Cecily remarked.

Arthur lifted his head and saw she was holding her lantern up to a framed portrait hanging on the wall. It depicted a grey-haired man wearing a navy brocade coat with gold buttons. He had a thin face, prominent nose and dimpled chin.

Cecily rubbed the bottom of the frame, coughing as a puff of dust rose off it. "It says, *Captain W. Saint-Ocean.* Anyone recognize the name?"

Arthur studied the portrait. There was something familiar about the captain's face, but he didn't know what.

"Ne-ber her a him," Ren mumbled, several hairgrips poking out between her lips. "Thiv lock iv impobabble," she added, her shoulders sinking. She took the grips out of her mouth. "I can hear six wheels inside the mechanism, which should mean there are six numbers in the sequence, but I don't have the skills to crack something this complicated. Sorry."

Arthur was about to abandon the notebooks as well when he realized he was holding one open to the folded page. This time, he saw that the creased corner looked just like an arrow, and it was pointing to a particular word in the text: *five*.

He tapped his fingers against the desk, thinking. *Six notebooks. Six numbers in the combination.*

A sliver of a hypothesis began to form in his mind. He rushed back through the other notebooks and, using a pen and exercise book from his rucksack, jotted down the words indicated by the folded corner of every page. As he read them back in order, his skin tingled:

1 – *four*

2 – *two*

3 – *zero*

4 – *three*

5 – *five*

6 – *four*

"I think I've found something!" he announced, flashing Ren and Cecily his exercise book. "The pages in these notebooks were folded over to mark a sequence of six numbers; it could be the combination."

"Wow, OK. That's a *seriously* complicated way to leave yourself a password prompt," Cecily commented. She glanced thoughtfully around the room. "You know, this is starting to remind me of a locked-room challenge my friends and I did for my birthday last year. It's where you're shut in a room filled with props and clues and you have to solve a puzzle in order to break your way out."

Ren slumped back against the door. "So, what, you

think we're in some sort of *game*?" She pulled a face. "On …
Peacepoint Estate?"

"I agree it seems unlikely," Cecily replied. "But if it is
a game, we should be able to play our way out – try the
code."

Joining Ren at the door, Arthur read the numbers from
his exercise book one by one as Ren rotated the silver key.
On the last turn, nothing happened.

"Well," Ren said, "that was about as useful as—"

Then the door made a low humming noise and a jet of
blood-red gas spurted from the keyhole. Everyone flinched.

"What *is* that stuff?" Cecily asked.

The vapour twisted into a triangle-hexagon-cross symbol.
"I don't know," Arthur replied, "but that's the same design
I saw on the front of the *Principia* and on Cloud's collar."

As they looked on, the mysterious symbol changed
shape, twirling and separating into words. In a matter of
seconds, writing hovered in mid-air between them all:

WONDERSC△PE

REALM 33: VOYAGE OF THE CAPTAIN

Loot: 150 DIRT, Wonderskill and realm-key

Travel with wonder,

HXPERION

"Who or what is Hxperion?" Cecily said. "And do you think *Wonderscape* is the name of this game? I've never heard of it."

Arthur waved his fingers through the vapour. It was cold and wet, like snow. "No idea, but this red stuff is breaking every rule of science I know. For starters, it's a gas; it shouldn't be able to hold a defined shape."

"So how has it formed *words*, then?" Ren asked.

Before Arthur could respond, the vapour dissolved and a tea-stained paper scroll materialized in its place. Arthur caught it before it hit the ground and unrolled it so the others could see. It contained six lines of text written in the same handwriting Arthur had found inside the notebooks:

> *Set sail across a stormy ocean*
> *With one, who wrote the laws of motion.*
> *To join my crew you first must find*
> *A ladder of a weightless kind,*
> *Then onwards through a fateful pass*
> *Where ice must fall and fire blast.*

"It's a riddle," Arthur said, reading it through slowly. "You could be right, Cecily. This is all starting to feel like a game – that other message even mentioned *loot*. But … I still don't understand how this is all possible."

Ren gave the scroll a wary glance before trying the door handle. "This is unlocked. Shall I open it?"

There were no sounds coming from the other side. Clutching the scroll in one hand, Arthur tried to settle his nerves. His insides felt like tangled spaghetti.

"Whatever's happened to us," Cecily said gingerly, "we don't seem to be able to return to Peacepoint from inside this cabin. We need to learn more about this game we're trapped in." She lifted Cloud up from the floor and gave him a hug. Judging by the amount he squirmed, this was clearly more for her own benefit than the little dog's.

With a deep breath, Ren turned the handle and pushed.

3

The iron door creaked as it swung open, releasing an icy gust of wind. Arthur wasn't sure what he'd been expecting to find on the other side, but it certainly wasn't a dead end.

"What's this meant to be?" Cecily asked, stepping inside the cramped wooden chamber. "A walk-in wardrobe?"

The circular space was barely big enough for the four of them. Cloud barked his disapproval as Arthur shuffled to the far side and tipped his head back. Daylight fell through an opening ten metres above. Beyond it, a black mast soared into the sky. "I think the ship's deck is above us," he said, trying to suspend his disbelief for a moment. They weren't going to get anywhere by just standing around, asking questions. They had to focus on the things they could control. "We need to find a way to get up there."

Cecily cast a doubtful look around the chamber. "I'm no climbing expert, but don't we need something to grip on to? These walls are polished smooth. I suppose we could try tying our blazers together to fashion some sort of rope…"

Arthur considered their options. They couldn't drag any furniture in from the cabin, since it wouldn't fit, and Cecily was right about the walls. The only remarkable thing about them was a column of teacup-sized circles cut into the wood on one side. As an experiment, he ran a finger over one of the circles and realized he was able to push it in. It swivelled to reveal a flat, circular mirror.

"That riddle mentioned something about a ladder," Ren reminded them. "If we really are in a game, it was probably a clue."

Arthur unwound the scroll and read part of it aloud again. *"To join my crew you first must find a ladder of a weightless kind…"*

"But what kind of ladder is weightless?" Cecily questioned. "One that's floating about in space?"

Arthur rotated one of the wall mirrors, thinking. *What doesn't have weight?* It was a tricky question. Scientifically speaking, weight was related to the force acting on an object, normally gravity.

"What about air?" Cecily suggested. "That doesn't weigh anything."

Ren frowned. "You want us to use a ladder made of *air*?"

Cecily's cheeks flushed. "Fine. Not air."

Arthur's spinning mirror caught a ray of sunlight and sent its reflection dancing around the chamber like a firefly. It gave him an idea. "Actually, with all these mirrors, the ladder's more likely to be made of *light*." He crouched down and tilted the lowest mirror so it reflected a beam of light onto the opposite side of the chamber. It wasn't quite horizontal, so he angled the mirror until the beam was parallel with the floor.

As soon as he'd made the adjustment, Cecily shrieked and leaped into the air, juggling Cloud. "What was that? Something poked my leg!"

"Let me see," Ren said, squeezing around her.

As they switched places, Arthur caught sight of a thick iron rod sticking out of the wall at the same level as the beam of light. "Look – that wasn't there before," he told them. "Maybe we're meant to build a ladder of light, in order for the bars of a *real* ladder to appear?"

Once Arthur had stuffed the riddle scroll into his rucksack, the three of them shimmied around each other, adjusting the mirrors. Arthur felt awkward being in such close proximity to them both. Ren appeared to be angry with everything all the time and Cecily was just as intimidating as she had seemed at school. He could only hope they'd be nice to him long enough to make it through whatever it was they'd got themselves involved in.

"Ouch, that's my foot," Cecily hissed. "Mind where you're treading."

"You're not exactly respecting my personal space either," Ren grumbled.

Arthur felt his elbow dig into something soft and cringed. "Sorry!"

Every time a horizontal beam of light landed on the opposite side, an iron bar extended from the wall, building a ladder towards the ship's deck. To reach the higher mirrors, they were all required to start climbing the ladder before it was complete.

"What kind of game uses super-advanced technology like portals, but nobody's ever heard of it?" Cecily asked, halfway up. With Cloud tucked under her right armpit, she reached for a mirror with her left hand and rotated it until a new shaft of light crossed their path.

"I don't know," Arthur replied, balancing on the bottom rung of the ladder. *Wonderscape.* The name repeated in his head. "Maybe the players are part of a secret society and you have to be a member to join?"

Between them both, Ren huffed. "Yeah, but why would a secret society have an entrance on Peacepoint Estate? It doesn't make sense."

Cecily reached the top of the ladder first, closely followed by Ren. Arthur heard them both gasp as he clambered onto the deck after them.

Then his legs went weak.

Beyond the ship, open sea had been replaced by the choppy waters of an icy fjord. Colossal mountains rose up on either side, their cliff-faces streaked white by waterfalls rushing down from the snowy summits. The polished deck of the *Principia* was dotted with wooden barrels, gleaming brass telescopes and large coils of rope. Strings of violet flags decorated with plain hexagons fluttered between the three black masts that sprung from the deck.

There were a dozen tanned crew members on board, all wearing floor-length white lab coats. As Arthur scanned their faces, he saw with a shudder that they looked *exactly* the same. All the men were tall and bony with sharp cheekbones and the sort of long, pointy noses you would expect a drip to fall from at any moment. The women had flame-red ponytails, piercing green eyes and impossibly flawless skin, so smooth and shiny it could have belonged to a Lego figure.

Arthur's jaw went slack. Viewed together, the clones looked like some sort of special effect in a movie.

Cecily lowered Cloud gently to the floor. "Hello?" she called uncertainly. "Can somebody help us?"

Arthur tensed as one of the crewmen turned. Pinned to his lab coat was a name badge, which read: *First Officer*. He gave Cecily a forced smile before zooming towards her like he was riding a travelator.

Which he sort of *was*.

As the bottom of his coat flapped back, Arthur saw that in place of legs, the first officer had two metallic wheels surrounded by rings of translucent haze, that hovered above the deck. He also had a glowing *T* in the centre of his chin, like a light-up tattoo.

"They're … *robots*," Arthur realized, blinking. No wonder they looked identical.

Arthur, Ren and Cecily took a step back as the first officer stopped a metre short of them and folded his arms. "Welcome aboard, *stowaways*," he announced gruffly. Like his fellow male clones, he had an unflattering mullet of greasy black hair clinging to the back of his scalp. "Have you seen the captain? He's disappeared."

Arthur remembered the oil painting Cecily had found hanging in the cabin. "Err…" He hesitated, conscious he was about to speak to artificial intelligence. "Do you mean Captain W. Saint-Ocean?"

"That's him," the first officer replied. "The *Principia*'s sailed off-course, into this deadly fjord frequently subject to avalanches. Without the captain's guidance we won't make it through safely. Unless you can help?"

"*Us?*" Arthur jerked his head. "Sorry, but we don't know how to sail a ship. We're thirteen."

"Without the captain's guidance, we won't make it through safely," the first officer insisted. "The *Principia*'s sailed off-course, into this deadly fjord frequently subject to avalanches."

As he continued, Arthur thought he could guess what was happening. "He's repeating himself," he told Ren and Cecily. "He must be programmed to say the same thing over and over. Do you think this is another part of the game?" It seemed crazy, but there had to be a rational explanation for everything. Perhaps Number Twenty-Seven was abandoned because it was being used as a testing centre for the game, and the three of them had somehow got caught up in it?

"Hold on. Hold on. Let's think. The riddle said: *onwards through a fateful pass*," Cecily remembered. "I suppose this avalanche-fjord could be what it was referring to, but there must be another way for us to get back to Peacepoint without having to play along, surely?" When Arthur and Ren didn't reply, a look of panic flashed across her face. She swallowed and marched up to a crewwoman polishing one of the brass telescopes. Arthur noticed a glowing *V* tattooed on her chin, instead of a *T*, like the male crew members. "Excuse me, can we please leave this *Wonderscape* game? We don't want to take part; we just want to go home."

The crewwoman arched an eyebrow. "Your request cannot be processed," she said.

"What do you mean?" Cecily demanded.

"I mean, your request cannot be processed," the crewwoman answered haughtily.

Throwing her fists down at her sides, Cecily returned to Ren and Arthur. Her voice was wobbly with nerves. "What now?"

Arthur considered what might be happening at school. His teacher would have contacted his dad to ask why Arthur was late, which meant his dad would now be seriously worried. He had to get back to let his dad know he was OK. He regarded the watery path ahead. The fjord was no wider than a football pitch and went off into the distance so there was little room for manoeuvre. "We'll have to play along. Do either of you know anything about ships?"

Cecily cringed. "Not really. I've only seen one Pirates of the Caribbean movie and I think I fell asleep halfway through."

Craning his neck, Arthur assessed the masts. They had no sails wrapped around them, which meant the vessel couldn't be wind-powered. "The ship must have an engine," he reasoned. "I can't see a ship's wheel; maybe there's a control panel somewhere, which we can use to steer it away from danger?"

"How much danger do you think the ship's actually in?" Cecily asked nervously. "This is just a game, after all."

"Best to assume the worst," Ren said glumly. She indicated a stairwell leading below deck. "I'll search for an engine room. My mum's a mechanic, so I should recognize one if I see it."

"Is this the same mum that does locksport?" Cecily asked.

"None of your business," Ren snapped. And with that, she stormed off towards the bow and disappeared into the stairwell.

Cecily's jaw dropped. "Wow. She's ruder than the robots."

Arthur was secretly beginning to admire Ren's confidence. She wasn't shy or easily intimidated; she just said exactly what she thought. At the same time, she obviously didn't know the first thing about making friends. Perhaps that was the reason she sat alone in geography.

Just then, a shout rang out from up ahead. "AVALANCHE, TWO O'CLOCK!"

A hundred metres off the *Principia*'s starboard bow, a shelf of snow broke away from the mountainside. Arthur's legs shook as the powder came plummeting down the cliff-face and a deafening rumble filled the air.

"Take cover!" the first officer hollered, diving behind a wooden barrel.

Arthur searched the deck for a hiding place, grabbed Cecily's arm and hauled her into the gap between several coils of rope.

"Cloud!" she called urgently.

Ears pricked, the little dog charged towards them. Cecily pulled on his collar and bundled him onto her lap.

As the ship surged forwards, the sky turned white. Hail and sleet churned through the air, obscuring the view on either side. Crew who hadn't managed to find shelter were left grappling at the rigging as snow crashed onto the deck. A slab of ice, the size of a small car, plunged into the water off the port side, making the ship pitch.

Arthur's jaw chattered uncontrollably as he cowered between the ropes, hoping he wasn't about to turn into a human ice lolly. His toes felt like icicles and a layer of frost had crystallized on the sleeves of his wet blazer. He brushed a growing pile of snow off his head with a trembling hand and squinted into the maelstrom. A hunk of ice had appeared right where one of the ship's masts had been standing.

Almost in slow motion, Arthur watched the splintered mast come looming through the mist, falling straight towards them. His heart seized with terror. Someone shouted a warning but there wasn't time for him or Cecily to leap to safety. He felt her squeeze his shoulder as he braced himself, expecting the mast to land on top of them at any moment...

But it never hit the deck.

A few seconds passed and Cecily loosened her grip. "Arthur." Her voice was frail. "Look."

Arthur's legs were like seaweed as he pushed himself up and saw what had happened: the first officer and several other crewmen and women had caught the mast before it had flattened them. With some difficulty, they were resting it down at the edge of the deck. His chest stung with relief. They were alive, for now, but what *was* this place? It felt too real to be any kind of game.

Overhead, patches of blue sky pierced the fog as the snow began to fall more gently. The ship juddered against the settling waves. "ALL CLEAR!" the first officer shouted.

With pens and clipboards, the crew immediately set about assessing the damage to the ship. Cloud twisted free of Cecily's grasp and shook himself dry.

"This is *insane*," Cecily said, wringing out her skirt. "We could have been killed! What kind of a game is this?"

Arthur shook his head. "I don't know." He had run out of potential explanations to help rationalize everything.

Whatever they were playing, he just wanted it to be over as soon as possible.

"Are you ready for the report?" the first officer asked, floating over.

Arthur wasn't sure what he meant. "Err … sure?"

"Well, the hull is still intact," the first officer said, "but we've lost all function in the port side propeller and, as you can see, the foremast has been demolished. The intensity of that avalanche was measured at a six. We are halfway through the fjord."

"Right." Arthur gulped. They still had a fair distance to go and he'd bet everything he owned that another, more intense avalanche was waiting up ahead.

Cloud yapped and scampered over to the bow of the ship where Ren had emerged from below deck. Cradled in her arms was what appeared to be a shiny black bowling ball.

"I found the engine room," she said, glancing warily at the broken mast as she hurried across the deck. There was oil on her hands and a sweaty sheen to her skin. "The engine has that weird triangle-hexagon-cross logo on it and it burns these things as fuel." She placed the bowling ball very gently into Arthur's grasp.

Arthur braced himself for the ball's weight, but it was surprisingly light. Inside, glittering silver dust moved around like dancing ants, changing direction depending on how Arthur tipped the ball.

"Careful," Ren warned as he rotated it in his fingers. "Those things explode on impact."

"What?" He stopped moving.

"There's a store full of them in the engine room," she continued. "The crew load them into a combustion chamber, and when the fuel cells hit the sides of the tank they explode, generating the energy to power the engine."

"So why did you bring one up here?" Arthur protested. "I could have dropped it and blasted a hole in the ship!"

She shrugged. "I didn't think you'd be that stupid. Anyway, I found the *Principia*'s control system."

"Is it possible for us to steer it away from trouble?" Cecily asked.

"Yes and no," Ren replied. "The ship is currently set to auto-sail. Its control system is activated by the captain's fingerprint. Without him, there's no way for us to use it." She gathered Cloud into her arms and gave a wonky smile as he dragged his pink tongue up the side of her face. "It's almost like we're not meant to."

Clutching the life-threatening fuel cell, it occurred to Arthur that maybe Ren had a point. "Perhaps navigating the ship away from danger isn't the solution to all this. The first officer asked us to help the ship make it through the fjord safely, he didn't actually mention anything about steering."

"So if we're not supposed to guide the ship away from the avalanches," Cecily said, following, "then how do we prevent it from being destroyed?"

We protect it, Arthur thought. But he wasn't sure how.

He considered the broken mast. It was the falling blocks of ice that had caused all the damage, not the snow. *Where ice must fall and fire blast.* Thinking of the gunports in the *Principia*'s hull, he had a brainwave. "Ren, do you think we could use these fuel cells in the ship's cannons? If we can obliterate the ice before it collides with us, we might survive."

She placed Cloud back down. "It's not the worst suggestion ever. I'll go see."

"AVALANCHE!" a voice screamed. "TEN O'CLOCK!"

Arthur turned to port. Two hundred metres above them, a giant crack tore through the mountain's snowy crust. As it collapsed, the thundering boom of tons of falling ice came resounding towards them.

Time was up.

4

"Just make it work!" Arthur said, shoving the fuel cell back into Ren's arms.

Cecily took one look at the approaching juggernaut and cupped her hands around her mouth. "Attention, crew!" she hollered. "Everyone: standby the cannons! We'll be firing those things – " she signalled to the fuel cell that Ren was carrying away – "at any ice falling towards us. Get to your posts!"

The crew gazed at her vacantly for a moment, then saluted with their right hands and swiftly dispersed to fulfil her orders.

Arthur's mouth fell open. "How did you know they'd listen to you?" he shouted.

"I didn't," she called back. "It just felt like the right thing to do. Watch out!"

The avalanche was upon them. Snow and ice stormed around Arthur, blurring his vision and pelting his body from every angle. Echoing all around, the various voices of the crew bellowed into the maelstrom. Through the mist, Arthur spied Cecily scoop Cloud into her arms and retreat to their previous shelter between the rope coils.

"Over here!" the first officer yelled crossly.

Arthur ducked to avoid an incoming boulder of snow before skating across the puddled floor to where the robot was sheltering behind a barrel.

Crouching beside the first officer, Arthur had a clear view of the hull. The crew's heads flashed in the openings of the gunports as they loaded and aligned the cannons. Taking inspiration from Cecily, Arthur circled his mouth with his hands and shouted as loudly as he could, "Target the larger blocks of ice!"

A fuel cell came hurtling out of the hull at a forty-five degree angle, sounding like a rocket screeching through the air. Arthur watched as it collided with a falling slab of ice. Fire burst in the sky and a shock wave sent the ship listing to starboard.

As Arthur recovered his balance, hope blossomed inside him. "Aim higher! Fire quickly!"

One by one, the fuel cells launched into the air, blasting through the incoming snow. Arthur shouted directions when he could, but it was difficult to spot the dangerous blocks of ice until they were up close. He heard Cecily yelling similar commands on the other side of the ship.

Heavy rain hammered the deck as their shots made target. Eventually the sound of cannon fire grew less frequent and steam pooled around the *Principia* like a thick fog. Arthur's blood was pumping so hard he almost didn't hear the slap of Cecily's shoes as she came charging through the mist towards him. "Arthur, look!"

He sprang to his feet. The fjord had widened and the *Principia* was coasting into calm waters. Ren ran out from below deck, slamming a fist into the air. "We did it!"

Despite being drenched through to his underwear, Arthur couldn't help but grin as they came together. Cloud resembled a soaked dishcloth in Cecily's arms, but he was wagging his tail and gazing up at them with hopeful eyes, like a proud mascot. The game *had* to be over now – they'd won. Hopefully they could return to Peacepoint and get to school before any of their parents got seriously concerned.

"*Hu-hum.*" The first officer cleared his throat. "Are you ready for the report?" The rest of the crew lined up on either side of the ship as if preparing for an inspection.

"Fire away," Ren said, winking at Arthur and Cecily.

"Well, there's no fuel left in the engine and we are drifting aimlessly," the first officer related stuffily. "*But* the ship has passed safely through the avalanche zone, which means you have completed the realm-challenge."

Arthur felt relieved to hear the word *challenge*. It seemed to confirm they were in a game. As the first officer finished his sentence, a football-sized sphere appeared, hovering in front of Arthur. It was made from the same red vapour as the earlier message from Hxperion. "Not that stuff again,"

Cecily said guardedly. "What is it this time?"

Arthur reached out. As his fingers made contact, the sphere dissolved and a small hexagonal prism fell into his palm. It looked exactly like the one hanging from Cloud's collar, except it was made of white quartz instead of obsidian, and there were no initials etched on the end. Before he could examine it properly, Ren elbowed him in the ribs. "Something's happening – look!"

A beam of sunshine had appeared on deck. It moved like a spotlight towards the stern of the ship, where there materialized a man of medium height and build, with uncombed grey hair and a thin, equine face.

Arthur stared. It was the man from the portrait: Captain W. Saint-Ocean.

The captain brushed a few water droplets off his otherwise spotless navy coat. Beneath it, he wore a ruffled white shirt, woollen shorts, long white stockings and black-buckle shoes. "Congratulations, wanderers," he said in a solemn voice. "You have successfully completed Voyage of the Captain."

As he strolled over, it occurred to Arthur where he'd seen the captain's likeness before: in a science textbook.

"That's odd," he murmured to Ren and Cecily, tucking the quartz prism safely in his pocket. "The captain looks exactly like a famous scientist I studied at school."

"Really?" Cecily whispered. "Who?"

Arthur was about to reply when he realized something.

"W. Saint-Ocean..." he murmured, picturing the name written at the bottom of the captain's portrait. "It's an anagram! The letters can be rearranged to spell the scientist's name: Professor *Isaac Newton*."

The captain lifted his chin. "Yes?" He stopped just in front of them. "I'm Professor Isaac Newton. And who might you be?"

Arthur wasn't sure whether the captain was trying to crack some sort of joke or if he really believed that. "I'm Arthur and this is Ren and Cecily," he introduced uncertainly. For clarity, he added, "Obviously you're not *the* Isaac Newton. He's been dead for hundreds of years."

"Ah." The captain gave a wry smile. "That's not *exactly* true."

5

"You're right about one thing: I did die hundreds of years ago," the captain said. "King George gave me a state funeral, actually." He spoke abruptly, tugging on the bottom of his coat to straighten it. Arthur noticed the edge of a brandy-leather notebook protruding from his pocket. "But I am also alive *now*, standing before you."

Arthur's brow twisted like the knots in the *Principia*'s rigging. The captain couldn't possibly be telling the truth. What was he suggesting? That he'd risen from the dead?

The longer Arthur considered the matter, the more doubts niggled at his mind. Trouble was, the points on his "reality" compass had shifted so dramatically in the last hour that he didn't know what to believe. If it was possible to walk through a doorway on Peacepoint Estate and end up on a ship, then maybe it was conceivable this man *was* Isaac Newton?

"I would explain everything if I could," the captain continued, throwing a cagey glance at his first officer, "but the secrets of the Wonderscape must stay secret. Now, I assume you're all eager to claim your loot?" He swept his gaze over their dripping wet school uniforms and did a double take. "First Officer?"

The crewman whizzed forward. "Sir?"

"These three aren't wearing Wondercloaks! Which Wonderscape realm have they come from?"

The first officer glanced at Arthur, Ren and Cecily. "I don't know, sir." He pulled a reporter's journal out of his top pocket, flipped to the first page and flashed it at Newton. "These were the coordinates of the Wonderway they entered through."

"*What*?" The captain's voice crept higher as he read. "That's not feasible." He circled them slowly, studying their features as if they were bacteria in a Petri dish.

At the same time, Arthur scrutinized him. There was no denying that the captain was the spitting image of Isaac Newton, and if he was also the author of those notebooks, then the strange old-style English would make sense. Arthur didn't understand *how* any of it was possible, but he found himself starting to believe it. He recalled the first two lines of the riddle: *Set sail across a stormy ocean with one, who wrote the laws of motion*. It was, without doubt, a reference to Newton. Writing the laws of motion was one of the scientist's most famous achievements.

When the captain finally made it back round to face them, his expression was tense. "You're not supposed to be here," he concluded.

"*Finally*! Someone who understands!" Cecily's breath painted the cold air as she stepped forward. "Please, you have to help us. We went through a doorway that we suspect might have been a portal, in order to rescue this dog." She held Cloud higher to illustrate, his paws hooked over her arm. "And then we discovered that our mobile phones weren't working and we were somehow on this ship. And now we need to get back home so we can get to school."

"*Portal... Mobile phones...*" Newton jotted the phrases in his leather notebook, rubbing his chin. "I may be able to explain your situation, but first I must insist that you get rid of those wet garments. It's for your own safety. Come with me."

Arthur wasn't sure why their wet clothes would affect their safety, other than perhaps giving them a cold, but if following so-called Isaac Newton meant the possibility of warming up and getting answers, he wasn't about to protest.

With the first officer at the rear, Newton led Arthur, Ren and Cecily below deck. The *Principia*'s cramped wooden interior smelled of motor oil and seaweed. Arthur kept his elbows in as they walked single-file along a narrow hallway decorated with hexagon-patterned wallpaper, and then turned into a tight stairwell. Somewhere in the belly of the vessel he heard the faint melody of a sea shanty being sung by deep voices. At the bottom of the stairs was a long passage with six doors, each one labelled with a hand-drawn sign. Arthur recognized the handwriting from the note-books. It was Newton's.

"As you've no doubt noticed," Newton said, guiding them past a door named *LABORATORY 18*, "the *Principia* is no ordinary ship; she is a scientific research vessel."

Cecily whispered in Arthur's ear, "I can't have been concentrating during my Isaac Newton lesson. What's he famous for again?"

"He's one of the greatest scientists of all time," Arthur replied, keeping his voice down. "He discovered gravity."

"Gravity?" She stared in amazement at Newton's back.

Reflecting on the scientist's accomplishments, Arthur had to pinch himself. It was amazing to think that just one person had changed the way humans understand the universe. Without Newton's work, other scientists wouldn't have developed flight or space rockets, and everyone would probably still be communicating via telegraph because satellites wouldn't exist.

"I redesigned the ship," Newton continued, "to help me voyage through the Wonderscape, learning more about nature and the cosmos. The *Principia* might appear plain but she is in fact as complex as a watch movement, precision-built by mimics."

"Mimics?" Arthur echoed.

Newton signalled to the first officer. "Short for mimetic androids; the Wonderscape is full of them. There are two types: the T-class and the V-class." He paused and added,

"They can be a little bad-tempered. Don't take it personally."

Arthur glanced at Ren and Cecily, who both shrugged. Bad-tempered robots were the least of their problems.

Newton stopped two-thirds of the way along the passage and opened a door labelled, LOST. "This is where I store the items that have been left behind by others, in case they come in useful for my studies. You should all find something that fits. When you're done changing, my study is the last door on the right. I'll meet you there." As Newton turned to leave, Arthur noticed him retrieve his notebook and turn to an empty page. He was writing as he walked away, with the first officer at his side.

"Do you really think he's *the* Isaac Newton?" Ren asked, opening the LOST door. "I mean, how can he be? He's dead."

Arthur rubbed his temples as they walked inside. Everything was so mind-boggling, it was bringing on a headache. "I don't know *how*," he admitted, "but the more the captain tells us, the more I think he's telling the truth. It's not just that he looks and acts like Newton, it's that he seems to have the same knowledge and skills."

"So what, he's some kind of zombie?" she suggested.

Arthur stared at her. "*No*, obviously not. But something strange is going on."

The lost property room was the size of a school canteen and contained enough clothes to dress a small army. Alongside trunks of jumpers, there were wardrobes of jackets and coats, drawers of coiled belts, chests bursting with

T-shirts, tightly packed rails of dresses and even an entire hat stand full of straw Panamas. The air smelled of washing powder and linen, like in a launderette.

"This place is incredible," Cecily said, marvelling. "Who knew a centuries-old scientist would have such an amazing fashion collection?" A line appeared on her forehead as she stroked the arm of a nearby dress. "Although … we've completed the game now, right? So why do we have to get changed?"

"Newton said it was for our own safety," Arthur reminded them anxiously. He was starting to worry why there didn't seem to be an obvious way for them to get back to Peacepoint. "I guess we'll just have to go along with it for now, until we hear what he has to say." He surveyed the rails quickly. Everything was meticulously catalogued with paper tags. From what he could gather, footwear had been organized by size, shirts by colour, and trousers by fabric type. It appeared Newton had written the chemical formulas of the materials as opposed to their common names – Arthur was pretty sure the rail of shorts labelled $C_6H_7O_2(OH)_3$ was known as cotton to most people.

He found a shoe rack of dry footwear in his size, moved past the flip-flops, plimsolls and stilettos, and grabbed a pair of air-soled trainers.

"It's going to take ages to decide what to wear," Cecily remarked, inspecting a rail of corduroy skirts. "There's so much choice."

"What about trying something dry that fits?" Ren suggested, rummaging through a chest of trousers. She selected a pair of black utility ones with lots of pockets and disappeared behind a screen to change.

After moving aside a couple of boxes of books, Arthur tramped over to a trunk marked $C_{16}H_{10}N_2O_2$ and lifted out a pair of jeans. The corner of a colourful piece of paper protruded from the pocket, so he tugged it out.

It appeared to be a ticket. The background featured the image of a multi-domed silver building surrounded by trees. This was overlaid by iridescent letters, which read:

WONDERSCAPE EXPO 2469

25TH JANUARY, WONDERDOME, REALM 89

Meet the founders of Hxperion: Milo Hertz, Valeria Mal'fey and Tiburon Nox

Ten new realms previewed today!
Plus, a very special announcement...

ADMIT 1 ADMIT

ADMIT 1 ADMIT

"Whatever this *Wonderscape* is, it's a big deal," Arthur realized, holding the ticket up so Cecily could see. "There's an Expo held for it." Arthur's dad had taken him to a comic book and film Expo last year. It was a huge fair showcasing all the latest releases, with tons of merchandise stands, meet-and-greets with famous actors and artists, and the chance to get a sneak peek at stuff yet to be released.

Cecily shook her head. "I still don't understand how a game this popular has been kept secret, and how we've stumbled into it from a house on Peacepoint Estate. Plus, if all these clothes have been left behind by previous players, then *tens of thousands* of people must have been aboard the *Principia* before us."

Feeling even more confused, Arthur slid the Expo ticket into his rucksack for safe-keeping. Searching through the trunk, he found a pair of jeans in his size and slung them over his arm.

"How far away do you think we are?" Ren called out as she was getting changed.

For a split second Arthur didn't understand what she meant. Then it hit him. "You mean, from *Peacepoint*?" As he started to consider the possibilities, his chest grew tighter. The only way to explain the second sunrise they'd seen was that they'd moved to a different time zone. And that meant...

He slammed shut the lid of the trunk and slumped on top, feeling unsteady. Whatever this game was, it was using some sort of freaky next-level science. Walking through that weird portal must have transported them *somewhere else on Earth or even further*. The thought terrified him.

"You OK?" Cecily asked him, replacing her blazer with a leather jacket.

No! But he was too shy to tell Cecily the truth. "I'm fine," he lied. In reality, his heart was pumping really fast, like it might explode out through his ribs. They could be hundreds of miles away from home right now and they still had no idea how to get back. All he could think about was how far away his dad was…

She assessed his face sceptically. "If you're not feeling well, you should try taking deep breaths." She demonstrated by inhaling slowly through her nostrils and then exhaling through her mouth.

Arthur did his best to copy her. The more he repeated the process, the easier it became. After a minute, the tension in his chest dissipated. "Good advice," he mumbled. "Thanks."

With a smile, she went back to admiring the blouse she was holding. "I don't think it really matters how far away we are," she replied to Ren. "Only that there *is* a way back. Isaac Newton is a genius. If anyone can help us, it's him."

Arthur appreciated Cecily's positivity, he really did. The issue was: the very fact they were seeking help from a walking, talking *Isaac Newton* showed just how much trouble they were in.

6

"You two ready yet?" Ren asked, emerging from behind the screen. In addition to the combat boots and cargo trousers, she wore a belted black gilet over a long-sleeved thermal running top. Combined with her pale skin, dark eyeliner and silky hair, she looked like a highly practical vampire.

Arthur reached blindly into a box of T-shirts. "Gimme a sec."

Minutes later, he and Cecily were changed. Under her leather jacket she wore ripped jeans, a vintage *California* logo T-shirt and a green cashmere cardigan. She'd even found a dog lead for Cloud that matched his ruby-red collar. Arthur had paired his blue-wash jeans and trainers with a plain white T-shirt, red jumper and thin waterproof jacket. It wasn't what he'd normally wear, but it was dry and surprisingly comfy.

He fiddled nervously with a loose thread on the sleeve of his jumper as they walked along the corridor towards the study. Although Newton had promised to try to explain their situation, Arthur had a horrible feeling he wouldn't like what the scientist had to say. It troubled him that no one had showed them how to return to Peacepoint yet, as if there was no easy way.

As they stepped through the cabin door, he blinked with surprise. The space was larger and brighter than he had expected. Crystal chandeliers bejewelled the ceiling, spilling light onto a selection of comfy leather armchairs, wooden desks and laboratory tables. The tiled floor was patterned with more hexagons and the walls were lined with bookcases, except for a section of the hull that had been replaced by thick glass, giving a floor-to-ceiling view of the inky water outside.

"Professor?" Arthur called, venturing in past a table of peculiar chemistry equipment. There were hovering test tubes; Bunsen burners crackling with candy-pink flames; and even a sealed beaker of orange gloop that appeared to be climbing the walls of the jar, trying to break free.

"He's not here," Ren said. "We'll just have to wait."

Cecily held a magnifying glass to her eye, making it bulge to the size of an apple. "What is all this stuff?"

Evidence of strange experiments covered every surface. The remains of a dissected mimic hand lay carefully organized on one desk, along with a tea-stained pile of papers, a pair of tongs and a singed woolly hat. Alternate pockets of sweet and sour chemicals lingered in the air. Arthur passed a table of microscopes with drawers underneath labelled

Wondernews Archives, and wondered what they meant.

In the middle of the room stood an imposing rectangular frame, as tall and wide as a bookcase. "Newton said that the *Principia* is a scientific research vessel," Arthur reminded them, circling the structure. "This must be where he does some of his research." The frame was painted black, but it seemed blacker than anything Arthur had ever seen before – like it was drawing all light towards it.

Right then, the study door slammed open and Newton barrelled into the room, carrying a heap of black material. "Apologies for keeping you," he muttered. "I couldn't find the right shoes."

As his feet came into view, Arthur did a double-take.

The man who had discovered gravity was wearing a pair of fluffy pink unicorn-head slippers.

"Nowadays I do my best thinking when I'm wearing novelty footwear, for some reason," he explained hastily. "And your particular dilemma definitely requires my best thinking." He hung the fabric over the back of an armchair and hurried to a brightly coloured contraption in the corner of the room. Decorated with neon flashing lights, it looked a bit like an old Wurlitzer jukebox, except there was a holographic catalogue glowing behind the glass.

"Lesson one: everything around you *is* real," Newton said. He flicked a finger through the air and the catalogue responded to his movements. The pages were animated with videos and scrolling text. "There's no virtual reality in the Wonderscape. Everything functions using a combination of molecular assembly, self-reconfiguring modular robotics and nanotechnology. Of course it might seem like *magic* to you, for reasons I'll get to later."

Arthur shook his head, overwhelmed with information. He was right about the freaky next-level science. He'd heard of nanotechnology before, but that was in *comic* books. He glanced worriedly at Ren and Cecily as they joined each other opposite the jukebox. This probably meant that getting home would be far more complicated than they'd hoped.

Newton gestured with his hands and a set of doors in the lower half of the jukebox slid open. He crouched down, lifted out a small china plate and placed it on a nearby table. Sitting on top was a wholemeal tuna sandwich, neatly cut into four triangles and garnished with a salad of fresh green leaves and juicy tomatoes.

Cecily frowned and whispered in Arthur's ear. "I thought he was meant to be serving us an explanation, not afternoon tea."

Arthur wasn't sure what Newton was up to, but he spotted the word *STORE* lit up at the top of a catalogue page. The jukebox had to be some kind of vending machine.

Newton ordered several more dishes and placed them alongside the sandwich. When he was finished, a sizeable buffet covered the table, featuring everything from rollmop herring and salmon sushi, to smoked mackerel kedgeree and steaming lobster bisque. The jukebox even dispensed a doggy bowl of water for Cloud, who plonked his bottom on the floor and began lapping at it.

"Cuisine aboard the *Principia* is limited to seafood," the scientist told them resignedly. "Some of these new-fangled dishes are really rather good, but I'd much prefer a simple meat stew. Anyway, please help yourselves."

The fishy odour was so pungent it made Arthur's stomach turn. Ren and Cecily must have felt the same because they quickly shook their heads.

"Suit yourselves," Newton mumbled. "Sometimes a snack can ease the pain of bad news, that's all."

Bad news? Arthur got a sinking feeling as Newton dashed over to the floor-to-ceiling window and removed a white marker from his pocket. "Now, I haven't given a lecture since my days at the Royal Society, so I might be a little rusty." His pen squeaked as he squiggled something on the glass and stepped back.

It was the strange triangle-hexagon-cross symbol again.

"This is the logo of Hxperion, a company that designs and builds in-reality adventure games, or I-RAGs for short. You are currently in the Wonderscape, the largest and most extraordinary I-RAG ever created."

Arthur had played enough games to know that an RPG was a role-playing game and an MMO was a massively multiplayer online game, but he'd never heard of an I-RAG before. He moved closer to the glass, staring at the

Hxperion logo. No wonder they'd seen it everywhere.

"The Wonderscape is divided into realms," Newton continued, drawing a series of interconnected circles. "Players are called wanderers. In each realm, they face a series of challenges, which they must complete in order to earn loot and progress to another realm."

"But what are *you* doing in a game?" Cecily asked. "You're a scientist."

Newton's expression soured. "Every realm of the Wonderscape is themed around a different hero from human history. Cleopatra's realm, I've heard, is an amazing recreation of Ptolemaic-dynasty Egypt, and apparently there's no better way to see Ancient Greece than to visit Alexander the Great's realm. If exploring is your thing, you can join the famous Viking Leif Erikson on his journey to North America, or climb aboard *Vostok 6* with Valentina Tereshkova, the first woman in space. Only if you complete all the challenges in a realm are you personally congratulated by the hero – an attraction that has made the Wonderscape incredibly popular, and Hxperion very powerful."

Arthur felt the hairs on the back of his neck stand up as he considered the implications of what Newton was describing. He couldn't believe it was really possible to visit all those places and meet all those amazing people. But why hadn't he ever heard of the Wonderscape before? He spent loads of spare time scouring the Internet for rumours of new games; it didn't make sense.

"So much for playing video games from the comfort of your sofa," Ren quipped.

Newton batted his pen. "Those ancient things? People of the twenty-fifth century want something more thrilling than that. I-RAGs are the most popular form of entertainment these days."

"Sorry?" Arthur said, thinking he'd misheard. "Did you just say the *twenty-fifth century*?"

Newton's cheeks flushed. "Ah, my mistake. That just slipped out."

"Just slipped out?" Arthur tried to bite back his frustration. "What exactly are you saying? That we're in a different *time*?"

When Newton didn't immediately answer, Ren gave him such a harsh glare he squirmed and returned his pen to the glass. "Wonderscape realms are located on different planets in the Known Universe," he explained hastily, sketching a large spiral with a rectangle in the centre. "At the moment, you are in Realm Thirty-Three, on Earth. But wanderers move from one realm to another. That's where *this* comes in – the gateway you walked through to get here."

Arthur recognized Newton's drawing. The spiral represented that twisting quagmire of blue smoke he'd felt thrumming with energy at Number Twenty-Seven – the portal.

"It's called a Wonderway," Newton went on. "As far as I can determine, it bends space–time so that users are able to travel the cosmic distances between Wonderscape realms in just a few seconds. Based on your entry coordinates, I believe the Wonderway you travelled through did the reverse – it enabled someone to travel vast expanses of *time* in only a few centimetres of *space*."

Arthur gazed into the dark water beyond the glass, feeling like he might drown in the enormity of Newton's words. He tried to steady his breathing like Cecily had taught him. "So right now we're … in the future?"

"2473," Newton clarified. "Here, sit down." He pulled three chairs out from under a laboratory table and Arthur, Ren and Cecily flopped into them like a trio of rag dolls. Cloud bounded into Ren's lap and buried his head between her knees.

Thinking back to the Expo ticket, Arthur now realized why it was called EXPO 2469 – because that was the *year* it took place. And no wonder he'd never heard of I-RAGs before; in the twenty-first century they didn't exist. A thousand questions streaked through his mind all at once, like a shower of comets. "What's 2473 *like*?" he asked, focusing on one at random.

Newton winced, cleaning the glass with the end of his sleeve. "It's best you don't know. Trust me, it can be unsettling to learn about an era more advanced than your own. You need to return to your own time as soon as possible."

"But *how*?" Cecily questioned. "By travelling through another Wonderway?"

"Wonderways are activated using realm-keys, an item found in loot," Newton explained. "You will have already received one by completing the Voyage of the Captain, but *that* realm-key will only open a Wonderway to another realm in the Wonderscape. I suspect that in order to get home, you will need a special type of realm-key, one that has been reverse-engineered to open a Wonderway through *time*. Let's call it a *time-key*."

A time-key. That was their ticket home. Rerunning the avalanche challenge in his mind, Arthur remembered the quartz prism he'd collected at the end. It was the only item any of them had received. He patted his pocket and pulled it out. "Do you mean *this* is a realm-key? An ordinary one?"

"That's right," Newton replied. "It may seem unassuming, but it's actually an advanced piece of technology."

"It looks a bit like the gem on the Fuzzball's collar," Ren observed. Giving Cloud a scratch under his chin, she unclipped the obsidian prism and handed it to Newton.

The scientist appraised it cautiously, then held it under a magnifying glass. "Fascinating," he muttered. "Realm-keys can only be used once, but *this* has been designed for multiple journeys. It has the same basic structure as a realm-key but with an entirely different space–time frequency." He lifted his head from the magnifying glass. "It could be a time-key. I think we should test it."

The unicorn heads on Newton's slippers nodded as he dashed over to the huge black frame standing in the middle of the floor. Maybe the scientist was just excited, but the speed at which he moved was starting to make Arthur feel uneasy...

The metal frame had a hexagonal hole cut in the bottom, exactly the right size to fit a realm-key. Beside it was a holographic keypad. "Is *this* a Wonderway?" Ren asked, approaching slowly. "It doesn't look like the one we walked through on Peacepoint."

"This one hasn't been activated yet," Newton explained, tapping a few numbers on the keypad. "To do that, you first enter your destination – a realm number – and then insert a realm-key. For time travel, I suppose you input a date." Arthur didn't get a chance to see which date Newton had entered, as the number pad vanished once the scientist had slotted the obsidian prism into the keyhole.

The effect was immediate. The black Wonderway turned sapphire-blue and then burst at the edges, transforming into smoke. The floorboards beneath it trembled as the vapour churned in an anti-clockwise direction, forming a whirlpool. Deep in his bones, Arthur felt wave after wave of energy discharging from it, just like before.

Cecily's braids whipped around her shoulders as a wind picked up, sweeping around the room. "Is it working?"

"So far so good," Newton said, scribbling observations in his notebook.

Arthur's hope soared. Being in the future was thrilling, but he just wanted to go home. In a few moments he, Ren and Cecily might be back inside Number Twenty-Seven...

But then a flurry of green sparks erupted from the centre of the whirlpool, like a firework had detonated inside. Arthur was forced to clamp his hands over his ears as a deafening screech cut through the air and the obsidian key shot out of the vortex and spun to a halt on the floor. The blue smoke vanished into a point at the centre and the solid Wonderway frame returned.

As the wind settled around his ankles, Arthur's insides turned leaden. They weren't going home after all.

"There must be a problem," Newton said, stating the obvious. He collected the prism off the floor and placed it back under his magnifying glass. "When the Wonderway opened in your time, was there any evidence to suggest something had gone wrong?"

"You mean, like exploding gnomes?" Arthur asked delicately.

Newton raised an eyebrow, looking carefully at Cloud's prism. "Hmm. My suspicion is that this *is* a time-key, but it was damaged the last time it was used. You will need to get it repaired before you can use it again."

"Can't you repair it for us?" Cecily asked.

The scientist shook his head. "I don't have the right equipment or expertise. There is probably only one person who does: the time-key inventor. Whoever they are, you will need to find them *quickly*." He returned to the glass and scribbled down a formula that was so long, it ran over six lines. After substituting all the Greek letters for numbers, and completing a series of calculations, he circled an answer: 57.

"Imagine a jar of bubblegums. Each bubblegum is in exactly the right place, but as soon as you pull one out, the rest fall into different positions. Travelling through time has the same effect on the order of the universe – it scrambles everything." Newton tapped his finger against the glass. "That's why the universe is always seeking to rebalance itself. And, according to my calculations, fifty-seven hours after your arrival, it will autocorrect, deleting you and any other anomalies present. So, given the time you arrived here, let me see..." He removed a golden pocket watch from his trouser pocket and glanced at its face. "You now have fifty-three hours and twenty-seven minutes to get back to the twenty-first century."

Arthur froze. *"Fifty-three hours?"* He calculated quickly. "That's a little over two days from now! What happens if we're late?"

"If you're still here when the time runs out?" Newton scrunched up his nose. "Very messy. Your bodies will most likely break down into protoplasm."

Arthur opened his mouth to respond but found he had no words. No wonder Newton had been hurrying! He glanced at Ren and Cecily, who were both staring at him.

Fifty-three hours. That was it. That was all the time they had to find this mysterious time-key inventor and get home ... before the universe turned them into *slime*.

7

Arthur grasped the edge of a laboratory table to steady himself. His whole body was shaking and he didn't know how to make it stop. Finding the time-key inventor in a place as vast as the Wonderscape seemed … well, *impossible*.

"I can't believe any of this is happening," Cecily uttered, hugging her elbows as she sat on a stool. "Everything feels like it should be a dream, only I know it's real."

Pacing by the glass, Ren snorted. "*Dream?* I think you mean nightmare. We're over four hundred years from home and if we don't make it back in time, we're going to turn into protoplasm – that's basically *snot*, isn't it?"

Arthur thought it best not to reply. His face felt numb. This morning he had been worried about being late for school; now he might never see school again. For a painful moment his mind turned to home. His mum had passed away when he was two, and he had no cousins or aunts or uncles, so for as long as he could remember his family had just been him and his dad. He pictured his dad's face when they'd said goodbye earlier: his wonky glasses, kind smile and curly dark hair. Arthur knew that if he ever wanted to see his dad again, he had to think of a plan, *fast*. "We need to figure out who the time-key inventor is," he said, clenching his fists. "What clues do we know about them so far?"

"They're a genius?" Cecily offered.

"Maybe not," Ren said. "Why would a genius give a time-travel device to a *dog*?"

She had a point. Arthur couldn't understand why anyone would leave something that powerful hanging around Cloud's collar.

"All right, well, they must know a lot about Wonderways and realm-keys," Cecily reasoned. "Perhaps they work for Hxperion? And those initials scratched onto the base could be a maker's signature – *HW*."

At this, Arthur rustled around in his rucksack and pulled out the EXPO 2469 ticket. "According to this, we know the names of three Hxperion employees, at least: Milo Hertz, Valeria Mal'fey and Tiburon Nox. It says here they're the founders of the company."

"And siblings," Newton chimed in from the other side of the room. Since informing them of their fate, he'd left them to discuss things while he busied himself with an experiment involving a vat of colour-changing jelly, a small mirror and a hot-water bottle. "They were all adopted. Tiburon is the oldest; Valeria's in the middle and Milo is the youngest. According to my research, they were each responsible for one major innovation in the Wonderscape. That's how the Hxperion logo was formed: a hexagon to represent Milo, who invented realm-keys and Wonderways; a cross for Tiburon, who developed mimics; and a triangle for Valeria, who created Wondercloaks."

The word *Wondercloak* spiked Arthur's interest, but he brushed it aside. He was more concerned with his own impending doom. "Do you know where we might find them?"

Newton stiffened, as if finding the founders was *not* a good idea. "Tiburon and Valeria each have their own operational headquarters in the Wonderscape, but the two locations are top secret. As for Milo Hertz – nobody knows where he is. He fled four years ago."

"Fled?" Cecily repeated. "What do you mean? He ran away?"

Newton walked over to a table of microscopes and opened one of the *Wondernews Archives* drawers that Arthur had been curious about earlier. The scientist selected a trio of small glass slides, switched on three microscopes and placed one slide under each. "Here, these will show you what happened."

Arthur didn't understand how a microscope was going to explain anything. The last time he'd peered through one at school, he'd seen a squirming mass of bacteria that had put him off probiotic yoghurt for life. Still, he followed Ren and Cecily over and hazarded a peek through one of the eyepieces.

Happily, there wasn't a writhing organism in sight. It was as if Newton had placed a miniature TV screen under the lens, because Arthur found himself watching a video. A female news presenter dressed in a waist-length tartan cape was reporting from a venue packed with people. "So *Wondernews* is a news channel?" Arthur asked.

"Not always," Newton answered. "Its format is different in every realm. Here, it's a news channel viewed through microscopes."

Arthur briefly speculated how else *Wondernews* might be presented; perhaps in Cleopatra's realm you read it as a newspaper from a sheet of papyrus? Somehow, the microscope was able to emit sound. He tuned his ears into the reporter's voice.

"This popular event attracts hundreds of thousands of fans every year," she said in a serious tone, "but attendees I've been speaking to are now confused and worried. Footage of the incident, which has been shared widely, was recorded by several fans at the opening ceremony."

The report cut to an auditorium heaving with people, all wearing waist-length capes. There was obviously something weird about the garments, because the designs kept shifting. Some had the appearance of tumbling sand or windswept grass; others were decorated with fluttering insects or ink blotches that slid around, changing colours. Arthur recalled Newton's mention of a Wondercloak, and guessed that might be what they were.

Rising in front of the crowd was a wide stage illuminated by overhead spotlights. Its heavy velvet curtains were printed with the EXPO 2469 logo – the same as on Arthur's ticket.

As the crowd chatted happily, there was a clang backstage and an angry voice shouted, "MILO!"

A muscly young man with hunched shoulders and a mop of scruffy dark hair shot out from behind the curtains and sprinted across the stage. He was dressed in a hexagon-patterned Hawaiian shirt, baggy denim shorts and sandals, and covering his back was a floor-length cloak that looked like it had been stitched together from green oak leaves. His tanned skin glistened with sweat and his grey eyes were drawn wide. Clutched in his arms was a bundle of black jersey with a couple of drawstrings – a hoody.

Seconds later, a group of T-class mimics skulked through the curtains and zoomed after him. They each carried a strange sword with a black blade that appeared to be smoking.

The audience hushed. People turned to each other, pointing and whispering.

Pursued by the T-classes, the man hurtled through a door on the opposite side of the stage and disappeared.

Here, the video ended. Arthur lifted his face away from the microscope to find Ren looking confused. "The beefy guy running away from the T-class mimics was Milo Hertz," she said, connecting the dots. "And that was the last time he was seen? I wonder why they were chasing him."

"He vanished right before the Expo opened," Newton said. "Authorities have been looking for him ever since; apparently, he left behind several unpaid debts."

"Sounds like he was in trouble; his brother and sister must be worried sick," Cecily remarked.

Curious, Arthur took another look at the video. This time he experimented with the two focus knobs on the microscope. One seemed to operate the play, pause, fast-forward and rewind functions; the other allowed you to zoom in or out.

As Arthur replayed the clip, he searched for details that might explain why Milo was running. During the fourth repeat, he noticed something reflected in the cover of an overhead spotlight, and zoomed in. There was an opening in the bundled hoody Milo was carrying, visible only from above. Inside, Arthur spied a patch of coarse white fur, a pointed ear and a slice of a familiar ruby-red collar.

He took a sharp intake of breath. "The hoody is Cloud! Cloud *is* the hoody!" He shook his head and tried to organize his words. "I mean, Cloud is inside the hoody Milo is holding."

Ren peered back through her microscope and adjusted the focus. "Arthur's right – and Cloud's wearing the time-key around his collar. Maybe Milo Hertz is the inventor?"

Cecily bit her lip. "But then whose are the initials *HW* on the time-key?"

As soon as she'd posed the question, Arthur realized their mistake. He gathered Cloud into his arms and twisted round the time-key – now back on the little dog's collar – so everyone could see. "I think we've been reading this upside down. They don't say *HW*; they say *MH* – for Milo Hertz." Cloud fidgeted in Arthur's grasp, so he plopped him down on the floor.

A line appeared on Cecily's brow. "But if Milo Hertz is the time-key inventor, then…"

"We're looking for someone who's been missing for four years," Ren finished gloomily. The three of them heaved a collective sigh. "How are *we* supposed to locate Milo Hertz in a couple of days when the authorities can't find him?"

"We have Cloud and the time-key," Arthur said hopefully. "That might give us an edge."

Cecily looked at Cloud thoughtfully. "I wonder how Cloud ended up on his own. If he and Milo fled together, then something must have happened to separate them."

"We might need to figure that out," Arthur said. He imagined how a detective would go about finding a fugitive. "First we need to establish *what* Milo Hertz was running from and *where* he was running to. Maybe we should retrace his final steps? The venue for EXPO 2469 was a building called the Wonderdome in Realm Eighty-Nine. We could go there and search for clues?"

Cecily nervously jiggled her foot. "But if we venture

further into the Wonderscape, we'll have to face more realm-challenges, and we only just survived those avalanches."

"Well, we're not getting home from aboard the *Principia*," Ren said tersely. "I vote we try the Wonderdome. It's our only lead."

Newton, who had been pretending to clean a rack of test tubes while he listened in, lowered his voice. "If you're going to journey through the Wonderscape, you must be careful. Your very existence here is proof that time travel is possible. If anyone discovers where you're from, they could see you as a threat ... or an opportunity."

"But isn't time travel how you and the other heroes are here?" Arthur asked, confused. "Surely everyone already knows about it?"

Newton lowered his voice. "I can't tell you that. The secrets of the Wonderscape are exactly that – *secret*. Hxperion has never explained anything. Part of the game's appeal is its mystery." He fetched the pile of black material that he'd hung on the back of an armchair when he'd first entered, and offered each of them a piece. "Your best chance to remain undetected is to disguise yourselves as wanderers. These Wondercloaks from lost property will enable you to play along."

Wondercloaks. Arthur's guess had been right. He shook the fabric and a short, hooded robe with bat-wing sleeves fell into his lap. It seemed ordinary enough, but as he pushed his arms inside, he heard Ren and Cecily gasp.

Gazing down, he saw that the outside of the material had changed. It now resembled the surface of sea water – deep blue and rippling with waves.

Cecily hurriedly tugged on her Wondercloak. The fabric shimmered and transformed into a field of golden sunflowers, swaying in a breeze.

"How—?" Ren spluttered, inspecting the surface of her Wondercloak. It had taken on the appearance of ever-changing architectural blueprints. The white lines slid around, plotting new structures as she moved.

"Wondercloaks adapt to represent whoever is wearing them," Newton explained. "The lining also features a diagrammatic map of the Wonderscape. You'll learn more about the garments as you continue your journey."

Filled with curiosity, Arthur folded back one half of his cloak. The material on the inside showed hundreds of different planets scattered across a starry sky. When he focused his gaze on one, the map zoomed in and he could see the planet's surface, with its own unique geography. Some were covered entirely in ice and snow; others had areas of rainforest or desert. A ring of white text circled each planet; and around one in particular the words were flashing red – *REALM 33: PLANET EARTH, MILKY WAY.* Arthur had to admit the map was seriously cool. If he wasn't in a life or death situation, he could probably have spent hours playing with it.

The ceiling gave a loud creak as the ship rocked. The

cabin door flew open and the first officer drifted in. "Four new wanderers have arrived on board," he announced curtly. "You must get into position, captain."

Newton's neck tensed. "I have to go, and so do you. Do not be afraid to ask questions. Always seek the truth." Then he nodded firmly, mustered a brave smile, and turned for the door. Arthur heard the gruff voice of another T-class mimic crying, "Welcome aboard, *stowaways*," as it opened and Newton walked out.

The first officer regarded them tetchily. His oily black mullet was still dripping wet from the avalanche and, not for the first time, Arthur questioned why anyone would choose to populate a game with an entire fleet of robots that ugly. "Travel with wonder," he uttered, before exiting and slamming the study door behind him.

Alone, Arthur, Ren and Cecily turned to the Wonderway.

"Realm Eighty-Nine, then?" Arthur croaked. His knees wobbled as he crouched in front of the Wonderway and tapped the number into the keypad. As he fetched the white realm-key from his pocket, he felt the Wonderway pulling on it like a magnet. He only had to move it a handspan away before it jumped out of his fingers, snapped into place and disappeared.

Much quicker than before, the black Wonderway frame transformed into a swirling vortex of blue mist. A wooden door filled with translucent paper appeared in the centre. It was painted with a large black comma.

"That door looks like a shoji," Ren noted, walking closer. "They're Japanese. My grandparents have them at their house in Kyoto."

Arthur was too embarrassed to admit that his Japan-related knowledge was limited to his favourite Japanese export, *Pokémon*, so he stayed quiet.

"Time to cross our fingers," Cecily said, yanking up the zip of her leather jacket as the sleeves of her flowery Wondercloak billowed. She grabbed Cloud's lead, marched over to the shoji and slid it open to reveal a grassy patch of land under a dusky evening sky. All around, a forest of maple trees trembled in the wind.

Arthur felt a dull ache in the base of his skull – another brain freeze – as he followed Ren and Cecily over the threshold. The shoji closed with a click behind him and as the Wonderway silently dissolved, Arthur squinted into the darkness ahead. There were buildings through the trees.

8

Behind the rustle of wind through the leaves, the clang of metal drifted over from a clearing in the forest. Arthur's view was obstructed by trunks and branches but he could see two massive wooden structures: one illuminated in red, the other in white. Giant beams of light rose from their rooftops, soaring into the night sky like beacons calling wanderers towards them.

"Stay close, boy," Cecily whispered, tugging gently on Cloud's lead. "We don't know where we are."

"That's an understatement," Ren muttered bitterly.

Arthur glanced across at them both and guessed they were quietly seething at him. He had already been angry with himself for not keeping the Wonderway open, but after everything they'd just learned, he was starting to feel a sense of bone-crushing guilt. He tried telling himself there was no way he could have known that the doorway was a portal to another time, but it didn't make him feel any better. The fact was, there was a high chance none of them would ever see their families again, and it was all because he'd chosen a book to hold a door open instead of something more solid...

A track led through the undergrowth. "We're probably meant to follow this," he said, kicking the toe of his trainers into the dirt. He tried to gather his thoughts as they set off. Fifty-three hours sounded like a long time to find Milo Hertz, but it wasn't. They still needed to sleep and eat, to *survive*. Pressing a few buttons on his watch, he set a timer so he could monitor how long they had left. He wondered if time even behaved the same in the future. They'd soon find out.

"At least we're not alone," Cecily decided, her gaze fixed on her new second-hand ankle boots. "We've got each other. That's something."

Ren grunted. "Yeah, it's us versus everyone else. If anyone discovers we've travelled through time, they might see us as an opportunity, remember?" The way she said it made Arthur shiver. He noticed that the blueprints on her Wondercloak showed designs for an enormous wall, like the material was feeling as guarded as she was. On Cecily's cloak, the sunflowers had closed their petals and the light across the field was dim. Newton had said there was more to learn about their Wondercloaks; maybe this was what he'd meant – that the cloaks reacted to the wearer's emotions.

Cecily moved a branch aside as they turned off the path into a leafy glade. Opposite, the land fell away into a deep ravine crossed by a wooden rope bridge. The two monumental red and white buildings stood in a clearing on the other side, each the size of aircraft hangars. They had ornate tiled roofs, and holographic projections covered the outer walls, although Arthur was too far away to see them clearly.

"If it wasn't for the holograms and lights, those structures would look like ancient Japanese temples," Ren observed. "I can't see anything that looks like the Wonderdome yet, can you?"

"No," Arthur agreed, craning his neck. "The Wonderdome is surrounded by trees in the picture on the ticket, so it could be anywhere in this wood. Let's cross over and investigate those other buildings; we might find a signpost." He took a step closer to the bridge—

"Watch out!" Cecily cried.

A rough stone boulder the size of a small car unexpectedly swung across Arthur's path, missing the tip of his nose by a few centimetres. He wobbled and fell backwards, landing with a thud on his bottom. "What the—?!" he spluttered. "What *was* that thing?"

"*Those* things," Cecily corrected him dismally. "There are four of them."

As Arthur scrambled to his feet, he saw that Cecily was right. Four swinging boulders blocked the bridge at different points, whooshing through the air like a set of giant wrecking balls. Miraculously, though, there were no ropes holding them up; they seemed to be floating.

A pounding drumbeat filled the air, making the three of them flinch. Arthur wasn't sure where the sound was coming from, but he got a sense it was another part of the game. It all felt eerily familiar. "I've tackled obstacles like this before," he said. "Or rather, my characters have in video games." It was a frightening thought: the trials his characters faced on-screen, he was now facing in *reality*. "We just have to time our runs to avoid getting hit."

"Are you sure that's all we have to do?" Ren said, peering into the ravine. "Because that's a long way to fall."

Arthur gazed over the edge and swallowed. The chasm was so deep he couldn't see the bottom. "Well, that's how I get my *characters* across," he answered honestly. "Then again, they have more than one life." He decided not to add that his characters also never got across on the first try. It wasn't as if the three of *them* could practise.

Cecily had started inching away. "I should probably tell you both now: I'm not good with heights."

"Not good like … you've got a phobia?" Arthur said.

She shook her head. "I mean, yes, but it's not just that. When I'm up high I get vertigo, which makes me dizzy and my vision blurry. If I lose balance when I'm running – " she clapped her hands together – "*smoosh*."

Arthur glanced worriedly at Ren and was surprised to see a degree of understanding in her dark eyes. He had the impression she was someone who didn't experience fear, but perhaps he was wrong.

"Is there something you can do to prevent it?" Ren asked. "Or anything we can do to help?"

Cecily took a deep breath. "Not really. I'll just have to stop myself looking down."

Arthur felt his confidence ebb. How were the three of them ever going to survive this place if they couldn't even cross a bridge without risk of death? Still, he made an effort to remain positive. Everyone double-knotted their shoe-laces and after studying the boulders' movements for a few minutes, they drew in front of the bridge. He and Ren positioned themselves shoulder to shoulder on either side of Cecily, so they looked like a trio of sprinters waiting to have their ankles tied on the start line of a four-legged race. Ren offered to carry Cloud, but Cecily insisted she keep him – for moral support, no doubt.

"Ignore the drumbeat; we have to move in time with the boulders," Arthur instructed. He tried to muster up some courage. After the whole book-in-the-door incident, he didn't want to let Ren and Cecily down again. "Ready?"

Cecily set her jaw, although she was shaking so much Cloud looked like he was sitting on a washing machine. "R-r-ready."

Arthur waited for the first boulder to swoop past. "Now!"

As one, they charged. But as their feet hammered the rickety bridge, it started to sway.

"Whoa!" Arthur spread his arms to help him balance, but it felt like he was running on jelly. Without warning, his toe caught the edge of a wooden plank and he went flying through the air, landing with a painful thud on his hands and knees. In his peripheral vision, he saw the boulder looming towards him...

"Arthur!" Ren grabbed him by the shoulders and heaved him up. They both dived forwards.

For a split second, Arthur thought they were going to become boulder jam. Then he felt a gust of wind on his back as the boulder sailed past behind them. Pulling himself up on the rope handrail at the side of the bridge, Arthur was aware of his heart beating almost out of his chest. "You just ... saved my ... life," he told Ren between breaths. "Thank you."

Her lips twitched. "You owe me."

After shifting places with Ren, Cecily was now on the outside, clinging to the opposite handrail with her head tipped back. "This is *horrible*," she said in a thick voice. Tucked under her arm, Cloud headbutted her fondly.

"There are only three left," Arthur called. "You can do it!" Watching her wrestle with her fear, he felt a surge of admiration. He thought of something his dad had told him once and felt a pang of missing him. *Bravery isn't about being fearless. It's about being scared and doing it anyway.*

They waited for the bridge to fall still before tackling the second boulder. This time, Arthur was careful where he put his feet. As soon as he reached the safe zone, he glanced across to check on the others.

"Made it," Ren said, panting. Cloud yapped in encouragement as Cecily focused on the sky. With a little more patience, they all dodged the third boulder and made it safely past the fourth. Collapsing onto the grass on the other side, Cecily buried her face in Cloud's fur. Ren kneeled to lay a hand on her shoulder.

As Arthur went to congratulate her for getting through it, a puff of red mist appeared at the end of his nose. He stumbled back as the vapour swirled first into the Hxperion logo, and then into words:

WONDERSC✛PE

REALM 89: RACE OF THE WARRIOR

Loot: 600 DIRT, Wonderskill and realm-key

Travel with wonder,

Knowing the message was important, he reread it quickly before it vanished. The words *DIRT* and *Wonderskill* stood out – Newton hadn't mentioned those. Next, a paper scroll appeared out of thin air and fell into his hands. The handwriting was elegant and flowing, with long swirly tails:

Yours is a challenge laced with fear;
Be sure to keep your teammates near.
The answer to this puzzling race
Lies in an unexpected place.
I am dauntless. I am fast.
Conquer me to win this task.

Cecily lifted her head and wiped her cheeks dry. "Another riddle?" she asked.

"It sounds like the challenge in this realm is some sort of race," Arthur told her. He stood on tiptoe to get a better look at the buildings ahead.

Although the white structure appeared deserted, a noisy crowd congregated outside the entrance to the red building. Arthur could just about perceive the people gathered there; several had hover-wheels for legs, and others had Wondercloaks draped over their shoulders. "It's not just mimics. There are wanderers from the twenty-fifth century."

"Then we'd better get our story straight in case any of them try to talk to us," Cecily said, getting to her feet. "Do you think we should change our names so they sound more futuristic?"

"We don't know what 'futuristic' sounds like yet," Ren noted, pulling up the hood of her Wondercloak. "Let's stay quiet and keep our heads down. If anyone tries to speak to us, we can just pretend we didn't hear."

Arthur wasn't sure of the best way to handle a possible

encounter. He agreed with Ren that they needed to keep a low profile, but that might make it more difficult to find the Wonderdome. What if they needed to ask directions? Eventually, they all agreed to investigate the white structure first. There was no one around there.

As they drew closer, the glare from the lights lessened and Arthur could see the holographic wall projections in more detail. They showed images of a high-speed car race in which several different types of vehicle were competing. There were dune buggies, monster trucks with wheels of green vapour, scooter-shaped hovercrafts, vans with massive jet engines and open-topped four-by-fours; all painted different shades of red. Only one white vehicle was featured in every shot – a long sleek-bodied sports car with dramatic curved fenders and angled slits for headlights. It looked so aerodynamic that Arthur suspected you could roll a marble from one end to the other with a single push. One of the darkened windows at the front had a column of Japanese writing down one side.

"I learned to speak Japanese when I was little so I could talk to my grandparents," Ren offered, "but I'm not great at reading it." She studied the image carefully. "I think the kanji written there is Byakko; it means 'white tiger' in English."

Arthur wondered if the name was significant; he had no recollection of hearing it before. Circling the perimeter of the building, they found no signposts or clues as to where the Wonderdome might be, but on the final wall, the holographic banners had been replaced with a trio of animated posters advertising the Wonderscape.

The first featured a beefy guy with a leaf-textured Wondercloak, floppy brown hair and easy smile. Arthur recognized him instantly as Milo Hertz. Dressed in another hexagon-patterned Hawaiian shirt, he was lounging in a deckchair with a Hxperion-branded frozen cocktail lifted in one hand. Behind him, sun glittered on the white shores of a paradise island. A slogan at the bottom read: *Come for the game, stay for the mai tais!*

The second poster showed a glamorous woman with a sleek red bob and the eerily smooth face of a V-class mimic, strolling past a row of elegant shop fronts. She wore a floaty emerald jumpsuit, a black bow tie with a jade triangle in the centre, and a long silver Wondercloak as reflective as a mirror. Flashing neon vending machines, like the one Newton had used, could be seen in the shop windows, alongside holographic mannequins dressed in a range of historical costumes. *Shop while you play!* the tag line read. *Exclusive access to the most unique retail experience in the Known Universe.*

"If that's Milo in the first poster, then I reckon this must be his sister, Valeria Mal'fey," Cecily said. "Newton didn't tell us that all the V-class mimics have been made in her image!"

Arthur couldn't help but squirm. Having thousands of robots drifting around with your face took "selfie" to a whole new level.

Ren nodded at the third poster, which featured a tall, thin man with the droopy features of a T-class mimic. He wore his long oil-slick Wondercloak over a flowing black tunic with a plus-sign brooch on the lapel. "And that has to be Milo's older brother, Tiburon Nox. *V* for Valeria; *T* for Tiburon."

With his spidery fingers steepled together, Tiburon stood in a mahogany-panelled study furnished with leather chairs and antiques. Beside him was a large table covered with the same Wonderscape map Arthur had seen on the inside of his Wondercloak. Hundreds of holographic figures were arranged on top. *Could you be the next Caesar?* asked the tag line underneath. *Test your tactics in the Wonderscape.*

Reflecting on the three posters, Arthur felt glad they were searching for Milo Hertz, and not one of his siblings. He looked the friendliest by far.

Arthur felt something vibrate against his back and quickly unshouldered his bag. His mobile phone had switched on inside. "Hey, my phone's working again." Unsurprisingly, it had no reception. He checked for new messages (there weren't any) then tested his camera by capturing a photo of the Wonderscape posters. Everything seemed to be functioning normally.

"Mine's back in business too," Ren said, tapping at her phone screen with her thumb. "I wonder why..."

With a shake of his head, Arthur added it to the ever-increasing list of mysteries they needed to solve. "We'd better keep them hidden until we know more about what's changed in this century. People might not use phones any more."

After stowing their phones away, the trio set off for the red building. The crowd outside had grown and as they ventured closer, Arthur's hands started sweating. He knew he had to act natural to avoid causing suspicion, but it was difficult not to stare at people from the *future*. Surprisingly everyone looked much the same as him, except they were taller and some wore strange glowing jewellery or hair accessories. He made an effort to keep his head low as they weaved through the masses, catching snippets of conversation.

"This morning's race was a classic," commented one voice. "Two vehicles crashed in the first sector and by the eleventh turn, the White Tiger was already ten seconds ahead of the rest of the field."

Another speaker chuckled. "I doubt it's even possible to beat the White Tiger. I've never seen a red team win."

Arthur wondered how, if no one had ever won the race, wanderers were able to progress in the game. There had to be another mechanism by which they were able to leave the realm...

He stiffened as a boy with freckles came jogging up to them. He wore navy overalls under his Wondercloak, which had taken on the appearance of lizard scales. His long black hair must have had some sort of anti-gravity effect applied to it, because it floundered away from his face like he was underwater. Arthur guessed it must be a twenty-fifth-century thing.

"The last race of the day is starting in an hour and a half," he told them eagerly, sweeping back his flailing fringe. "Who are you supporting? There's space in our viewing platform if you want to cheer for Hydraspeed?"

"Oh, uh…" Arthur tried to sound relaxed but his voice came out croaky. "We're all sorted, thanks."

"Suit yourself." The boy gave Arthur's rucksack a double take. "Cool bag. Where did you get it?"

"Err…" Arthur's heart pounded as he tried to think of a reasonable answer.

"Wasn't it a gift?" Cecily asked, staring at him.

"A gift – yeah, that's right."

With a shrug, the boy moved on to another group of bystanders. Arthur exhaled with relief as they passed through a set of immense doors in the front of the red building and entered a vast, floodlit space bustling with people. The roar of excited chatter reverberated around the walls, along with the buzz and whir of machinery. V-class mimics wearing stylish green overalls zipped through the cloaked masses, carrying tools and tyres. Overlooking the main floor were a number of balconies which extended outside the building. Glowing translucent elevators painted with green triangles hovered around like radio-controlled lanterns delivering people to every level. "What *is* this place?" Arthur asked, shrinking back.

"I don't know but act normal," Cecily whispered from one corner of her mouth. "No one else is gawping."

The walls were decorated with more holographic posters advertising Hxperion-branded clothing and merchandise. Arthur tipped his head to marvel at the high ceiling, which was painted with bloody battle scenes of warriors in samurai armour.

Beyond the main crowd, the concrete floor was divided into a grid of nine numbered paddocks with a different vehicle loaded in each. Teams of wanderers were busy examining engines, inspecting tyres or touching up the red paintwork. Arthur noticed that the closest group – four stern-faced blonde girls – had the words *Falcon's Fury* written on the back of their Wondercloaks.

"Must be some sort of garage where they keep the cars used for the races," Ren guessed, standing on tiptoes. "The crowd outside were talking about defeating the White Tiger, which might explain why all the red cars in here seem to belong to wanderers. The challenge is red versus white."

Arthur recalled a couple of lines from the riddle scroll: *I am dauntless. I am fast. Conquer me to win this task.* The subject had to be the White Tiger.

"Hey," Cecily said, pointing behind them. "Is that a map?"

They hurried over to the rear of the building, near where they'd first entered. Projected onto the wall was a Japanese woodblock-style illustration of the area, showing a vast, forested canyon with steep-sided valleys and jagged mountains. The red and white buildings were both situated on a plateau in the centre, accessed by a dozen rope bridges (lethal swinging boulders *not* included). A flag marking the start of the race was positioned behind the red building, although the track itself hadn't been drawn.

Large areas of the land had been shaded red and fenced by dotted lines. Arthur studied the key in the bottom right-hand corner. *"Restricted Zone,"* he read. *"Access to race winners only, except during the EXPO."*

"I wonder why only winners are allowed there," Cecily remarked.

Ren indicated to a round silver structure at the bottom of one valley. "Look – that's got to be the Wonderdome."

Arthur's heart sank when he saw it was located in one of the restricted zones. "So let me get this straight: if we want to visit the Wonderdome, we either have to wait until the EXPO is on in –" he checked the EXPO 2469 ticket – "January, if it's an annual event, or we have to win this race."

"We'll be snot by January," Ren offered helpfully.

"Then I suppose we've got no choice but to get racing," Cecily said, rolling up her sleeves. "If the race is part of the realm-challenge, it must be easy to enter. Where do you think we get a car?"

Recalling what he'd overheard, Arthur tensed. The White Tiger had never been beaten. Scanning the building for clues, he spotted a large holographic board on the opposite wall. It displayed a list of eight team names, including Hydraspeed and Falcon's Fury, with space for one more. Paddock Nine stood empty in the far corner. "Over there?"

As they crossed the floor, Arthur paid close attention to the wanderers his age that were rushing around. Anyone who wasn't dressed in overalls wore loose-fitting jeans and T-shirts, woollen jumpers and cotton dresses – the kind of items Arthur had seen in Newton's lost property. Arthur wondered what their parents thought of them playing such a dangerous game, and whether they were only allowed to visit the Wonderscape after they'd done their homework. There was no way *his* dad would be happy about him taking part. The game was far too risky and Arthur's dad was too protective.

The mimics, some carrying fire extinguishers and sand buckets, sported green-and-white chequered suits with the words *RACE MARSHAL* on the back. A few had wrenches or spray cans for arms as well as hover-wheels for legs. Notably, Arthur saw only V-class units zipping around; the T-classes and their robot mullets were nowhere to be found.

Ren dashed the last few paces to the free paddock. The area contained nothing but a rack of red spray paints. "Where do you think we get the car from?" she asked, walking around the edge.

Scanning the paddock, Arthur spotted a pattern of flat metal dots inlaid into the concrete in one corner, too smooth to be screw-heads. As he kneeled down to inspect them, a cloud of glittering silver particles spurted out. "Whoa!" He fell backwards as the dust condensed into a waist-high podium with a holographic screen at the top. "Where did that come from?"

"I don't know," Ren said, approaching the podium curiously. "How did Newton say things worked around here? Nanotech?"

Arthur couldn't remember, but Newton was right about one thing: the technology in the Wonderscape seemed like magic.

Beneath the screen hovered an M-shaped holographic controller. "Qwerty keyboards obviously don't exist any more," Cecily said. "How do you think we operate this thing?" Hazarding a guess, Arthur slid his hands around either side of the *M*, like he would his PlayStation controller. The screen immediately glowed into life and a video started playing.

"Welcome, wanderers!" declared Valeria Mal'fey, appearing in the centre. Her glossy red bob looked freshly styled, and over a crisp white shirt she wore a glittering jade pinafore dress embroidered with triangles. "You are about to enter a deadly race that will test your mind, body and spirit," she said in a smooth voice. "First, choose a vehicle design."

The video reduced in size and shifted into one corner of the screen to reveal a 3-D technical drawing of a sports car, rotating on a single axis.

Remembering that Ren's mum was a mechanic, Arthur

surrendered the controls. "Ren, you'll probably be better at this than me. What kind of vehicle should we have if we're to go faster than the White Tiger?"

Ren scrunched her mouth into one corner, scrolling through the different options. There were more than a dozen vehicles to choose from, most of which Arthur had spotted on the race posters outside. "That's odd," she said, hesitating. "The only cars available are self-driving vehicles."

"For a *race*?" Cecily jerked her head. "That doesn't make sense."

Arthur considered their task aboard the *Principia*. Perhaps this challenge was like Voyage of the Captain, and wasn't what it first seemed...

With a shrug, Ren nudged the controller towards a heavily modified rally car. It featured front and rear spoilers, aerodynamic body panels, a jet-propelled engine booster and superlight chassis. "This one seems designed for speed."

After Ren had confirmed her selection, Valeria's video returned to full size. "Interesting choice," she remarked, arching a perfectly shaped eyebrow. "But you must prove yourself worthy of a vehicle like that. You have six minutes on the clock – GO!"

Before Arthur could process what was happening, an intricately patterned black circle revealed itself in the middle of the paddock floor. A slot opened and several pieces of wood toppled out on a raised platform.

"This must be another challenge," he realized, kneeling to examine the pieces. They all had curved edges and were carved on one side with a twisting design that matched the pattern on the concrete. "Some sort of puzzle..."

Ren and Cecily dropped to the floor and started grabbing blocks. Arthur found two that fitted together and placed them over the corresponding outline on the concrete. He'd never been very good at wooden puzzles but the adrenaline seemed to focus his mind and with time ticking away, the design swiftly took shape. There was a hole in the centre surrounded by several rings of a twisting, maze-like track.

There was no countdown on the screen, so Arthur had to estimate how much time had passed when Cecily finally held the last piece. "I think that's probably three minutes spent," he said urgently. As she slotted it into position, he felt a shudder and the entire puzzle lifted from the ground, balancing on a pole in the centre. He jumped to his feet and caught one edge of the structure as it rocked towards him. A holographic ball materialized in the outer ring.

"This looks like one of those wooden labyrinths!" Cecily remarked, steadying the puzzle opposite. "I was given one in my Christmas stocking last year – it was a lot smaller than this."

"No kidding," Ren mumbled, straining to support her side. "What do we do?"

Cecily traced the route with her pupils. "We've got to tip

the puzzle in different directions in order to roll the ball into the centre. Left first."

"Whose left?" Arthur asked.

Ren leaned back. "This way."

"No!" Cecily used her weight to tug in the other direction.

Arthur was vaguely aware of people sniggering behind them. Apparently, their arguing was attracting an audience in the other paddocks. He followed the ball's route to the centre and pointed with his chin. "Slow down," he said, trying to keep his voice level. "The ball needs to move along that channel, there."

"You're wrong," Ren said, still pulling. "It has to go this way, otherwise it'll get stuck."

With all three of them working against each other, the ball eventually wobbled and rolled into a dead end. Cecily took a deep breath. "We're wasting time. One of us needs to lead, or else we'll never—"

But it was too late. As quickly as it had appeared, the holographic ball vanished and Valeria Mal'fey started talking again. "Time's up, I'm afraid," she said with an easy air of condescension. "What a *disappointing* performance."

With a clatter, a large slot opened in the floor and the puzzle table retreated into darkness. Arthur knew Valeria's message must be pre-recorded but it didn't make it sting any less. "Substantial modifications will need to be stripped from your vehicle," she decided. "Travel with wonder!"

The designs for a pared-down model of their rally car

appeared on screen. It now had a strange sausage-shaped body, a small electric engine and a handful of basic safety features which Arthur skimmed worriedly.

Without warning, the screen and podium reverted to a cloud of metallic particles that disappeared back into the metal dots in the concrete. Next, a floating elevator half the size of the entire paddock descended from the roof. The air trembled as the base of the elevator slid away and a small car fell with a thud to the paddock floor. Batting dust away from his face, Arthur saw that the vehicle was the exact same model they'd seen on-screen, built from plain sheet metal as if it had just rolled off a factory conveyor belt. Everything but the bodywork had been masked off in preparation for it to be painted.

Cecily circled it slowly, casting nervous glances at the much larger vehicles in the other paddocks. "Maybe with a little colour it'll look less like a tin can?" she ventured.

Arthur cringed. The only good thing about the vehicle was that it had blacked-out windows, so nobody would see them despairing inside when they lost. As he considered what might now happen to them, he started to feel sick. If they didn't win the race, they wouldn't find Milo Hertz and get the time-key repaired in order to travel home. He doubted they'd even survive much longer in the Wonderscape if they couldn't work together properly.

"We *have* to win this race," Ren reminded them. "It's the only way to gain access to the Wonderdome so we can retrace Milo Hertz's last steps. What are we going to do?"

"I'm not sure," Cecily admitted. "Why don't you two scope out the competition to see what you can learn? Cloud and I can stay here and do the painting."

The thought of splitting up felt risky, but with time running out, Arthur supposed it was the logical step. Walking side by side, he and Ren quickly made their way around the floor, ogling the other teams. Hydraspeed consisted of four heavily tattooed teenage boys, all with floppy anti-gravity hair like the supporter they'd met outside. The athletic blonde girls of Falcon's Fury looked like they might be professional race mechanics the way they moved around taking measurements and making minor adjustments. Their sleek sports car was painted to look like a falcon with flaming feathers of hot-rod red and orange. Both teams smirked as Arthur and Ren passed by.

"Everyone clearly did way better at that labyrinth puzzle than we did," Ren determined as they drew halfway around. "Look at all the modifications on their vehicles – the truck in Paddock Three has a jet engine!"

Arthur hung his head, feeling foolish. *Be sure to keep your teammates near*, the riddle had said. The labyrinth puzzle had been a test of teamwork, and they'd failed. No wonder everyone had been sniggering.

After a good twenty minutes exploring, Arthur and Ren were stopped by a V-class mimic wearing bright red lipstick, who scanned their Wondercloaks carefully. "Ah, you're from Paddock Nine. I've been looking for you."

Arthur glanced at the sleeve of his cloak and wondered if the pattern of rippling water revealed more than just his emotions. Perhaps because the V-class was a mimic, she could see something he couldn't. "I haven't had to tell any of the *other* teams this," she continued, "but you are required to register your team name with a race official, like me."

"Oh, right." Arthur hadn't spoken to a V-class before and after watching the real Valeria on-screen, it felt strange communicating with her mimic clone.

The robot took a pen and notepad from the pocket of her overalls and looked down her nose at them. "Well? What is it?"

Arthur thought carefully. They needed to choose a name that wouldn't draw attention; something that would help them blend in with all the others.

Just then, one of the Falcon's Fury girls came barging past, lugging a tyre over one shoulder. "Move, pipsqueak!" she bellowed, shoving Ren.

Ren glowered at her. *"Pipsqueak?"*

"Very well," the V-class said. "Good luck, Pipsqueaks. Travel with wonder."

Arthur flinched. "What? No, we don't want that as our team name!"

But it was too late. The word *Pipsqueaks* had already appeared on the holographic board at the far end of the building – and on the back of their Wondercloaks.

"You've got to be kidding," Ren said, clawing at her hood. "How are we meant to go unnoticed now?" The drawings on her cloak instantly shifted into the blueprints for a deep, dark well, big enough to hide in. Arthur assessed his own cloak. Between the team-name letters, the seawater was sloshing fretfully in all directions.

Annoyingly, after powdering her nose using a Hxperion-branded compact mirror, the V-class strutted away without further comment. At the same moment, a dog's bark echoed around the walls, and Arthur spotted Cecily and Cloud running over.

"Thank goodness we found you both," Cecily said breathlessly. "Cloud and I went up to one of those viewing terraces while we were waiting for the paint to dry and ... we *can't* enter this race. It's too dangerous."

"But – we've just entered!" Arthur said. "Our team name is up on the board."

Her eyes widened. *"What?"*

"Haven't you noticed it says *Pipsqueaks* on your back?" Ren asked brutally. "That's what we're called. Anyway, we *have* to compete in the race, you know we do."

"Pipsqueaks?" Cecily shook her head. "But..."

"Ren's right," Arthur agreed, checking his watch. "We've got no other choice. We'll be slime in fifty-two hours, anyway. The race can't be more dangerous than that."

Cecily's voice was hollow. "See for yourself."

They summoned one of the glowing elevators and rode

it up to the highest terrace in the building. A shoji slid open to reveal a crowded platform tucked under the eaves of the roof. After weaving through the mass of people, Ren and Arthur stopped at a railing and peered over the edge while Cecily stayed a few paces back to avoid triggering her vertigo.

Arthur immediately saw the reason for Cecily's concern.

Beyond the plateau where the red and white buildings were situated, the land plummeted into a steep valley. It was easy to spot the start of the racetrack in the trees, as it was marked by a row of chequered flags, flapping violently in the wind. The route then curved to the edge of the plateau and zigzagged down into the valley on a road that looked as if it had been cut into the sheer face of the rock. Arthur counted twelve hairpin bends before it straightened out, heading for the finish line below.

Despite the precariousness of the course, there were no safety barriers at the sides of the track. Threads of black smoke rose from piles of rubble scattered down the canyon side, and Arthur shivered when he realized what they were.

The remains of red vehicles.

9

"We're going to die," Ren said, squeezing the handle of Cloud's lead like it was a stress-ball. "And we're going to do it in a car that looks like a giant chilli hot dog."

The three of them stood in their paddock surveying Cecily's paint job. The rear of their long, round car was coloured a glossy maroon but the tone changed in a steady gradient towards the front, where it was a spicy orange-red. Arthur felt nauseous looking at it, and it wasn't just that it resembled food. He couldn't quite believe what they were about to take on. That racetrack, those corners, the speed…

A couple of V-class mimics wearing T-shirts saying *Pipsqueaks Rule!* stood watching them from the edge of their paddock. One had a flag in place of an arm; the other was so filthy with motor grease Arthur doubted she'd ever taken a shower. He guessed Hxperion provided two free supporters to every team so that the less popular ones always had someone to cheer for them. Holographic *Pipsqueaks to Win!* banners had also appeared on the sides of their paddock along with boxes of various budget team accessories, including branded helmets (the kind worn by bicycle riders and not high-speed car drivers) and water bottles.

Arthur could feel the stares of the other teams boring into the back of his head. A couple of wanderers in an adjoining paddock were whispering. The words *pipsqueaks* and *amateurs* sailed over. He swallowed down a ball of fear, knowing the wanderers were right. They *were* amateurs. They didn't have a clue about racing and it was probably going to get them killed.

Cecily lifted her chin, pretending she hadn't heard. "This red makes a bold statement," she argued, defending her handiwork. "It says: powerful, fresh, wild."

"It says: we have no idea what we're doing," Ren responded frankly. "In the end, it won't make us go any faster and that's all that matters."

"That's not true," Cecily retorted. "If I've learned anything from my parents' business, it's that when we look good, it can make us feel good inside. People come into their salon feeling *meh* but leave with a spring in their step. So if we have to descend the side of a perilous cliff-face – and deal with the worst vertigo ever, by the way – we should at least try to do it in style!" She took a deep breath and froze. "Wait... *What* did I just say?"

"Err..." Cautiously, Arthur retraced Cecily's own words. *"If we have to descend the side of a perilous cliff-face—"*

"Arthur!" she gasped. "That's it! I know something that

could help us in the race." She grabbed her mobile phone from her handbag and waved it in the air. "I've figured out who the hero of this realm is!"

Arthur threw himself in front of her to try to keep her phone hidden from view but Cecily seemed too intent on examining her phone case to worry. She pointed to one of the manga characters on the back – a beautiful woman with long, flowing black hair. The character was dressed in revealing white battle armour and carried a huge sword in one hand.

"This is Saisei," Cecily explained. "She's a character from *Samurai Deeper Kyo*, one of my favourite manga series. In the story, Saisei's a zombie but her true form is that of a real-life woman from twelfth-century Japan – Tomoe Gozen, the most renowned female samurai in history."

She pronounced the name *To-mo-eh*. Arthur found himself repeating it slowly in his head. "Is that who you think the hero is? Tomoe Gozen?"

"Well, Tomoe fought during the Genpei War," Cecily replied. "It was between two clans – the Taira, who wore red, and the Minamoto, who wore white. Tomoe was a leader in Lord Kiso's army on the Minamoto side."

Red versus white. Arthur glanced up at the samurai battle painted on the ceiling. "It's just like this race."

She nodded. "I thought Tomoe sounded cool, so I researched more about her. She was written about in this ancient Japanese epic called *The Tale of the Heike*.

She's described as a warrior who used to 'ride unscathed down perilous descents' – just like how I described the racetrack here."

"I never would have guessed you were so into manga," Ren remarked, appraising Cecily thoughtfully. "Me too." She paused and frowned. "I've just thought – remember that black symbol we saw on the door to this realm?"

"It was like a giant comma," Arthur recalled.

"Well, in Japanese it's called a *tomoe*," Ren said. She pointed decisively to Cecily's phone case. "All the clues point towards Tomoe Gozen; even the name of the realm-challenge: Race of the Warrior. It has to be her."

Arthur glanced contemplatively at the other paddocks. If no team had ever beaten the White Tiger before, then no one had ever won the chance to meet the hero. And that meant the Pipsqueaks might be the only people who knew it was Tomoe Gozen. "What else can you tell us about her?" he asked Cecily. "If the whole realm is themed around her, then the race probably is too. You're right, it could give us an advantage."

Cecily returned her phone to her handbag. "The Genpei War era was dominated by men – the samurai class were all men – but Tomoe still earned a position of leadership in their armies. She must have been fearless."

"So, then, *we* probably have to be fearless to complete this challenge," Arthur decided, gazing nervously at their tiny car. Two lines from the riddle set alarm bells ringing in his head: *The answer to this puzzling race, lies in an unexpected place.* If he could just figure out what that meant.

A klaxon sounded, reverberating around the building. Crowded on the balconies, the supporters hushed as a flashing message appeared on the holographic board at the far end of the room.

Media and non-essential personnel,
please leave the floor.

Race starts in
10:00

Cecily snatched Cloud's lead from Ren's hand. "Come on, we have to get ready."

The fan-mimics who had been cheering the Pipsqueaks' name abruptly changed character and zoomed into a paper elevator, which took off towards the roof. The atmosphere in the paddocks became feverish as the other eight teams rushed to put on their helmets and board their vehicles.

Ren threw a Pipsqueaks helmet at Arthur. "I need you in the front with me. Cecily's going to watch over Cloud in the back."

Arthur wasn't sure when those arrangements had been made, but he was too anxious to argue. He pulled the helmet over his head and stumbled to secure the strap around his chin.

"See you at the bottom, Pipsqueaks!" one of the girls

taunted from the Falcon's Fury paddock. "That is, if you make it in one piece!"

Arthur's jaw tightened as he opened the front-left car door and got in. Bundling Cloud onto the back seat, he heard Cecily mutter derisively under her breath. He might have also caught the barrage of curses Ren directed at the Falcon's Fury paddock, but when he shut the door, everything went quiet.

Soundproofing, he realized. *Nice.* He fastened a reassuringly mechanical seat belt and surveyed the car interior. The curved seats and floor were upholstered in a thick, woven black material and small mirrors had been fixed all around the windscreen to allow every rider a clear view of the car's surroundings. Arthur's trainers sat on a slanted footrest and above, where Arthur would expect to find a steering wheel and dashboard, there was instead a long silver panel punctured with two cup holders and a golf-ball-sized glass orb that throbbed with green light.

"That's the best I can do," Cecily grumbled from behind.

Arthur looked over his shoulder. Cloud was strapped into a makeshift doggy harness that Cecily had cobbled together using two seat belts, Cloud's lead and her leather jacket. He seemed comfortable and secure, which Arthur thought was a remarkable achievement considering the little dog's fondness for wriggling. Cecily gave Cloud a kiss on his head before fitting him with his helmet and whispering, "Good boy. It's going to be OK."

Arthur's throat tightened as he turned back around. It

was clearly not going to be OK. They needed a plan, and they needed one fast.

There was a burst of noise as Ren yanked open the front-right door, settled into the seat beside Arthur, and slammed the door shut again. "I hope I haven't just given people a reason to be suspicious of us," she admitted, her cheeks flushed. "I just called Falcon's Fury a bunch of names that are probably too stupid to still exist in the twenty-fifth century."

"Maybe not, if *pipsqueak* is still in use," Arthur commented. "Are you all right?"

"Not now I'm sitting in this deathtrap," she replied, securing her seat belt.

As if "deathtrap" was a cue to switch on, the glowing orb on the panel brightened and the holographic head of a half-human, half-lizard materialized. The creature had wide yellow eyes, scaly green skin and a mop of centre-parted dark hair.

"Good evening, Pipsqueaks," he said in a soft French accent. "I will be your driver for today's race. I advise you to wear your seat belts and helmets from now on. How are you feeling?"

Arthur's mouth went dry. The only reason he could think of to explain their driver's reptilian features was that he was based on some real-life *alien* from the Known Universe. "We're just great," he croaked, staring at the lizard-man's slit-shaped pupils.

"Pleased to hear it," the driver replied. Outside, the floor of the building had cleared, and technicians and supporters were making their way to the viewing terraces. "If you turn your attention to the front window, you can view our proposed route." The windscreen darkened and a flashing green outline of the racetrack and its surrounding terrain appeared. "I have plotted a course to ensure you reach the finish line safely."

Arthur tried to concentrate on the map but it was difficult not to be distracted by the driver's forked tongue flicking between his lips as he spoke.

"We will cruise along the centre of the road," the driver explained, "decelerate on entry into each of the twelve corners and take an easy line into the straights. I predict you will finish tenth overall."

"*Last*, then," Ren said, turning to Arthur. "What are we going to do?"

Arthur chewed on his bottom lip, searching for inspiration. The most predictable way to win a race was to drive the fastest around the track, but the riddle scroll had said the answer to the race was *unexpected*.

He pictured Tomoe Gozen riding into battle down the side of a mountain, then he remembered something he'd seen listed among the safety features of their car...

A horrible idea began to take shape in his mind. As he was thinking, he felt a tingle at the base of his skull, which worked its way over his head to his temples.

"Something's happening to your cloak," Ren said, tugging on his sleeve. "Look."

Numbers and symbols written in Newton's distinctive handwriting had appeared in the water on Arthur's Wondercloak. He wasn't sure how or why, but it was *doing* something to him. He suddenly realized he knew things, things he hadn't been aware of before. He made a series of quick calculations: wind speed, trajectory, total weight of vehicle and passengers, distance, landing time...

The ground shuddered. Something was going on outside but Arthur was only vaguely aware of it. "Driver? I need you to plot a new route."

The lizard-man turned in his direction. "Your route will be locked in under a minute," he warned. "What are your proposed changes?"

Arthur steeled his nerves. "I want you to ignore the racetrack and drive us directly from the start line to the finish line, over the side of the canyon at sixty-two point four decimal degrees north and seven point six decimal degrees east. We must be moving at a speed of one hundred and forty-five kilometres per hour when we drive over the edge."

The lizard-man's response was immediate. "Very well. This is your new route." The image on the windscreen changed to a dotted line that veered off the track just after the start line and plummeted directly towards the finish in the valley below.

"Are you *crazy*?" Ren sliced her palm through the air, pointing to the windscreen. "This isn't *The Fast and the Furious*! If we drive off the side of the mountain, we'll crash and explode into a million pieces!"

"Route locked in," the lizard-man announced with a toothy grin. "Travel with wonder!" The image of their journey promptly vanished from the windscreen, although the lizard-man's head remained.

Cecily gripped Arthur's shoulder. "What have you done?" she squeaked.

Hearing the terror in her voice, he tried his best to explain. "This is the only strategy that makes sense. It's like what we did aboard the *Principia* – destroying the obstacles rather than steering away from them. We have to come at the challenge from a different angle." He glanced again at his Wondercloak, which had returned to normal. "Also, I think my cloak just gave me the ability to do complex calculations. Don't ask me how."

It was at that moment he noticed what was happening outside. In front of them, the far wall of the red building had slid skywards, exposing the start of a wide road through the dark forest outside. The race-marshal mimics that Arthur had spotted earlier flanked the track every few metres. Small but powerful lights shone from their chests to illuminate the way, like some sort of iron-woman honour guard.

"This is it," Ren hissed. "The start line has to be on the other side of those trees."

Out of nowhere, music started playing inside the car – a fast-tempo orchestral piece with jerky violins, like part of the score to an action movie. Arthur assumed it was designed to make the whole experience more dramatic, as if it needed any help.

As the car rolled out of the building, the night sky appeared overhead. Leaves skittered across the windscreen, falling from the trees bowing in the wind. To Arthur's left, the other eight red vehicles advanced at the same steady pace. He couldn't hear the roar of their engines, but judging by the ear protectors everyone was wearing, the noise was ferociously loud.

Cold sweat beaded on the back of his neck as the start line came into view. A large bank of seating was erected on one side, filled with a sea of riotous supporters, all cheering and waving flags. Painted on the tarmac behind the start line was a grid of ten white boxes sitting two abreast. As the Pipsqueaks' car drove into the last box on the grid, Arthur spotted the White Tiger appearing from a side road and assuming its position at the head of the pack.

A gantry of red lights was suspended above the start line.

Watching the other vehicles move into position, Arthur shuffled in his seat, his nerves building like static electricity. "Which side actually won the Genpei War?" he asked Cecily, searching for a distraction. "Red or white?"

"White," she said, her voice trembling. "The side Tomoe Gozen was fighting for."

Once all the teams were in place, everyone revved their engines. Dust and debris blew out from under the hover-powered vehicles; multicoloured gases burst from various outlets on the other buggies, trucks and cars. Arthur's feet vibrated as the engine in their car purred into life. His pulse was thudding. He hoped above everything that he'd made the right decision and hadn't just doomed them to end their lives as another pile of rubble at the edge of the course...

One by one, the red overhead lights switched on.

Arthur's heart skipped a beat.

The lights went out.

And the race began.

10

They surged forwards, the G-force driving Arthur's shoulders back into his chair. The choking stench of chemicals cloyed at his throat as air from outside filled the car.

Ren clenched her jaw, clinging to the underside of her seat. "Everyone, hold on!"

Ahead, amethyst-purple exhaust fumes clouded the track as a saloon car with glowing wheels blasted through the grid. A red-camo motorbike swerved into the mist, its sub-zero engine leaving behind a trail of ice as it overtook a pair of monster trucks. The flaming feathers of the Falcon's Fury car blazed in the distance, approaching the first corner just behind the White Tiger.

Within seconds, the rest of the field had disappeared around the first bend and the Pipsqueaks were speeding along on their own.

"Get ready!" Arthur cried as they made a sharp turn off the road, heading into the trees. A dozen race marshals gave chase, their chest beams piercing the dark undergrowth like helicopter searchlights. The Pipsqueaks' car bumped and jerked over the rough terrain, making for a bruising ride. As the perimeter of the canyon appeared, so did the void beyond. Arthur spread his hands against the panel in front of him. "This is it!"

Everyone screamed as they sped up. The nose of the car lurched over the cliff edge and with a jolt they launched into the air.

Even though Arthur had been anticipating the fall, nothing could have prepared him for how it actually felt. His stomach jerked into his mouth; his helmet thumped against the roof of the car and as his bottom left his seat, his seat belt dug into his collarbone to pull him back into it.

Cecily shrieked.

Cloud barked.

The driver helpfully informed them that they were plummeting at a speed of one hundred and forty metres per second, and that the time until impact was seven seconds.

Blood rushed through Arthur's veins as the outside world spun past in a blur – the stars, the canyon, the tree-tops, the snaking racetrack...

...

...

There was a dull thud from somewhere inside the bonnet and their driver announced, "Parachute deployed!"

Arthur shook as the car tipped backwards. Heavy wires sprung from a spot behind each of the car's headlights and in two places at the car's tail. In the rear-view mirrors he saw they were connected to a huge red parachute branded with a black comma.

"Time until impact now twenty-six seconds," their lizard driver corrected.

As the earth stopped spinning, Arthur's focus recovered. Saliva bubbled in his throat and he fought back the urge to wretch. Cecily was hyperventilating behind him.

"Did you know our car had a parachute?" Ren yelled.

"I saw it on the spec!" Arthur replied, grateful he hadn't made a terrible mistake.

Below them, the racetrack grew bigger. Most of their competitors were rounding the tenth hairpin bend, with the Falcon's Fury girls second behind the White Tiger. Arthur doubted whether any of them had noticed the Pipsqueaks' car parachuting into the valley; they were probably concentrating too much on their own race.

"I think we're currently beating the White Tiger, but not by much." Ren pointed to a strip of straight road that went all the way to the finish line. "We're going to land over there. Prepare yourselves!"

As they drifted the last few metres to the ground, Arthur pushed down with his feet and rammed his hands against the dashboard, readying for impact. The parachute disconnected with a loud *click* and the car lurched, throwing his head back at the same angle as a Pez dispenser. Pain erupted in his neck and collarbone as the tyres hit the ground and the car crashed down. With a loud whir, the engine stirred into life and they bolted forwards.

"There are five hundred metres to the finish line," the driver informed them.

Arthur rubbed his jaw, wincing. He felt Cecily's hand on his shoulder and instantly felt a pang of guilt. Free-falling off the side of a mountain had probably been way worse for her. "Something's happened," she said shakily.

Hearing the tone of alarm in her voice, he twisted around and saw a scene of chaos through the rear window. The White Tiger was accelerating close behind them, but further back there had been an accident. The smoking remains of the car belonging to Falcon's Fury was lying trackside at the eleventh turn, surrounded by race marshals. The blonde-haired girls were nowhere to be seen. Arthur hoped they were OK. That rubble could have been them and he felt lucky his risk had paid off.

Gaining on them, the White Tiger hurtled around the final corner and eased onto the straight.

"It's getting closer!" Ren shouted.

As they streaked over the tarmac, still gathering speed, Arthur studied the rear-view mirrors. The snarling headlights of the White Tiger were growing bigger and bigger. The finish line was seconds away. An excited mob of supporters had amassed on either side of the track, cheering the cars home.

There was only one thing Arthur could think of to do. It

wouldn't make them go any faster, but it might make him feel better. He filled his lungs with air and bellowed the loudest battle cry he could, willing the car on. Cecily and Ren joined in, screaming together. "Ahhhhhhhh!"

And then in a flash, they crossed the finish line.

The action-movie soundtrack stopped abruptly and was replaced with a trumpet fanfare and recorded applause. "What happened?" Arthur asked, panting, as their car slowed. The White Tiger was braking beside them. He didn't know who had got there first. "Did we win? Driver?"

The lizard-man bared his pointed teeth as he spoke. "Congratulations, Pipsqueaks! You have completed the challenge: Race of the Warrior."

Arthur's head fell back against the headrest as he gave a weary sigh. *We did it!* said a voice in his mind. *We won!* But he was too overwhelmed to pay it much attention. A glance in one of the mirrors told him that Cecily's cheeks were flushed and she had Cloud pressed close to her side. He reached round and gently touched her knee. "It's all right. We're OK."

Ren dragged the heels of her hands down the sides of her face. "That was the scariest thing I've done. Ever."

Arthur had never felt so relieved and yet somehow so tense in all his life. His muscles felt like they'd morphed from iron to jelly and back again several times in the past few minutes.

Without warning, a gaseous red sphere appeared in the

middle of the car, hovering between the front seats. Ren reached across to touch it. As soon as her fingers made contact, the sphere evaporated and a white prism appeared in her palm. "Another realm-key," she said, tucking it into her pocket.

As they came to a stop in the middle of the tarmac, the White Tiger halted in front of them. The driver-side door lifted open vertically and a slim figure wearing a white leather racing suit and darkened helmet stood up and walked towards them.

"This isn't over yet," Cecily warned. "We've got to stay in character. No one can know where we're really from."

As the driver, or passenger – Arthur wasn't sure if they'd had a lizard-man too – of the White Tiger approached, hundreds of spectators ran onto the track behind them, throwing their flags into the air and high-fiving each other.

Without invitation, the figure in the white racing outfit opened a rear door on their car and climbed inside. Cecily unstrapped Cloud from his harness and lifted him into her lap as she shuffled over.

A voice mumbled something inaudible from inside the helmet, then, when no one responded, the figure pulled its helmet off.

"I said: *Congratulations*." The speaker was a beautiful woman with porcelain skin, a high-bridged nose and long black hair tied at the nape of her neck with a white ribbon. She bowed her head. "You're the first team to ever beat me."

"*Tomoe Gozen!*" Cecily exclaimed.

The driver's dark eyes glittered. "You know my *name*?"

"I read about you in *The Tale of the Heike*," Cecily ventured.

Arthur was glad she hadn't gone with, *I learned about you from a manga character on the back of my phone case.*

"I'm Cecily. This is Arthur and Ren."

"And who is this?" Tomoe asked, nodding at Cloud, who had wriggled out of Cecily's lap and padded across the seat to sniff Tomoe's hip.

"He's called Cloud," Cecily said, a little embarrassed, sliding him back over.

"I see." Tomoe tilted her head and absorbed the details of their faces, from the set of their jaws to the sweat on their skin. Arthur squirmed, feeling as though he was being read like a book. "Great warriors come in all shapes and sizes," she observed. As she pulled off her driving gloves, Arthur noticed several milk-white scars on her hands that he assumed she'd acquired during combat in twelfth-century Japan. He still didn't know how she and Newton were alive in the twenty-fifth century, other than it probably involved time travel...

Just then a hand pounded against his window and another banged loudly on Ren's door. Everyone except Tomoe flinched. Arthur made sure his door was locked before peering outside. While they'd been talking, the race supporters had caught up with them. The car was surrounded.

"Would you rather adjourn this meeting so you can

greet your new fans?" Tomoe asked, reaching for the door handle. "I'm sure the *Wondernews* press will be keen to interview you too."

"No!" Arthur, Ren and Cecily said in unison.

Tomoe settled back into her seat with a hint of amusement on her lips, as if she'd expected that answer.

"We'd prefer to keep a low profile, if you don't mind," Arthur explained. "We just want to visit the Wonderdome. Do you know how to get there?"

"The Wonderdome?" Tomoe raised her eyebrows. "I can show you the way, but as Hxperion weren't expecting anyone to win the race, the building won't be ready for visitors. It'll probably be next week before they grant you access."

Arthur's stomach dropped. "Next *week*!"

On the back seat, Cecily squeaked. "Then ... everything we've just been through was for nothing. How are we going to find Milo Hertz?" As soon as she'd said it, her hand jumped to her mouth and her cheeks flushed pink. Ren glared at her, but Arthur couldn't blame her for oversharing. After car-parachuting off the side of a mountain, she was doing well to speak at all.

"So *that's* it," Tomoe said with a smirk. "You want to solve the mystery of Milo Hertz's disappearance." She considered them thoughtfully. "You know, when I first arrived here, Milo had only been missing for a couple of days. Every wanderer in the realm was talking about it. Rumour was, he'd been seen arguing with Tiburon and Valeria backstage at the Expo before he ran away. Here, let me show you something."

Tomoe swiped her hand over the back of Ren's chair and Arthur blinked as the woven surface transformed into a tea-stained sheet of paper with a thick black border. Glimpsing a pattern of metal circles under the headrest, he figured it was something to do with nanotech again.

"Where I can, I learn about the Wonderscape by listening to the conversations and comments of wanderers who visit this realm," the warrior revealed, "but mostly I source information from this."

The page was divided in two horizontally. The top half was filled with black Japanese writing; the bottom, with black-and-white photos. Arthur thought it looked a bit like an ancient Japanese newspaper and realized it must be another version of *Wondernews*.

The warrior translated a section of writing at the top. *"Mysterious Flying Pipsqueaks become first wanderers to complete Race of the Warrior in Realm Eighty-Nine."* She flashed them a smile. "You've made the headlines already."

Beneath the writing was a photo of Arthur, Ren and Cecily in their paddock before the race. Cecily was signalling to their freshly painted car; Ren was scowling and Arthur … hadn't realized his cheeks looked so dark when he blushed.

"Who took that picture?" Cecily asked. "I didn't see anyone with a camera."

"All mimics transmit images back to Hxperion," Tomoe explained. "The V-class models communicate directly with Valeria Mal'fey. The T-classes, with Tiburon Nox."

Arthur wondered anxiously if Newton's first officer had transmitted an image of the co-ordinates of the Wonderway they'd arrived through back to Tiburon. If so, Tiburon might know that they were from a different time. "And Tiburon and Valeria, they look at *all* these images?"

"I think so," Tomoe answered, "although some things must go unnoticed for a while – a wanderer was recently expelled from the Wonderscape after Hxperion discovered they'd tried cheating, weeks ago."

Arthur crossed his fingers. With any luck their co-ordinates would stay undetected long enough for them to return home.

"This is what I wanted to show you," Tomoe continued. She tapped the top-right corner of the page and it changed to show a different article. *"Milo Hertz branded a 'lazy oaf' by his sister, Valeria,"* the warrior read, tracing her finger over the Japanese writing.

The photo below was of the three Hxperion founders at the Wonderscape opening ceremony. Arthur stretched across the middle of the car to see it better. Valeria was posing for photographers while she cut a holographic ribbon; Milo was spraying champagne above everyone's heads and Tiburon was standing like a heron behind them both, studying proceedings over the end of his long, droopy nose.

"The article features an interview with Valeria Mal'fey, taken right after Milo disappeared," Tomoe went on. "In it, she claims that Milo never took his role at Hxperion seriously; he was always missing meetings and shirking duties. She says she wasn't surprised in the least when he finally abandoned his responsibilities and ran off." Tomoe indicated to the last section of writing. "This final part is even more interesting. The interviewer asks Valeria if she knows where Milo is, and Valeria says no, but that she expects he still visits the Wonderscape from time to time, out of curiosity."

Arthur gave Ren and Cecily a sideways glance. If Milo Hertz *did* return to the Wonderscape occasionally, they probably had a higher chance of finding him. But all that stuff about him being lazy didn't sound right – how could a lazy person invent time travel? Something else Tomoe had mentioned was playing on Arthur's mind. "You said Milo disappeared a few days before you arrived here, but where did you come from? And how did you get here?"

"I came from *home*," Tomoe replied, glancing wistfully out of the window. "From Japan. The rest..." She shook her head and muttered tiredly, "Well, the secrets of the Wonderscape must stay secret."

Arthur's chest sagged. Newton had used the very same line to dismiss that question before.

"As it is getting late, I have an idea," Tomoe said. "Why don't you stay overnight at my house? In the morning, we will have a chance to get to know one another." She addressed the holographic lizard-man. "Driver?"

Before anyone could protest, the doors locked with a low buzz and Arthur felt the rumble of the tyres as they steered forwards into the crowd. Supporters slammed their fists onto the bonnet of the car, beating a rhythm as they chanted. Arthur thought they might be shouting, "Pipsqueaks!" but his lip-reading wasn't that good. It could also have been, "Big butts!"

In the rear-view mirror, he caught Tomoe Gozen scrutinizing their Wondercloaks. Perhaps she was intrigued because they were the first wanderers she'd actually spoken to, but it left Arthur feeling on edge. Without knowing her motives, he still wasn't sure they could trust her. If she learned they had time travelled, she might take advantage of them. With everything at stake, they couldn't take that risk.

As they drove clear of the spectators, they passed the blonde-haired girls from Falcon's Fury answering questions at the side of the track. They looked red-faced and sweaty, but uninjured.

"I don't know how they survived," Cecily commented from the back seat. "Their car was in pieces."

"Maybe it ejected them before they crashed?" Ren guessed.

"I expect they were rescued by V-class units," Tomoe said. "After all, they're trained in life-saving first aid and programmed to prevent casualties where they can."

Arthur thought of the grumpy crew of the *Principia*

saving him and Cecily from being squashed by a falling foremast and understood now why they'd done it.

"Ms Gozen," Ren said, shifting nervously in her seat. "Can I ask: why aren't you speaking Japanese?"

Tomoe instinctively touched her throat. "I *am*. And the wanderers we just saw were no doubt using hundreds of different languages from across the Known Universe. Your Wondercloaks translate everything you hear into your mother tongue – you must know that."

Moving the fabric between his thumb and forefinger, Arthur wondered what else the garment could do. He covertly caught Ren's gaze and drew a line across his throat, signalling for her to be quiet. They'd already revealed too much.

Ren smiled thinly at Tomoe before turning back round.

An uneasy quiet settled over the car as they wound along a narrow road, heading deeper into the valley.

Arthur couldn't relax. He examined his watch. Eleven hours had passed since they'd arrived in the Wonderscape, which meant they had a little under forty-six hours left in which to get home. Newton's warning echoed in his mind: *If anyone discovers where you're from, they could see you as a threat … or an opportunity*. He hoped news of the Pipsqueaks' win would blow over. They couldn't afford to make a name for themselves.

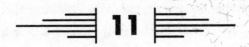

11

The car stopped at the foot of a pebble path that banked up through some trees. A V-class with a neat bun stood waiting for them at the top of the rise, her green overalls flapping in the wind. Tomoe collected her driving gloves and helmet from the space beside her, opened the car door and got out.

As soon as the door closed again, Arthur, Ren and Cecily huddled closer. "We've got to find out what Milo, Valeria and Tiburon argued about at that Expo," Ren whispered. "It could be the reason Milo ran away, and it might help us understand where he went."

"Do you think all that stuff Valeria said about Milo in the *Wondernews* was true?" Cecily asked. "Newton mentioned that Milo left behind several unpaid debts. Maybe he asked his brother and sister for money to help pay them and they refused?"

Arthur shook his head. "If he needed money that badly, he could have sold his designs for the time-key and made a fortune." Unsure what to believe, he retrieved the EXPO

2469 ticket from his pocket and reread the information on the front. It mentioned *a very special announcement* would be made; he wondered if their quarrel had been something to do with that. Trying to slot all the clues together felt like doing another build-a-labyrinth puzzle, only without all the pieces.

"I suppose we don't have any choice but to stay here overnight," Cecily said, peering outside. "We've got to sleep somewhere."

Ren grunted, struggling to unfasten her seat belt. "Am I ever getting out of this deathtrap?"

With a straight face, Arthur reached over and pressed the release button. Ren scowled in thanks, and together, they stepped out into the night. The temperature had dropped since they'd first arrived in the realm and Arthur was grateful that his Wondercloak provided extra warmth. Cloud wagged his tail as Cecily set him down on the ground, keeping the end of his lead firmly looped around her wrist.

Following Tomoe, they climbed to the peak of the hill. An enormous timber building with a thatched roof lay beyond. It had stables off to one side, and was surrounded by an intricate Japanese garden. Orbs of green-tinged light hovered between the plants and trees, illuminating the garden's elegant shapes like fireflies. Behind the wind, Arthur could hear the trickle of water and chirp of grasshoppers.

"Is this your home?" Cecily asked Tomoe, as they started

along a meandering path through the garden towards the building. "It's so peaceful."

Tomoe smiled. Arthur felt the pressure in his chest start to ease as he inhaled the cool night air. There were no strong perfumes; just the scent of clean water and fresh earth.

They entered the main building through a heavy wooden door and proceeded into a wide hallway lit by more hovering orbs. Everywhere Arthur looked, the walls were covered in displays of arms. There were fan-shaped arrangements of swords, huge wooden bows and ornate cases of arrows with different types of fletching. The scent of fresh straw and wood smoke lingered in the air.

Tomoe climbed out of her racing suit, revealing a loose white shirt and matching mid-calf trousers. A belt of green, gold and red silk was wrapped around her waist. Placing her boots against the wall, she collected a pair of straw-soled slippers from a rack by the front door and slid them on.

"It's customary to remove your shoes here when entering a Japanese house," Ren told Arthur and Cecily, keeping her voice low.

Thankful for the advice, Arthur pulled off his helmet and trainers and put on a pair of straw-soled slippers. As he waited for Cecily to untie the laces of her boots, he examined a set of boxy armour displayed in a glass cabinet beside them. It included a helmet, mask, sleeves, greaves and cuirass, all made of small iron or leather plates. "Was this your armour during the Genpei War?" he asked Tomoe, amazed anyone would be able to walk in it, let alone fight.

The warrior peered through the glass on the other side of the cabinet. Arthur shifted under her gaze, feeling like she was reading him again.

"It's lighter than it looks," she said. "A samurai rides on horseback and fights with a bow and sword. Our armour must be strong, but supple enough to allow movement." She pointed to the white-lacquered chords of leather and braided silk used to tie the armoured plates together. "The colour and design of these fastenings is unique to each warrior's family."

The lines around her eyes twitched and Arthur wondered if she was possibly thinking about her own loved ones, left behind in twelfth-century Japan. Eventually, she lifted her chin and gestured to the far end of the corridor. "Please, follow me."

Their destination was a few rooms away, past more weapon displays and several hanging scrolls of Japanese calligraphy. Tomoe shuffled her slippers off before padding inside. "Tatami mats," Ren noted, glancing at the floor. "It's customary to be barefoot for those."

Removing his slippers, Arthur followed Ren and Cecily in. He gaped when he saw the size of the room. Like a great hall, it was rectangular with a tall, coffered ceiling. Ancient suits of armour from across the world stood guard around the walls, glinting in the orb light. Some wielded sharp pikes or daggers; others heavy swords and bows. Their shadowy eyes watched Arthur unnervingly as he shuffled across the woven straw rugs on the floor.

A large window in one wall gave a view out into the surrounding forest. In the dark distant mountains beyond, an emerald-green pyramid jutted out of the rock. "What's *that*?" Arthur asked. He couldn't remember seeing it on the map.

"Valeria Mal'fey's operational headquarters," Tomoe answered, throwing a wary glance at the V-class who had followed them in. "She is always watching."

Arthur suspected Tomoe was referring to the robot, who was doubtless sending live images of all this back to Valeria. It made him uneasy that they were being spied on; they would have to watch what they said around the mimics.

"Is that why there are restricted zones in this realm?" Cecily asked. "Because it's where Valeria has her 'secret' headquarters for the whole Wonderscape?"

Tomoe gave a single nod. "She is the designer of this realm. Her signature is everywhere."

Her signature? At first, Arthur wasn't sure what Tomoe meant, but then he remembered what Newton had told them about the Hxperion logo being formed of three different shapes, each representing a different sibling. *The green triangles.* That's why he'd seen them on those floating elevators – they denoted Valeria. He thought of the hexagon-patterned wallpaper aboard the *Principia* and decided Milo

Hertz was probably the architect of Newton's realm.

"I suppose it's nothing like twelfth-century Japan," Ren commented sympathetically.

Tomoe sighed, gazing out into the darkness. "No."

Right then, the shoji slid open and another shiny-faced V-class entered, balancing a stack of futon mattresses on one shoulder. There was no way a human would have the skill or strength to do so, but Arthur supposed mimics had a whole repertoire of such party tricks.

"You three must rest," Tomoe said hastily. "And I must prepare for this new opportunity. I will call on you first thing tomorrow."

Prepare for what new opportunity? Arthur thought, as with a solemn bow the warrior retreated through the shoji. The V-class glided into the centre of the room and flung the futons in a pile on the floor.

"The lights will dim automatically when you fall asleep," she droned, inspecting her sparkly green manicure. "Travel with Wonder."

Once she'd gone, Ren pulled a futon off the mound. "Is it just me, or do you get the sense that Tomoe doesn't want to be here?"

"She seems sad," Cecily said thoughtfully. "Like she's lost something."

The secrets of the Wonderscape must stay secret... Arthur wondered what Tomoe and Newton were hiding. As he hauled his futon into position, his stomach gurgled so loudly the others turned to look at him. He grinned. "Apparently parachuting into the canyon burned more energy than I realized. Do you think Tomoe has a kitchen?"

"*Grrf!*" Cloud unexpectedly scampered to the other side of the room and pawed at the floor. Wondering what had got into him, Arthur went over to investigate.

"Hey, buddy," he said, kneeling down. Where Cloud was scratching, a section of the tatami mat was inlaid with a series of flat silver dots – the same kind Arthur had seen in their paddock earlier. "Strange," he muttered. Presuming they were activated in the same way, he swiped his hand across them and a puff of metallic dust spurted out. The particles quickly swarmed into a solid shape, transforming in both texture and colour, until standing in front of Arthur was a jukebox vending machine, identical to the one they'd seen on the *Principia*.

"Whoa! Lucky!" Ren exclaimed.

Arthur stared down at Cloud. *Was* it luck? It wasn't the first time the little dog had helped them. When they'd been trapped in the captain's cabin aboard the *Principia*, Cloud had uncovered the only exit. It got Arthur thinking...

"Maybe I'm wrong, but I don't think Cloud's taken a poop since we met him."

Ren frowned. "Weird change of subject, but you're right. He hasn't eaten anything either. Only drunk some water. Do you think he's all right?"

Arthur scratched Cloud between the ears. The dog

yawned, flashing his sharp incisors and pink tongue, then sleepily licked Arthur's hand.

He seemed happy enough.

Arthur checked him over, like he'd seen vets do on TV. His eyes were bright, his nose wet, his tail wagging. Arthur ran a finger around his collar to make sure it wasn't too tight. It was then that he felt some sort of energy pulsing inside, making Arthur's fingertips tingle.

Curious, he inspected the silver disc attached to Cloud's collar. On the front it still read: *Cloud. West Highland Terrier. Male.* It was attached not by a chain or links but by two heavy metal beads. Experimenting, Arthur twisted them both clockwise and heard two clicks.

Suddenly, there wasn't a dog sitting on Arthur's lap any more.

There was a pig.

Arthur yelled. "Ow – it's crushing me!" He tried to wriggle out from underneath the creature's sizeable rump as Ren and Cecily rushed to help.

The mystery pig was over a metre long with tough grey-brown skin covered in coarse hair. It had a wiry blond mane around its pink nose and tassels on its curly tail. A ruby-red collar – exactly the same as Cloud's – hung around its thick neck.

While Ren and Cecily pulled on its rump to get it to stand up, the pig wagged its tail and gave Arthur a friendly nudge with its snout.

"Cloud?" Arthur exclaimed, sliding his legs free.

The pig grunted.

"No way." Ren let go of Cloud's bristly back. "Is the Fuzzball some sort of alien?"

Arthur stared at pig-Cloud's collar. The disc now read: *Cloud. Bornean Bearded Pig. Male.* Thinking of the energy he'd felt thrumming inside it, Arthur shook his head. "No, I think ... he's a *mimic*."

"That explains why he hasn't eaten anything or gone to the toilet," Ren said. "But mimics transmit images back to Hxperion..."

They all tensed. Arthur thought carefully. "Maybe it's just the V-classes and T-classes that do that? If Cloud was a spy, Hxperion would have come after us by now."

Cecily kneeled so she was eye-level with Cloud. "And Cloud has been helping us this whole time. Besides, he's Milo's mimic, not Tiburon's or Valeria's." She smiled and then hugged Cloud's hairy snout. "Mimic or not, we still love you," she told him. "And don't worry, you make a cute pig."

Arthur marvelled at how advanced Cloud's engineering must be to allow him to transform from a small dog to a giant pig in seconds. Theories stirred at the edge of his mind – ideas he knew nothing about. When he examined his Wondercloak, Newton's handwriting was reflected on the surface of the water, just like it had done before the race.

"*Now* it makes sense why Milo fitted the time-key to Cloud's collar," Ren said, patting his wiry back. "He's a superintelligent robot; perhaps he was meant to guard it?"

Arthur thought carefully. "But Cloud trusted us with the time-key straight away. I wonder why."

Once Cecily had finished cuddling pig-Cloud, Arthur set about trying to understand how the collar worked. He played around with the two beads. Twisting the right bead on its own changed the words on the disc. The transformation was then activated by turning the left bead in the same direction.

He clicked the right bead steadily round, reading the different animal options:

Cloud. Brown Rat. Male.

Cloud. American Fuzzy Lop Rabbit. Female.

Cloud. Texas Longhorn Ox. Male.

Something about the selection of animals rang a bell in the back of Arthur's head but he wasn't sure why. Eventually, with his tummy still rumbling, he changed Cloud back into a West Highland terrier, so they could turn their attention to the vending machine.

"What's on the menu?" Ren asked.

"I don't know." Swiping his hand through the air, Arthur turned the pages to peruse the STORE catalogue. There were sections for first aid, consumables, garb, equipment and special items. In garb, you could pick up replacement Wondercloaks in case yours had been damaged, as well as thousands of outfits from different fashions throughout history. Arthur also spotted *I* ♥ *REALM 89* T-shirts and accessories. In equipment, it was possible to select from a variety of wanderer starter packs or pro-wanderer packs, which featured things like night-vision goggles, long-range binoculars, radio transmitters and basic tool kits. Curious, Arthur took a peek at the special items section. Realm-keys weren't listed, but you could order exit-keys, which the catalogue explained opened a Wonderway to the outside world, so you could leave the game. *That must be what happens to wanderers if they don't win a challenge,* he thought. *They have to leave.* Perhaps when a wanderer returned to play, they entered the Wonderscape via a different realm to avoid getting stuck in the same place...

"No wonder my request to leave 'couldn't be processed' before," Cecily muttered. "Let's order an exit-key. It might be useful."

But when Arthur made their selection, a message flashed behind the glass in an alarming shade of red:

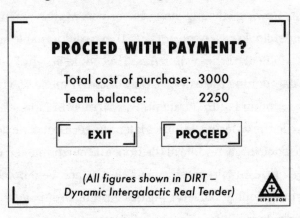

PROCEED WITH PAYMENT?

Total cost of purchase: 3000
Team balance: 2250

EXIT   PROCEED

*(All figures shown in DIRT –
Dynamic Intergalactic Real Tender)*

"Hang on," Cecily said. "Does that mean we have to *pay* for everything?"

Arthur groaned. He couldn't believe he'd come four hundred years into the future and the miserable fact remained that he might not be able to afford stuff. Still, he should have seen it coming; *Wonderscape* was a game, and Hxperion had to be making a profit from it somehow. Dynamic Intergalactic Real Tender was probably twenty-fifth-century money.

"I didn't see anyone walking around with cash or credit cards today," Ren noted. "DIRT must be a cryptocurrency. But how did *we* get over two thousand?"

"I think we each earned it," Arthur said, remembering the messages they'd received. "The loot for completing Voyage of the Captain and Race of the Warrior included a certain amount of DIRT. And if it's a cryptocurrency, it has to be stored digitally somewhere." He considered the water flowing steadily along his arms. "Maybe it's in our Wondercloaks? Newton told us they would enable us to play along like other wanderers. That could be why."

Abandoning the exit-key, they opted to spend 750 DIRT as a team on food. The menu was written in Japanese, so Ren did the ordering. Minutes later, she set a hot plate down on a stone in the middle of the floor and surrounded it with trays of freshly prepared vegetables. There were bowls of rice and dipping sauces, a jug of steaming broth and a dish of soft dumplings. She placed a selection of vegetables onto the hot griddle using a pair of chopsticks and let them sizzle. Soon the three of them were enjoying mouthfuls of the first Japanese food Arthur had ever tasted, and it was delicious.

"This is amazing," he remarked, bringing a bowl of soup to his mouth and preparing to slurp it down. "Thanks, Ren."

"Dinner at my grandparents' is better," she decided, "but this isn't bad."

After they'd eaten and cleared away, Cecily unwound her braids, before lying on the middle futon and staring up at the ceiling. With her turquoise hair spread against the pillow, she looked more like a mermaid than usual. "I'm exhausted," she admitted as Cloud curled up next to her. "I know time's running out, but we need to get some rest – or we'll collapse before we ever make it home."

Arthur glanced at his watch. They'd only been in the Wonderscape the length of a school day but it felt like longer. Perhaps moving between multiple time zones had given them something akin to jet lag.

Sitting on the futon to Cecily's left, he hugged his knees, thinking about home. His dad worked mornings as a cleaner at the local hospital and in the afternoon wrote movie reviews for this geeky website called The Nerd Cave. He was always at home when Arthur got in from school. "Do you think we've been reported missing yet? The school must have rung our families to ask why we didn't turn up for registration."

A line appeared on Cecily's forehead but she didn't say anything.

Ren huffed. "My mums will probably think I've gone truant again."

"Again?" Arthur asked.

Ren was staring into her lap, picking at a loose thread on her trousers. "There were some girls at my old school who used to tease me all the time," she explained, quieter. "I didn't like hearing what they had to say, so I used to bunk off. That's why I got expelled."

Judging from her body language, Arthur got the impression Ren didn't talk about the subject often. "Well, it sounds like your old school was full of morons," he said, making her smile. "I heard you got expelled because you rode a motorbike through the canteen."

"Me too," Cecily said. "And I agree about the morons."

A grin widened across Ren's face. "Is that really what people are saying? That makes me sound awesome."

"I also heard you got tattoos for your birthday," Arthur mentioned. "Is that not true?"

"These?" Ren held up her hand, showing the dark-brown diamond, spade, heart and club motifs on her knuckles. "They're henna. My eighty-year-old next-door neighbour drew them on me!"

The three of them burst into laughter. It felt good to release some of the tension Arthur had been carrying in his body since the race. For the first time, he felt like he was getting to know the real Ren, and she wasn't half as intimidating as he'd initially thought.

Ren threw a cushion at Cecily. "Hey, I'm sorry I snapped at you earlier when you asked about my mum. I'm just used to people judging my family before they even know us."

"I get it," Cecily said, smiling wearily. It didn't take a Newton-level genius to sense that something was wrong, but Arthur didn't press the matter. He imagined she was probably feeling as overwhelmed and as anxious as he was. She might even have the same horrible thought swimming around her head: that after everything they'd been through, they still might not survive this.

After removing their outer layers, they all slid under their Wondercloaks, using them as blankets. Cecily's sunflowers slowly closed their petals, changing from brilliant yellow to dusky gold; Ren's blueprints shifted to show designs for a baby's crib, complete with a bunny-shaped mobile. Arthur considered telling her about it when she woke up, but pictured the look on her face and decided he wasn't brave enough.

Too restless to settle, he inspected the inner lining of his Wondercloak, casting his eye over the countless realms of the Wonderscape. If Milo Hertz *was* returning to visit one of them, Arthur wondered which he'd choose. His gaze fell on a green planet covered in mountains and rocky canyons. The flashing label around the outside read, *REALM 89: PLANET ATARIA, KALLEDRON GALAXY*. With a deep sigh, he reflected just how far from home they were. Not only had they jumped four hundred years into the future, they'd also travelled to a planet *outside* the Milky Way.

The task of getting home felt even more daunting.

12

Arthur slept soundly but woke with a start. For a blissful, hazy second, he didn't recognize his surroundings – the distant coffered ceiling, the suits of armour standing guard, the dusty smell of straw – then the events of the previous day came flooding back to him and he sat bolt upright with a jolt.

The orbs in the corner of the room glowed with dim green light. Cecily stirred on the futon next to him. "Arthur?" She rubbed her face, looking bleary-eyed. "Are you OK?"

"Sorry," he whispered. "I didn't mean to wake you."

She propped her head up, resting on her elbows. "Is it morning? Have we overslept?"

"I don't know." He pulled back his Wondercloak and got to his feet. Sleeping in the same clothes he'd been wearing since they'd left the *Principia* hadn't exactly been comfortable, but at least he'd been warm. He slid open the shoji. The corridor outside was dark.

Examining his watch, Arthur saw they had thirty-seven

hours left to get home, meaning – he counted on his fingers – they'd slept for eight hours. "We have to get up!" he said urgently. "We still need to find Milo Hertz." He wasn't sure how they were going to locate the runaway now the Wonderdome was off-limits, but they could discuss all that once they were on the move.

Cecily quickly arranged her hair into a single French plait. Cloud bounded onto Ren's futon and dragged his pink tongue over her cheek.

"Wher—? Wha—?" Ren sprang up, flapping her hands around her face. Her gaze flicked from Cloud, to the futon, to the suits of armour. "Are we still trapped in the future?"

Arthur gave her a glum smile. "Afraid so."

She scowled and tightened her ponytail, then pulled on her gilet. As she reached for her Wondercloak, she hesitated. "Hey, are your Wondercloaks doing that too?"

The blueprints on Ren's cloak showed designs for a set of hazard warning lights. Arthur checked his sleeves and saw that the water was dark and churning with whirlpools.

"It's as if they're trying to alert us," Cecily said, examining the sunflowers on her own cloak, which were opening and closing very quickly.

There was a clatter in the hallway and Tomoe Gozen came charging through the shoji with a long sword gripped in her hand. She had a white ribbon tied around her head and a large wooden bow slung over her brightly coloured armour. "You're in danger," she said, dropping a sack of shoes on the floor. "Put these on and follow me."

"What do you mean?" Arthur spluttered, grabbing his trainers from the pile.

Cecily fumbled with Cloud's lead as she fixed it to his collar. "Why are we in danger?"

"There's been a slight problem," Tomoe replied. "I'll explain on the way. Hurry!"

They rushed out of the hall and into a long corridor displaying more of Tomoe's weapons collection. Arthur heard the whir of hover-wheels and the clash of heavy weapons in another part of the house. He got a sinking feeling in his stomach. "What's going on?"

"This way." Tomoe signalled left. "Stay close."

They hurtled around a corner …

… and came face to face with two V-class mimics dressed in green overalls. One had a nasty gash in her waist; the other was missing an arm and had a bouquet of spiky wires protruding from the empty socket. Judging from the way they glowered at Tomoe, Arthur reckoned they'd both had recent encounters with her sword.

"Is *this* the slight problem?" he asked in a high-pitched voice, backing away.

"We're taking a different route," the warrior decided hastily. Sliding open a nearby shoji, she steered the four of them into another room covered in tatami mats. This time they ran across with their shoes on.

Arthur glanced over his shoulder. The V-class units had

given chase, but thanks to their various injuries were wobbling all over the place. "Why are they coming after us?"

"Because I've broken one of Hxperion's rules and they think I've told you why," Tomoe said. She rounded another corner, opened a heavy wooden door and herded them into a cramped room containing a large ebony cabinet on one side and a folding screen made from six panels of painted silk on the other.

Rules? Arthur didn't follow.

"We should be safe here for a short while," Tomoe decided, bolting the door closed and hauling the ebony cabinet in front of it. "I need you to listen carefully." She signalled to the folding screen. Painted on the surface was a hilly green landscape dotted with trees and rivers. In the centre, two mounted samurai armies charged towards each other. "This shows the Battle of Tonamiyama, in the year 1183."

Cecily's face brightened. "I read about this! You led over a thousand samurais into battle. It was one of your most famous victories."

"Apparently so," Tomoe said flatly. "I have no memory of the conflict. The night before the battle I was approached by a *yamabushi*, a mystic from the mountains. He offered to give me a blessing." She scowled. "But I was tricked. The *yamabushi* was someone else in disguise. His 'blessing' put me to sleep and when I awoke, I found myself in the Wonderscape. Except..." Her voice faltered. "Except, I *wasn't* myself."

With her back to them, Tomoe lifted her long black hair so that the base of her skull was visible. Arthur spotted something glinting in her hairline and squinted to see what it was. His blood turned cold when he realized.

Tomoe's skin had a *zip pull*.

Arthur edged back in horror as the warrior tugged it open a few centimetres, revealing several paper-thin layers of metal and an intricate network of glowing wires – the inner workings of a complex *machine*. "You're … a *mimic*," he breathed.

Emotion shone in Tomoe's dark eyes as she turned back around. "*All* the heroes in the Wonderscape are."

Cecily's jaw fell open. "I, uh … *how*?"

Arthur was struggling to make sense of it all too. If Tomoe was a mimic, how could she also be the *real* Tomoe Gozen?

"There is much to say," the warrior continued. "You three are the first wanderers I've ever spoken to, and therefore the first people I've had the chance to reveal the truth to. It was too risky to talk yesterday; there were V-classes everywhere."

Arthur remembered something the warrior had said the evening before, about a new opportunity that she needed to prepare for. This must have been what she meant. Perhaps that was also why Newton hadn't told them the truth – because there was never a safe instance.

Ren started pacing up and down by the cabinet-barricade. "I don't get it. If you're a mimic – and Newton too – then how are you so *real*? You have the same personalities, memories and skills as the actual people."

Whatever class of mimic the heroes were, Arthur figured it was a lot more advanced than the others they'd met so far; except maybe Cloud. Ideas burst like fireworks at the edge of his mind as he endeavoured to puzzle it out. He felt the same tingle at the base of his skull as he had before the race, and looked at the sleeves of his Wondercloak to discover Newton's handwriting swirling in the water...

At that moment, the walls tremored like a heavy lorry had just driven by outside. Tomoe scowled. "Listen carefully: this body may have been manufactured by Hxperion, but the spirit inside it is *real*." She pounded a fist against her heart, making the three of them flinch. "I am Tomoe Gozen, First Captain of Minamoto no Yoshinaka. My memories, emotions, fascinations, dreams and passions – they're all mine. But I can't be myself."

Arthur didn't understand how that could be true. Then he felt the base of his skull prickle again and before he knew it, thoughts floated to the surface of his mind. They were all about *computational neuroscience*, which he'd never heard of before, but suddenly realized he knew a lot about.

"Inside our brains is a network of billions of neurons," he said to Ren and Cecily. "By sending chemical signals to each other, they enable us to process information. Computers work in a similar way, except they use transistors to send signals around a circuit."

Ren's gaze shifted to Arthur's Wondercloak; the water flowed with Newton's handwriting. "OK…"

"Our consciousness, which contains all our memories and personality, is stored in our brains, like files are stored on a hard drive," Arthur continued. "So what if it were possible to copy all the files in someone's brain and download them somewhere else? What if this stranger disguised as a *yamabushi* was sent back in time to make a copy of Tomoe's mind, bring it to the Wonderscape and download it onto a mimic?"

Ren stopped pacing. "That would mean the original Tomoe Gozen claimed victory in the Battle of Tonamiyama and continued her life on Earth, while the other version –" she glanced shyly at Tomoe – "moved here."

"And it would explain why Newton was wearing unicorn slippers," Arthur said. When the others frowned at him, he added, "What I mean is, the heroes in the Wonderscape aren't the same people they were on Earth. Waking up to realize you're a mimic trapped centuries in the future must change you."

"Is that true?" Cecily asked Tomoe, her voice tinged with disbelief. "Is that what happened?"

Tomoe rubbed the back of her neck. "This world and its science is far removed from the one I left. I do not know *how* this happened, but I do know *who* is responsible. The stranger who came to me disguised as a *yamabushi* – his eyes are everywhere in the Wonderscape."

Arthur could only think of two people who had their eyes everywhere, and one of them was a woman. Which meant... "Tiburon Nox," he said grimly. "*He* did this to you."

"And to every other hero, I assume," Ren said, tightening her fists. "At some point in his life, Professor Newton must have encountered Tiburon before waking up here as a mimic. Tiburon has torn them all away from their families and friends, from their whole lives!"

Cecily's nostrils flared. "How could anyone do something so cruel? They must feel so trapped, so alone. And all for a *game*!"

Arthur tried to imagine how he would feel if the "original" him was currently getting on with life at home with his dad, while *his* consciousness was imprisoned inside a robot body, forced to entertain people in a game. It made him flush with anger.

Just then, voices sounded in the corridor outside. Arthur thought he heard the words "trapped" and "wanderers".

Tomoe drew her sword. "We have run out of time." Using the tip of her blade, she reached above the ebony cabinet and slid open a hidden panel in the wall, revealing a square, shadowy tunnel the width of a wheelie bin. "This will lead you outside. Hurry."

Hearing the hum of hover-wheels near by, Arthur didn't need to be told twice. "You said you broke one of Hxperion's rules. What was it?" he asked, weaving his fingers into a basket in order to give Cecily a boost.

"I didn't attend the first race of the day. A V-class would have driven the White Tiger in my place," Tomoe said, passing up Cloud. "Every hero is expected to participate in realm-challenges; to keep the secrets of the Wonderscape; and to never, *ever* venture outside of their realm. Those are Hxperion's three conditions."

Cecily poked her head into the tunnel, scrunched her nose and crawled inside. Cloud trundled after her.

"And ... what will they do if they catch you?" Arthur asked, quieter. There had to be a reason the heroes were afraid of Hxperion, especially someone as fearless as Tomoe Gozen.

As Ren clambered onto the cabinet using the handle as a foothold, the ancient warrior gazed over at the silk screen with a haunted look in her eyes. "My two older brothers are generals in Yoshinaka's army. If I disobey Hxperion, Tiburon Nox will ensure they perish in the Battle of Tonamiyama, and their future lives will be unwritten."

Ren froze mid-climb. *"What?"*

Cold fingers traced the length of Arthur's spine. *Tiburon is controlling the heroes by threatening to go back in time and murder their loved ones?* It was so wicked and deplorable a scheme he could barely believe it. "That's... I mean... He's messing with history! He's a maniac!"

"With a time-key," Ren murmured bleakly. She threw a meaningful glance at Arthur, who instantly got her gist. If Tiburon Nox had been zipping backwards and forwards in time creating all the hero-mimics, he had to have a time-key.

Which meant Milo Hertz had made more than one.

"I've never faced such a powerful or dishonourable enemy," Tomoe admitted, giving Arthur a shoulder to lean on as he scaled the cabinet. "That's why I need your help. You see, to have a chance of vanquishing Tiburon, I must leave this realm with you. There is a Wonderway beyond my garden, on the edge of the forest. We can use the realm-key you've won to open it." She held her blade aloft. "Now you've talked to me, Hxperion will see you as a threat – that's why you're in danger. I'll head Valeria's forces off at the front while you sneak around the back and run across the garden. I'll meet you at the Wonderway."

13

The tunnel was dark, cramped and reeked of bird poo. Arthur presumed it didn't get cleaned much since the mimics probably weren't aware of its existence, and Tomoe was always off racing. Pinching his nostrils shut with one hand, he shuffled forwards on the other, tailing Ren.

Thoughts swirled like windswept ashes in his head. *The heroes are all mimics… Time is running out… Tiburon Nox has a time-key…* He wondered how Tiburon had got hold of it and whether it was somehow connected to Milo's decision to run away.

Light shimmered in the distance. "There's a shaft here that opens onto the sky," Cecily called from the front. "And a ladder. Can you back up a little?"

He and Ren reversed a few paces to give Cecily more room. Dust fell from the tunnel walls as she and Cloud wiggled into the opening and disappeared.

They emerged onto a flat square of concrete in the middle of the roof. Mossy black tiles sloped down on all sides towards Tomoe's garden, and in the distance a strange double-sun was dawning through the trees, casting long shadows across the warrior's plants.

"Erg!" Cecily moaned, holding one hand over her eyes and another out to balance. "Everything's spinning."

Arthur grabbed her arm just as she was swaying towards the edge. "Don't worry, I've got you."

Ahead, the road they had driven in on was obscured by forest. Arthur couldn't see or hear any sign of Tomoe Gozen, or the two wounded V-class mimics that had been chasing them earlier, which made him nervy. Over his shoulder, he spotted the top of a wooden ladder peeking above the guttering. "It must be this way. Come on!"

Then the roar of engines sounded from the road. "Get down!" Ren cried.

They dropped to their knees as a pack of open-topped buggies blasted through the trees and swerved into Tomoe's garden. Arthur recognized their design from a vehicle he'd seen in the race, but these were painted bottle-green, not red, and plastered with Valeria's triangle. Half a dozen V-class mimics dressed in race overalls sat in the back of each, clutching spanners, tyres or paint cans.

Once the buggies had come to a stop, the mimics filed out and rocketed straight to Tomoe's front door. Six units wearing khaki combat apparel emptied from the lead vehicle and started shouting orders. Glossy red pony-tails swung from their baseball caps, where the word

SECURITY was stencilled in glitter.

"Find the subordinate!"

"Use the weapons on the walls!"

Arthur noticed black utility belts strapped around their waists, containing perfume bottles, hairbrushes, lipsticks and compact mirrors. For a moment he wondered if they were intending to *style* Tomoe Gozen into submission, but then Cecily grabbed his wrist. "Are those make-up themed weapons?" she hissed, sounding horrified.

Squinting, Arthur realized she was right. The hairbrushes had razor-sharp spikes; the perfume bottles were actually grenades with gold pull rings, and the lipsticks were rounds of ammo. There was something extra chilling about the creepy creativity that had gone into their design.

"Something must have happened to Tomoe," Ren whispered, further along. "She was meant to head them off at the front."

"We'll just have to reach the Wonderway ourselves and hope she meets us there," Arthur decided. "Let's start movi—" But his sentence was cut short as an amused voice filled the air.

"*There* you are, Pipsqueaks!"

Down below, a figure stood silhouetted in the headlights of the lead buggy. She was dressed in a cropped fur coat and wide palazzo trousers, both dyed the same shade of seafoam-green. Fear closed Arthur's throat as he realized their chances of getting home might have just nosedived. That was Valeria Mal'fey.

"You have my congratulations," she called, waving a gloved hand. "The White Tiger has finally been beaten!" The liquid-silver surface of her Wondercloak rippled as she moved, distorting the reflections of two security mimics standing at either shoulder. "I'm sorry to have to interrupt your game, but one of the mimics in this building has malfunctioned and we're here to remove it. If you'd like to come with me, I'll get you to safety."

Ren looked across at Arthur and slowly shook her head. After what Tomoe had told them, he felt the same: going with Valeria would *not* improve their safety. He wasn't sure if Valeria was helping Tiburon with his evil scheme or not, but she definitely couldn't be trusted. Instead, he desperately tried to formulate an escape plan. If they made a run for it, he felt certain they'd be caught, and with the house swarming with mimics there was no point retreating into the tunnel. Mustering his courage, he shouted, "We're not going anywhere with you!" He hoped to at least buy them some time.

Valeria smiled, flashing unnaturally white teeth. "You mean, you *don't* want an exclusive behind-the-scenes tour of my headquarters?"

Right at that moment, Cloud twisted free from under Ren's arm and starting barking so furiously she had to seize him before he fell off the roof.

Recognition drew across Valeria's face like a shadow.

"I *know* you," she muttered. "You're *Milo's* pet." Her smile shrank at the edges. "Does my little brother have something to do with this? Are you three working for that traitor?" With a stomp of her heel, she pointed to the roof and screamed, "GET THEM!"

And just like that, making a run for it became the best plan Arthur had. "Go!" he cried, leaping to his feet. The others sprang up and scrambled towards the rear of the roof, but as they approached the ladder, the khaki baseball cap of a security V-class rose over the edge. Grinning maniacally, she was holding what appeared to be a glittery hair-clip-cum-throwing-star in one hand.

Arthur swivelled on his heels, unsure where to go. Ren lifted up a couple of roof tiles and hurled them in the mimic's direction. "Get away from us!"

"Grrf!" Cloud barked in support.

Glancing at their fluffy mimic companion, Arthur had an idea. "Stand back!" he said, crouching to adjust Cloud's collar. Twisting round the right-hand bead, he frantically searched for the name of a creature he'd seen last night.

"I don't think rat-Cloud or pig-Cloud can help us now!" Cecily shrieked, as the mimic advanced. But it wasn't either of those animals Arthur was searching for. His heart thudded as he found the one he wanted: *Cloud. Green-winged Dragon. Female.*

With a twist of the left-hand bead, the transformation activated.

Everything happened imperceptibly fast. Cloud's stubby legs lengthened; his body enlarged; giant claws grew from his fluffy paws and his white fur was replaced by emerald-green scales. Tiles cascaded from the roof and shattered down below as the dragon grappled for a foothold.

With a flick of her tail, Cloud thwacked the approaching mimic twenty metres into the air and it landed with a squelch in the mud of Tomoe's garden.

Ren cheered. "Yes, Fuzzball!"

Arthur grabbed Cecily's hand and dragged her up the side of Cloud's dragon-body. "Come on – this is our ride out of here!" Once Ren had clambered onto the tail end, they took off.

On the ground, Valeria roared, "You can't escape me! Not while you're in the Wonderscape!"

With her eyes squeezed shut, Cecily wrapped her arms around Arthur's waist. "Don't you dare let go!" she yelled in his ear.

"I won't. I promise!" Straddled across Cloud's back, Arthur tightened his grip on the now giant-sized ruby collar on the dragon's neck. Wind thrashed through his hair, making his cheeks glow.

I'm flying on a robot dragon.

I'm FLYING on a ROBOT DRAGON!

The situation was something out of a dream, but Arthur had never felt more awake. Adrenaline coursed through his body, his senses on high alert. He could hear Cloud's ragged breathing and smell her strange dragon odour in the air, like a mix of burnt toast and black treacle. As they soared higher, he pressed his knees into her thick hide, feeling the ridges of her scales digging into his thighs.

Despite being the size of a lorry, Cloud flew with expert grace, swinging her long tail for balance and flapping her eight-metre-wide wings to lift them higher. Far below, Tomoe's house shrunk to the size of a matchbox.

For a few minutes, they glided in circles above Tomoe's garden with nothing but the thud of Cloud's wings to keep them company. Then Ren cried, "The Wonderway! Over there!"

Arthur didn't turn to see where she was pointing; one false move and he'd slip off Cloud's back and fall hundreds of metres. Instead, he stretched forwards and patted Cloud's leathery cheek. "Can you see what Ren's spotted, girl?" It felt strange calling Cloud a girl, but Arthur was getting used to strange in the Wonderscape.

The cat-like pupils in Cloud's yellow eyes flitted. She gave a thundering roar, which made Arthur's ribs shake, and swerved to the left. "Hold on!" he shouted, clinging to the horns on her spine.

Cecily screamed as they banked lower. Ahead, between the edge of Tomoe's garden and the forest, was a clearing wide enough for a dragon to land in. As they flew closer, Arthur spotted a huge black frame standing in the trees – a Wonderway.

Cloud beat her wings as they hovered into the space, dust swirling into the air.

"Prepare to land!" Arthur called, reaching for the disc on Cloud's collar. He twisted the bead on the right until the disc read *West Highland Terrier. Male* again and once they were close enough to the ground, he clicked the left-hand bead to trigger the transformation...

At which point, he narrowly avoided doing the splits, as a fluffy white dog padded out through his legs.

"Watch out – we've got company!" Ren cried.

An angry shout came from behind. Arthur turned to see the two wounded V-class units from earlier had been joined by a third. While they carried axes, she had a spiky iron club raised threateningly above her head.

The Wonderway wasn't far. Arthur had started to make a run for it when he heard a loud whinny and a huge black horse came galloping through the trees.

Tomoe Gozen was riding towards them, her long sword gripped in her right hand. Tugging the horse's red bridle with her left, she charged the mimics and swung her blade, striking all three of them at once.

The two axe-wielding mimics staggered back. The V-class with the club swiped at Tomoe's legs, but the warrior easily parried her blows.

In a blur of black hair and silver sword, Tomoe dismounted her horse and delivered two, three, four hits to the mimics, moving with dancer-like grace. Arthur was mesmerized. Tomoe seemed to predict the V-classes' every move, dodging aside just in time, and then aiming directly for their weak spots. She handled her mammoth sword as if it weighed no more than a feather.

In a few seconds, it was over. With one final blow, Tomoe struck the remaining mimic at the waist and she dropped to the ground to join a scrambled mess of other V-class body parts. Despite her exertion, Tomoe wasn't even out of breath when she turned to face them. She sheathed her sword across her back and walked over. "There are far more than I expected," she told them gravely. "The plan has changed. Which among you collected the realm-key?"

Arthur glanced at Ren, who nervously stepped forwards. Tomoe laid a hand on her shoulder. "Use the talent only when you need to," she advised cryptically. Her eyes drifted to Arthur and Cecily. "I didn't intend for this, but I must ask the three of you to continue my mission. You have to stop Tiburon and free the other heroes."

"*What?!*" Arthur said, his heart racing. They couldn't possibly defeat Tiburon on their own! Apart from anything else, they were already busy trying to prevent the universe from turning them into slime. "Why can't you come with us?"

Her brows drew together. "I have fought many battles and I know when the odds are against me. If I don't take a stand here, we'll all be overrun and *none* of us will make it to the Wonderway. Better that you three escape, at least."

Arthur gulped. Judging by the seriousness of her tone, there was no opening for argument. Cloud started whimpering, so Cecily bundled him into her arms and let him bury his head under her Wondercloak. "It's all right, boy," she murmured softly. "We're going to be OK." But as she stared at Arthur, her face flushed with panic.

The growl of a chainsaw sounded in the distance. Tomoe spun round towards the house, her hair swinging behind her.

The ground rumbled as a mob of V-class mimics stampeded over the hill, their hover-wheels churning up the plants and soil in Tomoe's garden. At the head of the pack were a couple of security mimics brandishing perfume-bottle grenades; the others had made do with spears, axes and swords from Tomoe's house.

"These are for you," Tomoe said, hastily removing a leather quiver of arrows from the back of her saddle, and passing it to Ren. She unshouldered her bow and handed it over too. "Use them well."

Ren cradled the items in her arms like they were made of highly breakable china. The bow was taller than her. "Thank you," she spluttered, "but I don't know archery."

"Yes, you do," Tomoe said, leaping back onto her horse. "Now shoot fast and aim for the joints, that's where mimics are vulnerable. And remember: heroes come in all shapes and sizes!" With a defiant smile, she pressed her heels into the horse's haunches and stormed into the fray.

"Wait!" Ren called after her, slinging the strap of the

quiver over her head. She pulled out an arrow and waved it at Arthur and Cecily. "What am I meant to do now?"

Arthur noticed the blueprints on Ren's Wondercloak change into the design for a large black comma. Remembering how the water on his cloak had swirled with Newton's handwriting earlier, he made an educated guess. "I think when you and I collected those realm-keys, we also received something else mentioned in the loot – a Wonderskill."

"Skill, as in a talent?" Ren questioned.

He nodded. "It's something to do with our Wondercloaks. I think mine allows me to access Newton's knowledge of science and algebra – it's the only way to explain how I know all these new things. Perhaps your Wonderskill is Tomoe's archery abilities? Try shooting at something."

"Preferably her!" Cecily shrieked, pointing to a charging mimic, who had slipped past Tomoe and was about to hurl a spear in their direction.

A determined scowl burrowed into Ren's brow as she clasped the bow in both hands. The blueprints on her cloak shifted into plans for a target board.

In one swift movement she notched an arrow, drew the bowstring and aimed. The arrow gave a soft *shhft* as it fired. Arthur traced its path through the air. At the edge of his mind, the equations for kinetic energy, momentum and force whirled around, but he didn't reach for them.

With a dull thud, the arrow buried itself into the mimic's

hip joint. Her hover-wheels jarred, she toppled off balance and flipped head first into a pond.

But there wasn't time to celebrate. "Run!" Cecily cried.

By the time they'd made it to the Wonderway, Arthur could hear the clash of Tomoe's sword behind him. Ren retrieved the realm-key from a pocket in her combat trousers and kneeled at the foot of the black frame. "Which realm should we travel to?" she asked, her fingers hovering over the keypad.

In all the chaos, Arthur had forgotten that they hadn't decided where to go next. "Err…"

While he hesitated, Cloud wriggled free of Cecily's grasp and landed in the dirt. He shook himself clean and scampered under Ren's hand, tapping the keypad confidently with his nose: *105.*

"Cloud, what are you—?" Ren spluttered. But it was too late. The realm-key shot out of her fingers and disappeared into the hexagonal hole at the bottom of the Wonderway.

The frame instantly transformed into a mass of spiralling blue smoke. This time, the door in the centre was a tent flap made of oiled khaki canvas. It was decorated with strange gold writing and as a warm breeze blew under it, a few grains of sand skittered to the forest floor in Tomoe's realm.

"The realm-key's gone," Ren said urgently. "We'll have to go through, wherever it leads."

Arthur glanced over his shoulder. Tomoe's horse was

surrounded by mimics and she was swinging her blade in all directions, her face straining with effort. He wished there was something they could do to save her but he felt helpless.

Ren notched another arrow. "There could be more mimics on the other side."

With no other option, Arthur tore his gaze away from Tomoe and lifted the tent flap. Before either Ren or Cecily could go first, he stepped through the opening.

14

The highest temperatures Arthur had ever experienced were during a heatwave a couple of summers ago, when the grass in his back garden had turned yellow and the tarmac on Peacepoint Estate had started to feel sticky underfoot.

But this new realm was even more sweltering than that.

Sweat trickled down his forehead as he viewed the landscape. Rolling turmeric sand dunes stretched in all directions as far as the eye could see. To his relief, there was no one and nothing else around. Arthur thought deserts were supposed to be dry, but the air felt humid, like inside a bathroom after someone had taken a steamy shower.

He stripped off all non-essential layers and stuffed them into his rucksack before turning up the bottoms of his jeans to air his ankles. He would have taken his Wondercloak off too, but it was the only thing that actually made him feel cooler – undoubtedly another of its advanced features.

"Where have you brought us, Fuzzball?" Ren asked.

Arthur watched Cloud wiggling his rear end, preparing

to spring into the sand. "He knew exactly how to operate that Wonderway. That must be how he's been travelling on his own."

"He could have chosen somewhere cooler; this is gross," Cecily muttered, her face glistening as she tied her leather jacket around her waist. Ren folded up her sleeves and stuffed her gilet into her quiver.

Whatever planet they were on, it must have been around midday, because the sun was high in the sky. Arthur flapped open his Wondercloak and checked the lining for a planet ringed by flashing text: *REALM 105: PLANET TYR, HORSETAIL GALAXY*. According to the image on the planet's surface, there was more than desert in this realm. Arthur could make out cities with towering skyscrapers and huge industrial ports. Sand shifted beneath his feet as he climbed to the top of a dune and squinted into the distance.

"See anything?" Cecily called, helping Ren redo her hair.

Arthur shielded his eyes from the glare of the sun. A cluster of dark rooftops and umbrella-shaped palms shimmered near the horizon. "There's a settlement of some sort, but it's a bit of a trek."

"Then let's get going," Ren said, replacing her bow across her shoulders. With her fringe pinned back, you could see her whole scowl for once. "The sooner we get there, the sooner we can find out why Cloud brought us here. He must have had a reason. Also, you never know when a V-class will pop up. We should keep moving."

With a shiver, Arthur assessed their surroundings for places mimics might jump out from. He hoped the Wonderscape worked differently to some of the video games he had played, where the bad guys spawned randomly out of thin air.

"Do you think Valeria will be able to track us?" Cecily asked worriedly. "Perhaps she can tap into our location via our Wondercloaks?"

Arthur rubbed the edge of his cloak between his fingers. "Maybe, but if we take them off we'll only draw attention to ourselves. I haven't seen a single wanderer who wasn't wearing one."

"That, and we won't be able to use our Wonderskills any more," Ren pointed out. "And they've saved our lives at least twice so far."

With a sigh, Cecily reluctantly agreed to keep hers on. As they set off, Ren swung round her gifts from Tomoe Gozen to examine them in more detail. Arthur noticed the leather quiver had gold kanji written on it.

"What does it say?" he asked, trudging forwards.

"I'm not sure what the exact translation is: 'bravery of the tiger' or maybe 'tiger's courage'." She glanced over at him. "It's strange – whenever I touch the bow, I feel this force surge into me from my Wondercloak. I've never held a bow before today, but somehow it's like I've been an archer my whole life."

"Probably because Tomoe Gozen was," Arthur said. "You've inherited her talent for archery, just like I've gained Newton's knowledge of maths and science." He concentrated on his memory of Ren's speeding arrow, and facts about motion, wind speed and acceleration bubbled to the surface of his mind. When he inspected his Wondercloak, there was Newton's handwriting, shining in the puddles on his arms. "It's like our Wondercloaks temporarily give us their abilities. That must be why they're called Wonderskills."

Cloud was panting as he trotted beside Cecily, the drying mud from Tomoe's garden crumbling from his paws. "It's a pity we can't use one of your Wonderskills to help us locate Milo Hertz," she said. "I've been thinking: Tiburon might not be acting alone. One of his siblings could be helping him."

"Yeah, and I don't think Valeria and Milo can be on the same side," Ren decided. "She called him a traitor. Perhaps that's why they argued at the Expo?"

"We have to hope Milo's on the side of the heroes," Arthur said. "After all, he's the one we're searching for."

"Is that *all* we're doing now?" Cecily asked. "I know we've got to get home but Tomoe Gozen said it was up to us to continue her mission. She sacrificed herself so we could escape; we can't let it have been for nothing, *can* we?"

Thinking of the legendary warrior, Arthur's heart sank. He wondered what had become of her after they'd gone. With any luck, she'd retreated into the forest on her horse and was still evading capture. Her request had been so unexpected, he still hadn't had time to process it. "What's happening to the heroes is awful but how are the three of us supposed to stop Tiburon and help them escape? If we slip up, Tiburon has the power to go back in time and kill *our* loved ones. Plus, he's got unlimited resources and an army of robots on his side. All we've got is Cloud, a couple of Wonderskills and the imminent threat that we'll soon turn into protoplasm."

"That's the problem," Cecily said, her voice hollow. "We've already got an important mission of our own. Perhaps if Tomoe had known, she wouldn't have asked?"

Ren's jaw tightened. "But she did ask. I know the odds are stacked against us, but we're possibly the only wanderers who know the truth. We can't just ignore that and abandon the heroes. Plus, Tomoe Gozen believed in us. That's got to count for something."

They trudged on in silence for a few minutes, mulling it over. Arthur stared at his footprints disappearing into the sand and imagined what would happen if they made it home *without* helping the heroes. He'd probably feel guilty for the rest of his life. "Ren's right," he said eventually. "We've got to find a way for us to get home *and* save the heroes. Milo Hertz could help do both. Our priority should still be to find him."

Ren looked down at Cloud. "In that case, we better figure out why Milo's Fuzzball brought us to this realm."

Travelling across a desert, it turned out, was very sticky

work. After traipsing over his third dune, Arthur was perspiring so much the inner soles of his trainers started to squelch. Sand got everywhere – inside his socks and jeans, down his T-shirt and under his fingernails. Fortunately, he'd filled his Pipsqueaks bottle with water from the vending machine the previous evening, although he still had to ration it. It took over two hours before they were close enough to see their destination in more detail, at which point it became obvious that it was a lot bigger than Arthur had first thought.

The various rooftops – some made of corrugated steel, others decorated with colourful tiles – continued far into the distance and between the golden minarets of mosques there were flashing signs for hotels and restaurants.

Eventually, as the light was dimming, the dunes levelled out and the sand sprouted with thorny evergreen bushes and pale brown grass. Sweaty and exhausted, they spotted a long caravan of camels plodding towards what seemed to be the entrance to the city – a wide stone archway between two round towers. Fine-clothed T-class mimics wearing turbans were riding on top.

"Do you think they can see us?" Arthur hissed. He bent his knees, ready to run. "Maybe we should find a place to hide?"

"Behind *what*, genius?" Ren replied. "We're in a desert. There's nothing but sand."

Arthur was about to suggest that they could always

make like meerkats and burrow when Cloud yapped and scampered off towards the camels.

"I *knew* I should have kept him on his lead," Cecily whispered, stomping her foot. "Come on, we have to follow him – he's got the time-key!"

Hoods up and heads down, they reluctantly slipped alongside the caravan. Cecily hastily grabbed Cloud, re-attached his lead to his collar and tucked him under her cloak.

"Well, they're not jumping off those camels to attack us," Ren observed. "I wonder why."

Arthur peered up at the closest T-class, whose droopy grey cheeks were like melted plasticine. He cast his cold blue eyes over Arthur, but didn't pay him any attention. "Maybe Valeria hasn't told Tiburon about us yet?" Arthur suggested, keeping his voice low. "The T-classes get their orders directly from him. We need to stay alert."

The camels snorted as they lumbered on. Hanging from their saddles were baskets of dates, jugs of sloshing liquid and leather coffers filled with grains.

As the four of them passed through the archway, they were greeted by the chaos of a noisy marketplace bustling with T-class mimics, wanderers and animals. Stalls sold everything from spiced cooked meats and ring-shaped bread dotted with dark fruit, to tablecloths and teapots, and stood between enclosures of grunting cattle and honking ostriches. Arthur briefly wondered if the vendors traded in DIRT, and if you could pay for goods with your Wondercloak. The air stank of camel dung and heavy incense, both of which made his nose tingle.

Up on his tiptoes, he spotted a quiet side road in the shade branching off from the main thoroughfare and guided Cloud, Ren and Cecily over. As they squeezed between tightly packed groups of wanderers, there seemed to be only one topic of conversation on everyone's lips:

"The hero is a writer; everyone says so."

"They *say* he's a cartographer."

"Nonsense. He flew airships; he was an aeronaut."

"His ship was definitely named *Lulu*."

"It was called *Lola*."

"Don't be ridiculous, its nickname was *Leeloo*."

By the time Arthur had broken through the crowd and reached the quiet side street, he'd heard people say that the hero was an anthropologist, an academic, a poet, a holy man, a historian *and* an astronomer. The name of his mysterious ship had tens of variations, all beginning with the letter *L*. Arthur didn't have the foggiest who it could be.

The four of them paused between a souvenir shop offering Hxperion-branded T-shirts and biographies of Wonderscape heroes and a kiosk selling deep-fried balls of swirling pink gas, called timefritters. Judging from the holographic poster hovering above the awning, the balls seemed to explode in your mouth like nuclear-grade popping candy. Arthur wouldn't have been surprised if they caused choking, knowing how dangerous everything in the Wonderscape was.

Cloud whimpered and tugged on his lead, aiming his nose towards the end of the road. "All right, all right," Cecily said, gently pulling back. "We get the message. You want to go that way."

"Look there," Ren said, pointing over the rooftops in the same direction.

A few roads away, above a wide thatched roof, a message was written in red vapour.

WONDERSC△PE

REALM 105: LAND OF THE EXPLORER

Loot: 250 DIRT, Wonderskill and realm-key

Travel with wonder,

HXPERION

Although the other messages they'd seen had disappeared, this one seemed to be permanent. *Which means it's probably been placed somewhere important*, Arthur thought.

The air buzzed as another riddle scroll dropped out of

thin air and landed at Ren's feet. She unfurled it for them all to see. Unlike the previous two, it wasn't handwritten, but typed in a neat font:

> *Yonder lies a world to explore,*
> *Accept my challenge and take the tour.*
> *Search the ocean, city and sand*
> *To seek what is hidden in this land.*
> *Over the rooftops I travel free;*
> *Your task is simple: find me.*

"No wonder everyone's gossiping about the hero," Cecily remarked. "The realm-challenge is like a giant game of hide-and-seek – wanderers have to *find* him."

Ren grumbled. "We're already on a man-hunt. We don't need another one."

Cloud held his chin high and wagged his tail as he trotted forwards, leading them through the city. Arthur wondered if the reason the little dog had brought them here was related to this mysterious hero, or if there was something else important about this realm.

Trailing behind, they passed a wagon filled with honey jars that appeared to be moving of its own accord, and a booth selling spices in floating brass bowls. They dodged a troop of strange armoured peacocks and turned into a vast clearing with the thatched building in the centre. Despite the structure being big enough to house an entire department store, it had no doors or windows. Instead, the curved walls were plastered with *postcards*. In the middle of them all was a handwritten notice using red ink on parchment that read:

IGC Restrictions and Guidelines

— Postcards cost 20 DIRT each

— Messages must not exceed 300 characters

HXPERION

"IGC," Arthur mumbled. "What could that stand for?"

Cecily rubbed the corner of a postcard between her thumb and forefinger. "I think it's *in-game communications* – see, it's printed here. And they're not made of paper either."

She was right. Even though the postcard had the appearance of paper, Arthur noticed its surface flickering with light.

He bent back a couple more of them to examine both sides. They all had the same design: the front featured a photo of the wanderer or wanderers sending the postcard, and on the reverse was the scribbled name of a recipient and a message. Where a postage stamp would be placed on a twenty-first-century postcard, there was a printed date and time.

Cecily smirked at a photo of four particularly shiny-faced wanderers. "Four hundred years have passed and they still don't have an anti-sweat filter," she mused.

Scanning the images, the three of them found it difficult not to smile. The wanderers all had their arms round each other, laughing with glowing faces or pulling silly poses with their Wondercloaks. The writing on the reverse made for an interesting read:

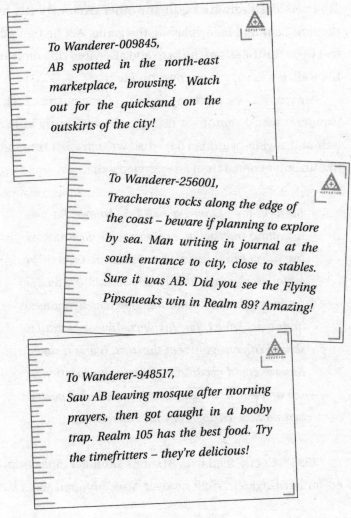

To Wanderer-009845,
AB spotted in the north-east marketplace, browsing. Watch out for the quicksand on the outskirts of the city!

To Wanderer-256001,
Treacherous rocks along the edge of the coast – beware if planning to explore by sea. Man writing in journal at the south entrance to city, close to stables. Sure it was AB. Did you see the Flying Pipsqueaks win in Realm 89? Amazing!

To Wanderer-948517,
Saw AB leaving mosque after morning prayers, then got caught in a booby trap. Realm 105 has the best food. Try the timefritters – they're delicious!

"Exploring this realm sounds lethal," Arthur commented. "No wonder it's a challenge to find the hero." For a moment, he imagined what it would feel like to experience the Wonderscape as a regular wanderer, without the threat of their impending slime-doom, or the knowledge of Tiburon's dastardly tricks. In any other circumstance, he thought he might enjoy playing the game. AB, he figured, had to be the initials of the hero and after studying more of the wall, it was easy to uncover his identity.

"Amaros Ba," he read on the back of one postcard. The wanderer who'd sent it – a teenage girl with curly brown hair and a wide-brimmed hat – had written what sounded like an entry copied from an encyclopaedia:

> Born on the planet Tyr in 2335, Amaros Ba was a prolific interstellar explorer who documented his adventures across the Horsetail Galaxy in a manuscript called the Tyrian Guide to Travel. He could speak over a hundred different languages, and was famed for his incredible navigation skills. With one glance at the stars, it was claimed Amaros could accurately pinpoint his location in the universe. His many passions included poetry, aeronautics, cartography and astronomy.

"2335!" Cecily read over Arthur's shoulder. She counted on her fingers. "We'll be over *three hundred years old* before this guy's even born! Providing we actually get home, of course."

Arthur raised his eyebrows. This realm belonged to a hero from their future – a man from another planet, no less. No wonder they hadn't been able to decipher his identity. For a split second his skin tingled and he had the feeling of being very small and very insignificant. Then Ren burped.

"Sorry," she said, covering her mouth. "You two might want to see this. I think Cloud's found something."

The little dog was sitting by a section of the curved wall. *"Grrf!"* he barked, pawing at the messages that covered it.

Arthur ventured closer to investigate and discovered a rusty iron handle peeking through the postcards. "I think you're right," he told Ren, pulling on it. "It's some kind of door but it feels stuck. Can you give me a hand?"

With Ren's help, he tugged open a sliding panel, revealing a tall concrete tunnel behind. As Cloud bolted inside, Arthur followed him in. In the dim light, he could see a stone door at the opposite end.

And there was a purple hexagon stencilled on it.

Behind him, Cecily gasped. "That's Milo Hertz's symbol! Is it locked?"

"I don't know," Arthur replied. "There's no handle on this one."

The *clomp, clomp, clomp* of Ren's combat boots echoed around. "Let me take a look."

But then Cloud pressed his nose against the bottom of

the door and a holographic screen shimmered across the stone. Written in the centre was the phrase *PLEASE ENTER PASSWORD*, followed by twelve spaces. A Wonderway-style keypad materialized beside it.

Arthur gazed down at his ankles. "I don't suppose you know the password as well, do you?" The little dog stared up at him blankly.

Cecily slumped against the tunnel wall. "It might be something simple and easy to remember, perhaps? What about *Wonderscape* or *Hxperion*?"

Ren shook her head. "Neither of those has twelve letters."

"What about a word that meant something important to Milo?" Arthur suggested, thinking of the password for his school email account: *MaryGillespie2504*. It was his mum's name and birthday.

"Yeah, but *Wonderway* and *Cloud* are still too short," Cecily pointed out.

Thinking of Cloud, something snagged in Arthur's memory. "This might be unrelated, but I'm pretty sure I counted twelve animals on Cloud's collar yesterday."

With a frown, Cecily beckoned the dog over and lifted him into her lap. "Dog, pig, tiger, rat," she read, twiddling the right-hand bead on his collar. "Rabbit, ox, dragon, snake, horse, monkey, rooster and sheep. How many is that?"

"Twelve," Arthur answered. "I was right. Maybe each animal represents a character in the password, like some sort of code? We've just got to work it out." His legs ached as he dropped to his knees and tore out a wad of dry-ish pages from one of the exercise books in his rucksack. He handed Ren and Cecily a few sheets each, along with a pen.

Cecily clicked the top of hers and started scribbling feverishly. "OK, so the password could be the first letter of each animal name?"

Ren inputted it into the keypad but nothing happened. Arthur stared at the list of animals he'd written down, thinking. An idea nagged at the back of his mind, but he couldn't quite bring it into focus.

"Maybe it's to do with the number of legs the animals have?" Cecily theorized. "Rats have four, snakes have zero, roosters have two..." She jotted down a string of twelve numbers and held them up. "Anything?"

This time, Ren tapped the combination in and a message appeared: *ONE ATTEMPT REMAINING.* She groaned. "We'd better make our next guess count. The dragon is the only animal on the list that doesn't exist in reality. Maybe that's a clue?"

Arthur thought about legendary dragons. He knew of St George and the dragon, and the multi-headed Greek Hydra. He remembered his dad reading him tales of dragons in Chinese mythology and Norse stories too.

Hang on, Chinese mythology.

In a flash of inspiration, he looked back at the list. "That's it!" he blurted. "These animals are all from the Chinese zodiac. Did you ever hear the legend of The Great Race?"

Cecily and Ren shook their heads. Cloud settled himself into a comfy position with his tail curled around his bottom and peered up expectantly, as if he was hoping Arthur would tell the story.

"I don't remember all the details," Arthur admitted. "My dad used to read it to me when I was little, but the ruler of all the gods in Chinese mythology is this guy called the Jade Emperor. One day, he holds a competition to see which animal in the kingdom should become his personal guard. Twelve animals take part – the ones on Cloud's collar. In order to reach the Jade Emperor, the animals must race across a river. Everyone thinks the ox will win because he is a strong swimmer, but the sneaky rat jumps on his back and lands on the other side first, winning the whole competition. The order in which the animals crossed the river decided the position they would appear in the zodiac."

Cecily chewed on the end of her pen. "So each animal might represent a different number – the position in which they finished the race. Do you remember their order?"

Arthur cringed. He hadn't heard the story for years. "After the rat and the ox came the tiger followed by the rabbit – they were both fast, so they beat the others. Then I think it was the dragon and the snake, and I'm pretty certain the pig was last, but between them I'm not sure."

"Well, I was born in the year of the rooster," Cecily said. "I know because my aunt has this Chinese calendar magnet stuck to her fridge. And my cousin who's only three months younger than me is the year of the dog, so those must come one after another."

"That leaves the monkey, the horse and the sheep," Ren figured. She scrunched her nose. "Surely horses swim faster than sheep?"

"I don't know, sheep can be pretty fast when they want to be," Cecily commented.

If it weren't for their impending slime-doom, Arthur might have laughed. As it was, he took their debate on the swimming prowess of farmyard animals very seriously. Eventually, they hashed out what they thought was the most likely order the animals had crossed the river, so that each creature represented a number between one and twelve. Then Cecily scrutinized Cloud's collar again. "The animals here are in a different order. Cloud normally takes the form of a dog, so perhaps we should assume that's the first? If so, the second is pig, then tiger, rat..."

Arthur scribbled down the corresponding numbers in a sequence of twelve and Ren filled them in on the screen. Although some of the numbers had double digits, they fitted into the twelve spaces perfectly. Ren took a deep breath before entering the final number. "All right, fingers crossed."

The screen flashed. For a heart-stopping second, Arthur thought they'd entered the incorrect password and were about to set off some kind of alarm. But then two words appeared in the centre:

PASSWORD ACCEPTED

15

The door slid open with a low hiss and closed behind them. On the other side, a set of winding steps descended into darkness. Arthur took out his mobile phone and turned on the torch. One good thing about not using it for two days was that it still had some battery life.

As the three of them followed Cloud down, the air turned staler. It smelled like the back of Arthur's wardrobe: musty winter coat with a hint of damp trainer. Judging by the cobwebs breaking across his body he doubted anyone had been there for a very long time, and he wondered what they might find. Perhaps they'd discover a clue to Milo Hertz's location, or even Milo himself? It was important they found him soon; *both* of their missions relied on it.

At the bottom of the stairs they stepped onto a stone floor. The air hummed and soft purple light glowed overhead.

They were standing in the corner of an enormous hall filled with rubble. Chunks of masonry were missing from the walls; there were holes in the ceiling, blackened potholes in the flagstone floor and scorch marks on just about every surface. The far wall was covered by flickering holographic screens and beneath the wreckage was the remains of a friendly office, equipped with comfy floating armchairs, and desks with shattered coffee mugs and shrivelled pot plants. Water dripped from several holes in the ceiling, echoing like a snare drum.

With his nose pressed against the floor and his bottom in the air, Cloud set off to sniff the site, doing his best bloodhound impression.

"This has got to be Milo's headquarters," Cecily whispered, treading carefully over the debris. "But what happened? It looks like it was attacked."

"Yeah, by mimics," Ren said ominously. "I bet these burn marks are exactly the kind of thing that would be made by the V-class and T-class units' weapons."

Arthur shuddered. It was one thing seeing the mimics with weapons, but another entirely to witness the damage they could cause. And to think all that power was being wielded by Valeria and Tiburon alone...

He felt a waft of air overhead and ducked as four black drones the size of crows shot out of a hole in the ceiling. Their chunky cuboid bodies were like a cluster of obsidian *Minecraft* blocks with strange googly eyes. Hovering sinisterly, they began scanning the ground with long green sensors.

Ren drew her bow. "More robots."

"What are they?" Cecily asked, inching back. "Do you think they'll try to kill us?"

"Those are the top two questions," Arthur agreed, nodding frantically. His muscles tensed as he checked the hall for exits. If the robots had been sent by Valeria to hunt them down, they'd need a quick escape.

But the drones paid them no attention. Within moments of completing the scans, the bodies reconfigured into masses of smaller cubes. Two of them transformed into dustpans while the other pair changed into brushes. Then they set about sweeping the floor.

Cleaner bots, Arthur realized. Their presence must have activated them. Slowly, his nerves started to subside. Navigating the ruins, he tried to imagine what might have transpired. It struck him as odd that the mess had been left untouched. Perhaps that was why the space felt haunted, like the wounds inflicted had never fully healed.

As the three of them ventured further in, more technology hummed and glowed into life. Dust crumbled from the rubble as devices buried underneath struggled to the surface. Arthur jumped as a cloud of glittering nano-particles burst in one corner and fashioned itself into a jukebox vending machine. Violet light shone under furniture and around the edges of the room, giving the place a funky hotel-lobby vibe.

It wasn't until they'd reached the centre of the hall that they could finally examine the holographic screens. Most of them were flickering so badly it was impossible to discern what they had once displayed, but a couple showed live CCTV-style footage of the city. One was the view outside the concealed tunnel entrance, by the IGC building.

The largest functioning screen resembled an airport departures board. A section on the left featured a list of numbers marked by either a hexagon, triangle or cross; and a column on the right displayed either *OPEN*, *CLOSED* or *PENDING*. Each number had a name written next to it.

"Those must be the realms of the Wonderscape," Cecily said, staring at the screen. "There are over two hundred of them!"

Arthur's gaze drifted down the grid. Some names he'd never heard of; others sounded familiar but he wasn't quite sure who they were. Of the ones he knew, there were doctors, musicians, dancers, inventors, athletes, chemists and campaigners, among others.

"William Shakespeare, Marie Curie, Edith Cavell," Ren read. *"Albert Einstein…* I can't believe all these incredible people are trapped here, forced to do Hxperion's bidding."

"And Tiburon's threatening to kill their families," Cecily added in a wobbly voice. "It's barbaric!"

As Arthur contemplated the scale of Tiburon's cruelty, his mouth went dry. The heroes, he realized, were similar to the three of them – lost in a time they didn't understand and unsure if they would ever get home and see their loved ones again. But he had Ren and Cecily, while the heroes were all alone. Tightening his jaw, he felt a renewed surge of determination to help them all. "The symbols probably denote who designed which realm," he guessed. "That's why there aren't any hexagons towards the end of the list, because Milo had fled by then."

At the bottom of the screen was an M-shaped controller like the one they'd used in Tomoe Gozen's realm. Ren gave it an experimental nudge and a pinprick of light traced her movement on-screen. "This doesn't tell us where Milo is," she said, moving her hand away from the controller. "Shall we search this place for clues? It's where Milo worked before he ran away. We might find something useful."

"Can we have a drink and something to eat first?" Cecily asked, clambering over a section of rubble. "I don't know about you two, but I'm running on empty." Arthur had noticed she was scrambling towards the vending machine. Its flashing neon lights seemed to activate an alarm in his head saying, *You haven't eaten in waaay too long.*

He checked his watch. It had been seven hours since they'd woken up at Tomoe's house and they hadn't stopped since. "Let's restock our supplies and take a break before we begin," he decided. "There aren't any mimics here. I think we're safe."

Cecily took charge of the shopping while Arthur and Ren found a reasonably unharmed bench and heaved it up against one wall. Cloud flopped on the floor, his pink tongue lolling out of his mouth.

"I'm not exactly sure what everything is," Cecily admitted, carrying back an armful of strange cuisine. There was a star-shaped loaf of bread streaked with what looked like blue jam, a box of glowing purple dumplings and some cube-shaped fruits with cracked skins. She'd also purchased three litres of water contained in a squidgy pouch. Ren poked a hole in it with the corkscrew attachment on her multi-tool and they refilled their Pipsqueaks bottles several times, guzzling as much as they could.

"Here," Arthur said, sharing out the bread. "This stuff has a weird marshmallow texture, but it tastes good." As he bit into the dough, his memory returned to last weekend when he and Dad had made pancakes. They'd played rock, paper, scissors for the last one, and even though Dad had won, he'd given Arthur the final pancake anyway. A lump formed in the back of Arthur's throat as he considered the possibility that he might never see him again.

Ren nudged him with her elbow as she peeled one of the cube fruits. "You all right?"

The water on Arthur's Wondercloak had turned a dismal shade of grey and was dotted with circular ripples, like a puddle in the rain. "Just worrying about my dad," he said honestly. "It's just the two of us and if we don't make it home..."

She gave him a weak smile. "I'm trying not to think about that."

Cecily huffed and dropped her chin into her hand. Her

sunflowers bowed their heads like a hearse had just driven by. "You wanna know something embarrassing?" she said wearily. "My parents might not even know I'm missing. I was off sick with flu for a week last year and they didn't call me for three days because my aunt hadn't been able to get hold of their PA."

Arthur lowered his hunk of bread. Whenever he was ill, his dad took the day off work to care for him. He hadn't realized how lucky he was.

"Their business is *everything* to them," Cecily continued. "They sometimes work seven days a week, and they're away so often doing fashion shows or photo shoots I spend more time with my aunt and cousins." Her voice cracked. "They're a really nice family, but I'm an outsider there."

She paused, her eyes welling with tears. Without thinking, Arthur shuffled closer and put his arm around her shoulders. He felt Ren's hand on Cecily's back and realized she'd done the same from the other side. "Your parents probably think they're doing the right thing," he reasoned gently. "They're working hard to give you the best in life."

"I know," she said quietly, "but I'd rather see them every day, like you do with your dad."

Arthur didn't know what to say. It hadn't occurred to him that someone like Cecily, with her nice house and expensive holidays, would be envious of what he had.

Hoping to cheer her up, he searched for Cloud. The little dog was digging in a pile of rubble on the opposite side of the hall, wagging his tail. As he pawed at an old chair leg, Arthur caught a glint of silver in the heap. "Hey, do you two see that?"

Cecily sniffed and dried her cheeks. "Where?"

Arthur rose to his feet and walked over. He covered his hand with the edge of his Wondercloak so as not to cut himself on any sharp edges, and began tossing aside pieces of debris. Working quickly, he freed a misshapen mimic head from under the junk. It had no skin or hair, just a bare skull and lifeless eyes.

He passed the head to Cecily, while he and Ren dug a badly damaged arm and separate chest out of the pile, as well. Several gashes in their metal casing allowed a glimpse through to the mimic's advanced inner circuitry.

"I can't tell by the shape if it's a T-class or a V-class," Cecily remarked, cradling the mimic's battered head in her hands. She brushed dust off its chin, revealing a spiky figure inlaid into the surface of the metal. The letter *M*.

"Of course," Arthur hissed, frustrated he hadn't thought of it sooner. "This must be one of Milo's mimics, an M-class!"

Ren scrutinized the chest part she was holding. "Perhaps they were shut down when Milo ran away?"

Arthur felt something tugging on the M-class's arm and peered down to find Cloud chewing on the mimic's index finger. "You can't eat that," Arthur said, trying to shake Cloud off, but the dog persisted. He growled and chewed harder, grinding his back teeth together.

There was a loud hiss, and then the M-class's fingertip

opened like a clam shell, revealing a small red lever inside.

Arthur flicked it down and Cecily flinched as the mimic's head started moving in her hands. The muscles in his forehead twitched; he blinked rapidly and rolled his tongue around the inside of his mouth like he was trying to dislodge a crumb of food stuck in his back teeth. Eventually, his eyelids stopped fluttering. "Good evening," he said, a little uncertainly. "Is there anything I can help you with?" He spotted Cloud sitting on the floor and spluttered, "*Cloud?* Is that you?"

The little dog licked the mimic's fingertips.

"Yes, I missed you too," the M-class said affectionately.

Before the two could catch up, Arthur spied movement on one of the CCTV screens. A mob of V-class mimics was filing into the hidden concrete tunnel, each carrying what looked like a sleek gold can of hairspray, but was probably filled with atomized C-4 explosive. They started to spray the edges of the stone door.

"They're going to blast their way in!" Cecily squeaked.

Ren instinctively dropped the mimic's chest onto the floor and drew her bow, but Arthur covered the top of her quiver with his hand. "There are too many of them. We have to hide."

"Then we'd better take these body pieces with us," Cecily said, tapping the M-class's chest with the toe of her shoe. "The mimic might be able to give us a clue to Milo's whereabouts."

16

With Cloud's lead gripped in one hand and the M-class's metal arm dangling from the other, Arthur rounded a corner and skidded to a halt in front of a wall of debris. Ren had the M-class's torso tucked under her arm, while Cecily clutched his head.

"Dead end," Ren said, wheezing. "Where to now?"

Milo's headquarters seemed to go on for ever. Arthur bent over and took a mouthful of air. Cecily, he noticed, wasn't even panting but then he'd seen her practising with the school cross-country team, so he wasn't surprised.

The sound of hover-wheels echoed near by; the V-class mimics were close. Arthur scanned the corridor and spied a large air-vent covered by a metal grate, low down in one wall. "In there, hurry!"

Ren unscrewed the grate with her multi-tool and they crawled in, pushing the M-class body parts ahead of them. Once Cloud was safely tucked inside, Arthur and Ren lifted the grate back into position and poked the screws through from the other side to hold it in place. They just had to hope the mimics wouldn't notice. Cecily propped the M-class's head, torso and arm next to each other, against the vent wall. His grey eyes swivelled around in their sockets, but he stayed quiet.

It didn't take long for voices to arrive.

"The suspects made a purchase in this building sixty-two minutes ago," a V-class sneered. "They may have left by now. What are your orders?"

Arthur tensed, realizing Hxperion did have a way to track them – by monitoring their DIRT transactions. They would have to remember not to use a vending machine again. He, Ren and Cecily went like statues as footsteps crunched over the dusty floor. Arthur glimpsed a pair of knee-high green boots through the slats of the grating. *Valeria.*

"I don't care what it takes, I want those brats found," she growled. "Triple the patrols and scour the realm. It looks like vandals may have already broken inside; we can't let anyone obtain any information lying around. Destroy the place."

"Excellent idea," the V-class agreed. "Anything else?"

Dust blew into the vent as a set of hover-wheels floated past, stirring the dirt on the floor. Arthur's throat tickled and heat rushed to his cheeks as he desperately tried not to cough.

"I think it's time to contact Tiburon," Valeria said calculatingly. "Do *not* ask him for help. Just let him know what's happened."

"That way, you'll be doing him a favour," the V-class said approvingly.

Arthur heard the grin in Valeria's voice. "Yes, exactly." Her tone became grave. "Wherever Milo is hiding, he must have recruited those three to scout out my headquarters. *Typical.* Now that I've grafted for years to turn around Hxperion's fortunes, he wants to swan back and enjoy the fruits of my labour. Well, I won't allow it! My brand, my fortune, my empire … everything I've built is in jeopardy," she said, adding with a sniff of indifference, "including all of you."

Valeria's anger seemed to linger in the hallway even after she and the V-class mimics had gone. Once the noise of their hover-wheels had faded, Arthur's shoulders sagged with relief. He waited as long as he could before clamping a hand over his mouth and letting loose a hacking cough. His lungs felt like sandpaper. "Sorry," he whispered, wiping tears from his eyes. "I couldn't hold it in any longer."

Cecily sat cross-legged, hugging her knees. "If Valeria tells Tiburon, he'll be after us too," she said grimly. In the dim silvery light of the vent, her eyes shone with worry. Arthur offered her a brave smile, although deep down, he knew their mission to save the heroes and get home had just got a lot more hopeless.

"Even Valeria doesn't know where Milo ran off to," Ren noted. "It's like he's vanished."

Arthur's head throbbed, trying to work it all out. Hoping for answers, he turned his attention to the M-class they'd found. "I'm Arthur," he said hesitantly. "This is Ren, Cecily and Cloud. We're trying to find Milo Hertz. Can you help us?"

The mimic's cheeks twitched. "Your request cannot be processed," he said, but then his face broke into a smile. "No, only joking. I'm M-73; pleased to meet you!"

Arthur blinked. None of the mimics they'd met so far had come close to cracking a joke. He glanced sideways at Ren and Cecily. Perhaps the M-class units had a few eccentricities not present in the V-class and T-class models…

"A large percentage of my memory has been destroyed," M-73 revealed. His pupils flicked to the fluffy white terrier, lying with his head in his paws on the floor of the air vent. "But if you're Cloud's friends, I do have two remaining recordings that may help you."

There was a whirring sound like a car window opening, and a slot appeared in M-73's chest which was still propped up beside his head. Nestled within a web of glowing wires and moving lights was a fist-sized glass pebble. It reminded Arthur of the fuel cells from the *Principia* because there were particles of dust glittering within it.

"In order to view my recordings, you will have to touch this and close your eyes. It is my neuro-processor. Once it is removed, this body will shut down."

Cecily hesitated. "You want us to take out your *heart*?"

"It isn't as primitive as a human heart," M-73 explained. "If you place my neuro-processor inside an undamaged mimic body, I will be reborn." A finger on his dismembered arm pointed towards the hole in his chest, while his head gave them all a reassuring smile. "Go on, take it."

Arthur didn't feel great about it, but he nodded. Reaching forwards, he gently pulled the neuro-processor out of the tangle of circuitry. The hole in M-73's chest closed immediately, and within seconds the life disappeared from his pale grey eyes.

"Here goes," Arthur said, holding the gem out so Ren and Cecily could lay their hands on it. After he'd shut his eyes, he felt a rush of blood to the head, and on the inside of his eyelids there appeared moving images…

M-73 was floating at considerable speed along a corridor of flint-grey stone with a row of doors on either side. Framed photographs of different M-class units holding *Employee-of-the-Month* trophies covered the walls, and purple light glowed at the edges of the ceiling. Arthur guessed from the décor that the mimic was somewhere in Milo's headquarters before the attack. Reflected on the polished floor, Arthur could see M-73 as he had been back then – a tall, strapping mimic with cropped dark hair. Unlike Milo Hertz, he moved with his shoulders back and chin up, like a proud soldier.

Stopping at one of the doors, M-73 held out a finger and pushed it against the stone. As the slab slid open, Arthur jerked his head in surprise. The room inside was as big as a house, set out on two open-plan levels. Through the railings of a mezzanine above, he spied the edge of an unmade bed and a table stacked with dirty plates. Downstairs, an incredible workshop filled the floor.

Arthur recognized a few pieces of apparatus lying on the clean surfaces of the workstations – a pink-flamed Bunsen burner, a set of floating test tubes and a beaker he'd spotted in Newton's study. But most of the equipment was new to him. A transparent machine filled with red gas buzzed loudly in one corner; holographic screens glided in and out of focus, and glowing liquids gurgled away in racks of conical flasks. It was like a cross between a live-in scientist's laboratory and a wizard's lair.

Angry voices sounded at the back of the room. "Boss?" M-73 called, whizzing forwards. He passed a dog bed, where Cloud was asleep. At the rear of the lab, a large black hoody was slung over a well-worn leather office chair, tucked under a desk. Hanging above was a noticeboard filled with scribbled notes, highlighted newspaper cuttings and annotated pages ripped from books. The portraits of a dozen people stared out from a number of postcards pinned around the board's edge. One showed a Japanese woodblock print of a dark-haired woman in samurai armour riding a black horse with yellow eyes: Tomoe Gozen.

Milo Hertz, Valeria Mal'fey and Tiburon Nox were standing around a dark Wonderway frame, talking. Milo looked *exactly* like M-73, except he had legs instead of hover-wheels and there were dark circles under his pale grey eyes. Arthur couldn't help but like him instantly. His hunched bearing and the shy way he peered out from under his hair made it seem like he'd just woken up one morning in that wrestler-sized body and never got used to it. He was dressed in jeans and a Hawaiian shirt, this one featuring pineapples.

"Hey, M-73," Milo said, raising his hand. "Thanks for coming. Valeria wants me to go over some profit projections she sent us last week," he said tiredly. "Can you get me a copy?"

Valeria's rust-red hair was slicked against her scalp like a layer of grease. She wore an acid-green trouser suit with wedge heels. "It's quite simple, Milo," she said drily. "They're going *down*. The Wonderscape's been open for five years and player numbers are stagnating. Do I need to remind you that we invested *all* of our parents' inheritance in the company? Unless we increase profits, we'll lose everything."

Tiburon Nox towered next to her, his oily black Wondercloak dripping from his shoulders. "We're not beating our rivals any more. Warstar's share prices have risen, as have Techmax Games's." In the greenish glow of the orb lights, he looked positively ghostly. "I want people to associate one name with in-reality gaming: Hxperion. Anything less than the best is not good enough."

"What we need," Valeria said, tapping her chin with a perfectly manicured finger, "is to give our consumers something they've never experienced before, something unique to the Wonderscape."

"We already have a unique selling point!" Milo insisted. "Our realms are themed around heroes from human history."

"Yes, that was a good idea of yours – to begin with," Valeria conceded. "But five years on, it's just tired interior décor."

Milo shrugged, his pineapple shirt stretching across his muscles. "Isn't it enough that people are enjoying the game and we continue to get great reviews? The Wonderscape is making people happy – that's the whole reason I agreed to be a part of this business, to inspire people."

"Inspiration has no net value," Tiburon said, gazing down his long nose at his younger brother. "I, however, have been pioneering a new mind-transfer technology, a way to copy the contents of a human brain into a mimic. It's something we could use to enhance our current operations." He snorted. "I'd like to see Warstar compete with *that*."

Milo stared at him. "*Mind transfer?* Tiburon, are you serious? That's not ethical."

"You treat your M-classes like people anyway," Tiburon sneered. "I find it distasteful myself."

"What's distasteful is that they all must have *our* faces," Milo retorted.

"It's called *branding*, Milo," Valeria scolded, as if she'd had to remind him of it a thousand times before. "The more our faces are seen, the more widely we are known." She signalled to Tiburon. "At least Tiburon's trying to find a solution. You're refusing to acknowledge the problem. Whatever happens, we need to announce a new feature of game play by Expo 2469, or Hxperion will be in serious trouble."

The vision abruptly disintegrated into clunky grey-scale pixels. Arthur blinked several times, but it didn't correct the problem. When the image finally sharpened, he found himself watching a different recording in Milo's live-in laboratory.

This time, the place was a wreck. The floor was covered in broken glass; drawers and cupboards were hanging open and apparatus lay smashed on the worktops. Racing to his desk, Milo Hertz was clutching Cloud, wrapped in a black hoody. Arthur recognized Milo's outfit as the one he'd been wearing when he ran across the stage at Expo 2469.

Milo placed his bundle on the floor and Cloud wriggled out from inside, the obsidian time-key still dangling from his collar. "M-73, are you all right?" Milo asked, wiping sweat from his brow.

M-73 wobbled forwards. "There were T-classes here, boss," he explained anxiously. "They found the time crystal you were working on yesterday and got away with it. I tried to stop them."

"It's not your fault," Milo reassured the M-class. Kneeling at the foot of the Wonderway, he tapped a number into the keypad and inserted a realm-key from his pocket. The frame burst into a swirling mass of blue vapour with an arched wooden door in the centre. "Tiburon confronted me at the Expo. He'd been spying on the lab and had found out about the time crystal I hid here. When he spotted the other crystal on Cloud's collar, I had to get out of there."

"What shall we do now?" M-73 asked urgently.

Milo fiddled with something on Cloud's foot. "First, we have to get this crystal out of Tiburon's reach." He gave Cloud a serious look, staring into his fluffy white face. "Listen, you need to protect this crystal. I've activated your tracking device; get as far away from here as you can and await my instructions; I'll be in contact as soon as I'm able."

There was a loud *bang* from somewhere behind M-73, and he swivelled round to see Tiburon Nox marching through the crumbled doorway of Milo's quarters. Ten T-class mimics flanked him like a troop of ghostly bodyguards, each carrying a smoking sword – the same weapon Arthur had seen them wielding in the *Wondernews* video.

"Cloud, go!" Milo urged.

The little dog nudged the wooden door open with the tip of his nose and bounded through. It closed behind him with a *click*; the blue mist evaporated and the black Wonderway frame returned.

Tiburon whispered something in the ear of one of his T-class units, who did an about turn and whizzed away.

"You're too late, Tiburon!" Milo cried. "You won't find him."

The corners of Tiburon's mouth wrinkled. "I wouldn't

be so sure, brother. I have spies everywhere. And it's a good job I do, or else I wouldn't have discovered *this*." Dangling from the tip of his bony finger was a glittering black time-key. Arthur could just about see the initials *MH* etched on the hexagonal base. "When, precisely, were you going to tell me you'd developed a method of *time travel*?"

Milo's jaw tightened. "I didn't mean to invent it and I wasn't going to share it with you. It's dangerous. It needs to be destroyed." He went to snatch the time-key off his brother, but Tiburon swiped it away, out of his reach.

"You invented it by accident?" Tiburon said, sounding amused. "How typically unambitious of you. Don't you realize what could be achieved with this technology? It won't be dangerous if I control it."

"That's exactly what I'm worried about," Milo murmured. He glanced warily at Tiburon's T-class units. "History isn't something to be messed with."

Tiburon growled, "And neither am I." His knuckles turned white as he tightened his fist around the time-key. "With this tool, Hxperion can pulverize its competition and build a grand legacy. We can be the most powerful organization in the Known Universe."

"Playing with time isn't like playing chess," Milo argued, staring down his brother. "I won't let you do this, Tib." He pounded a large fist onto the desk behind him, making the whole thing shake. A glass of water fell off the side and shattered.

Tiburon's nostrils flared. "Then I'm afraid you leave me no choice." He whispered to one of his T-class units, and four of them approached Milo.

"What are you doing?" Milo asked, edging back.

Tiburon moved to the Wonderway and tapped a number in the keypad. "Placing you somewhere you won't be able to stop me."

Milo glanced fearfully at the Wonderway. There was no door inside, just a curtain of thick blue smoke. "That's a *closed* realm."

"Yes. One of mine, in fact – that's how I'm certain there'll be no way for you to leave. I was going to open it at the Expo, but I decided it should remain closed."

The T-classes glided towards Milo, their hands outstretched. Milo stumbled back into his desk as they grabbed him by the shoulders and searched his pockets. "M-73, help!"

M-73 zoomed forwards to intervene, but his path was blocked by another three T-class units wielding smoking blades.

"You can't expect me to just walk through there," Milo exclaimed as the T-class units emptied several realm-keys from his pockets.

After whispering something in the ear of another T-class, Tiburon's voice went cold. "I don't expect you to walk. Goodbye, brother."

Milo's eyes flashed with terror. "No!" But the T-classes

tossed him through the wall of smoke as if he weighed no more than a sack of newspaper.

Looking on, Arthur felt Tiburon's betrayal like a stab to the chest. How could he do that to his own brother?

Tiburon waited until the Wonderway had closed before turning to address his T-class mimics. "My brother has fled," he said coolly. "Make sure the press are tipped off about his troubled finances. Oh, and destroy this place and anything that moves inside it."

Before storming out of the apartment, he browsed Milo's noticeboard and ripped down several postcards. "I'll give our investors something no I-RAG is offering," he muttered angrily.

As the T-class mimics swarmed M-73, the recording faded to black. Arthur's pulse was racing when he opened his eyes. "We've had it wrong this whole time! Milo didn't run away, he was *trapped*!"

Ren glanced in the direction of the main hall. "I might be able to open the closed realms using that controller," she said thoughtfully. "But we still need to figure out which one Milo was sent to."

Arthur tucked M-73's neuro-processor inside his rucksack for safekeeping and glanced at his watch. Countdown to protoplasm was now twenty-eight hours away. If they wanted to save the heroes and get home, they had to reach Milo before the clock ran out. Arthur swallowed and kicked off the grate. "Time's against us. Let's go."

They raced back into the main hall. Ren hurried to the controller at the foot of the large screen and started working. Arthur noticed Cloud's ears flatten as he cowered by Cecily's legs. "I don't mean to panic everyone," she said nervously, peering up, "but is that what I think it is?"

Arthur threw his head back. Strapped to the ceiling was a large green device in the shape of a triangle. It featured vials of coloured liquid, wires, and a holographic countdown panel with under five minutes remaining.

He might not be an expert, but Arthur had watched enough action movies with his dad to know what the device was.

A bomb.

The bomb's ticking echoed around the hall. "We need to leave, now!" Arthur hollered.

"Just a few more seconds..." A bead of sweat trickled down Ren's forehead as she focused on the screen, using the controller to make changes to the long list of realms. Her jaw trembled. "I have to get *all* the realms open, otherwise we've no chance of reaching Milo Hertz."

Arthur briefly considered taking a photo of the list with his phone, but then he checked the holographic countdown panel on the bomb. They had less than four minutes before it detonated and he reckoned they'd need most of that just to clear the building.

"All right – *done*!" Ren threw back the controller, and on the largest holographic screen, every red *CLOSED* status changed to a green *OPEN* one. "Let's go!"

Cecily grabbed Cloud and the three of them charged towards the exit. Arthur's thighs burned as he bolted up the stairs two at a time and hurtled through the stone door.

They ran as fast as they could away from the IGC building, their feet pounding the hard earth. The streets were darker now and as they raced past various stalls and shops, Arthur noticed the T-class units were holding weapons – the same smoking swords he'd seen before. When they were two streets away, a deep *boom* reverberated through the air; the ground shook and dust crumbled from the walls of buildings.

The bomb had detonated.

Arthur's heart was thudding as he skidded to a stop in an empty alleyway off one of the main thoroughfares. "Did you see the T-classes? They're all armed!"

Ren drew her bow, panting. "Valeria's message must have got through. Tiburon's looking for us."

Thinking of the ruthless man they'd seen in those recordings, panic built in Arthur's chest. If Tiburon had locked his own brother in a closed realm of the Wonderscape to keep him quiet, there was no telling what he'd do to them. Perhaps there was a fate worse than being turned into slime...

The sunflowers on Cecily's Wondercloak bristled. "What are we going to do? We're trapped."

The streets were quieter now that most of the stalls had been cleared away, but there were still plenty of mimics and wanderers milling around – and anyone who'd read yesterday evening's *Wondernews* might be able to identify them as the Pipsqueaks. Arthur spied a hooded figure watching them from under the awning of a closed shop. The figure's face was in shadow but Arthur could make out a person of medium-height, wearing a long black cloak and leather gloves. "We need to get out of the city," he decided. "The longer we remain around others, the more danger we're in."

"We could fly away on Cloud," Ren suggested, "but it might attract too much attention. It's safer to leave on foot."

"If we're heading back into the desert, then we'll need torches," Cecily said, reaching for her phone. After a moment's hesitation, Arthur and Ren did the same. It was worth the risk of their phones being seen.

They set off at a frantic pace towards the stone archway on the edge of the city. Fiery braziers crackled on every corner and laughter and music drifted through the streets. Above the jumbled rooftops, the sky was speckled with millions of pinprick stars. Arthur had never seen so many shining so brightly before, and wished he wasn't fleeing so he could stop and appreciate the view.

Turning into the main market square, he caught sight of the hooded stranger that had been watching them. The figure was half hidden behind a group of mimics unloading Persian rugs from a wooden cart. "I think we're being followed," he told Ren and Cecily. "Over there, behind the carpets. It could be a spy for Tiburon or Valeria."

Ren took a sneaky glance. "If we leave the city now, they'll only follow us into the desert. Let's double back on ourselves and try to shake them off."

They broke into a run along a side street, their phone-torches flashing across the ground. After weaving through a crowd of wanderers, they shot past a parade of noisy restaurants and dodged into an alleyway. Arthur glanced over his shoulder. "I can't see them. Let's get out of here."

Emerging back into the main square, they rushed under the stone archway and ventured into the desert. The air was cool and quiet, and the shadows of the dunes looked like giant's footprints. Arthur's calves ached as he trudged through the sand, trying to get as far away from the city as possible. "I'm parched," he admitted, halfway up another dune. "Do you think it's safe for us to stop for some…"

His words faded as an enormous gold dome rose over the top of the dune. Arthur tripped and fell to his knees as the dome climbed higher and narrowed into the shape of a balloon, carrying a large metal basket. If he tilted his head at the right angle, he could see a grid of pale blue light wrapped around them both, like some sort of holographic shield. With a deafening growl, a column of deep purple flames shot into the balloon's neck and lights flickered in a complex pattern under its surface.

Arthur was kneeling there, gawping, when a pair of large hands grabbed him from behind and a rough hessian sack was thrown over his head. "Oi, get off me!" he yelled, trying to wriggle free.

Cecily screamed and Cloud growled. Ren, Arthur was

pretty sure, managed to punch her captor because he heard her yell, "Take that!"

Arthur felt himself lifted off his feet. The roar of the balloon's burner grew louder as he was thrown against a cold, shuddering surface. The next thing he knew, the sack over his head was ripped off, and he was staring up at a man with beady dark eyes, a well-groomed moustache and bushy brows.

"Greetings," the man said, with an expression of easy amusement.

Ren and Cecily, who Arthur was relieved to see sitting beside him, both spoke at once.

"Who are you?"

"What's your problem?"

The stranger glanced at Ren, who had delivered the second question. "Apologies for kidnapping you, but you were attracting too much attention on land and I had to get you to safety. There wasn't time to discuss the matter."

On land? Arthur staggered to his feet, only just noticing where they were. He caught his breath as he stared up into the golden balloon. A complicated system of circuit boards, wires and transparent pipes twinkling with nanotech particles covered the inner surface. Arthur was no mechanics expert, but it looked like the purple flames were collected by a huge flume before being dispersed throughout the components. It had to be some kind of engine.

"No *way*," Ren whispered, tipping her head back as she

pushed herself up. "You'd better stay down, Cecily. This will trigger your vertigo."

Standing on tiptoe, Ren and Arthur peered over the edge of the basket. Below, the desert was very nearly pitch black. A caravan of camels lit by flaming torches made a dot-to-dot through the dunes on their way to the city. Arthur felt his face flush. Not once in his whole life had he ever imagined he'd be soaring this high.

"Quite a view, isn't it?" their kidnapper said, behind them. "You can see all the way to the eastern shores of the realm from here."

Arthur turned around to study the man in more detail. Under a battered knee-length leather coat, he wore a pair of loose-cuffed trousers and a colourful shirt. A pristine white turban covered his hair.

It was then that Arthur spotted a hooded black robe slung over the side of the basket. A Wonderway stood in the opposite corner, with Cloud curled up beneath it. A cluster of levers and strange controls sprouted from a box on one side, which was fixed with a brass nameplate that read: *LULU*.

"You're … Amaros Ba, aren't you?" Arthur blurted. "*You're* the one who was following us."

Right then, a wispy red ball materialized in front of where Cecily was still sitting. She had barely grazed it with her fingertips before it dissolved and a quartz realm-key dropped into her hand.

Amaros Ba smiled. "I'd say congratulations, but technically *I* found *you*, not the other way round. I've been watching you since you arrived. I had a hunch there was something different about you right away."

Makes sense, Arthur thought. According to the information on that postcard, Amaros Ba had spent his life documenting the people and places he saw on his travels, which meant he was probably very good at observing things.

"How do you know we're not safe in the city?" Ren asked curtly, folding her arms. She obviously hadn't forgiven him for kidnapping them.

Amaros pulled a notebook from inside his coat and opened it to a position marked by a leather bookmark. "Firstly, your clothes are stained with dirt like you've been wearing them for days. Secondly, you were able to gain access to Milo Hertz's old headquarters. And thirdly, every single mimic in the realm is after you." He shut the book. "All of this led me to believe that you were likely enemies of Hxperion, on the run."

Arthur raised his eyebrows. The explorer really had noticed everything – including the secret entrance to Milo's headquarters. "Talking of mimics, why isn't there one with us now? Don't they watch over you like hawks?"

"They used to," Amaros replied, grinning. "But with a T-class trailing me everywhere, I stuck out like a sore thumb and it became too easy for wanderers to find me and complete the realm-challenge. After several thousand wanderers complained, the T-classes were given new orders to spy on me less frequently."

"You're lucky," Arthur said, thinking of Tomoe Gozen. "I'm not sure the other heroes enjoy as much freedom."

The explorer's bushy brows drew together. "You three seem to know a great deal more about the secrets of the Wonderscape than most wanderers," he observed. "Who are you, and how do you know Milo Hertz's password?"

Arthur glanced at Ren and Cecily, wondering if it was safe to trust Amaros Ba with the truth.

Cloud trotted over to Cecily and licked her hand before settling himself in her lap. "I think we should tell him," she said, stroking Cloud's head. "We need all the help we can get – and Cloud doesn't seem too worried."

With them all in agreement, Ren took it upon herself to recount the we're-from-four-hundred-years-ago speech. She told him everything that had happened to them, and what they'd learned so far. Amaros Ba made notes as she spoke, an expression of genuine fascination on his face.

"So now that you've opened all the closed realms, the next part of your mission is to learn which one Milo was sent to," he said, rubbing his beard. "I may have something that can help you on your quest." Reaching into a pocket on his cloak, he withdrew a palm-sized tin. Inside it was a stack of small transparent patches, veined with copper. "These are skin-mounted inhibitors – *shadow patches* to most people. You wear them on the back of your wrist."

"What do they do?" Ren asked as Amaros handed her one.

"T-class and V-class mimics identify wanderers by scanning the data stored in their Wondercloaks," Amaros explained. "Mimics can see how much DIRT a wanderer has spent, which challenges they've completed and where in the Wonderscape they've been. Shadow patches feed false data into a Wondercloak, effectively giving the wanderer a new identity."

Arthur remembered the V-class in Tomoe's realm studying his Wondercloak as if she was reading something. Now he knew why. "So if a mimic sees us, they won't know we're us?"

Amaros grinned. "Exactly."

"You can't have got these from a vending machine," Ren commented suspiciously, pressing the patch onto her skin.

Arthur placed his shadow patch on the opposite wrist to the one he wore his watch. It was soft and rubbery like silicone. The transparent part faded into his skin, leaving only a few metallic lines visible.

"No, these aren't available from Hxperion. They're only distributed by a few *select* traders," Amaros answered with a wink.

The Wonderscape must have a black market, Arthur realized. It was such a big place, it didn't surprise him there would be criminal activity going on right under Hxperion's nose.

Cecily wobbled as she stood to collect her shadow patch, lifting three fingers to her temples. "Erg, head rush," she murmured, reaching with her other hand for the basket wall to steady herself.

"I expect that'll be the Wonderways," Amaros said. "Do you have dizziness as well?"

She appeared to wait till the feeling of light-headedness had subsided before replying. "A little."

"If you travel through too many Wonderways too quickly, you experience desynchronosis," he explained. "You need to rest."

Arthur wished they could. He yearned to be tucked up in his own bed at home. Even setting his alarm for school the next morning felt strangely appealing.

Unexpectedly, a bright light streaked through the air a few metres from the basket. It was followed by a screeching whistle that made Arthur wince. Amaros lunged for the controls as the craft lurched. "We're under attack! Take cover!"

Arthur risked a peek over the side of the basket. In the desert below, a trio of T-class units were operating some sort of rocket launcher. He dropped to his knees and clung to the basket walls, his blood pounding.

"They're trying to bring us down," Amaros shouted. "We've got to climb out of their range." There was a thunderous roar as he opened the burner and a blast of purple flames appeared over their heads.

"It's T-classes!" Arthur yelled at Ren and Cecily. "They must have followed us!"

Another two missiles hurtled past in quick succession, missing the top of the balloon by a whisker. Arthur scanned the basket for parachutes in case they had to make an emergency escape. His whole body was shaking.

As they drifted higher, the ship passed through a layer of misty cloud. Droplets settled on Arthur's skin.

"That's it," Amaros said, lowering his voice as the burner switched off. "That's as high as I dare go."

At that moment, a postcard fell out of the sky and landed on the floor of the basket, between everyone's feet. Arthur bent down to pick it up but as he touched the paper, it unfolded into a holographic screen that hovered in the air like a glowing window.

"Hello, wanderers," Tiburon Nox said, smiling.

Arthur froze, staring into Tiburon Nox's cold blue eyes. He was dressed impeccably, his mullet neatly combed and a gunmetal plus-sign brooch fixed to the collar of his buttoned-up black shirt. The shoulders of his oil-slick Wondercloak glistened at the sides of the screen.

"Apologies for the interruption to your gaming experience," he began in a measured tone. Grabbing hold of the basket walls, Arthur peered over the edge. The bright lights of similar holographic displays were dotted across the dunes. Every wanderer in the realm was watching this message.

"You may have noticed, in the last few hours, mimics in some realms have been arming themselves. On behalf of Hxperion, I want to reassure you that this is all part of a planned security drill." His lip twitched into a slight sneer and Arthur caught a flash of the Tiburon he'd seen in M-73's recording. "As you know, Hxperion prides itself on staying one step ahead of any ... *threats* which may have an impact on your visit. Drills such as these allow us the best chance of deleting such threats, should they arise." The numbers *33, 89* and *105* flashed up in the corner of the message. "The drill is concentrated in these realms, for now."

As quickly as it had appeared, the screen folded in on itself and the postcard vanished in a puff of red gas. Arthur was left blinking dazedly at Ren and Cecily. "Realms Thirty-Three, Eighty-Nine and One Hundred and Five – they're all the ones we've been to. These *threats* – he's not talking about outside forces, is he? He's talking about us."

Ren angled her head so she could see Arthur's watch. "Well, in twenty-six hours he needn't bother deleting us," she noted grimly. "We'll be goo by then anyway."

"If they're following this ship, then the shadow patches won't help us." Arthur felt his chest tightening and tried to steady his breathing. Things had gone from bad to worse.

"But they *will* when you reach another realm," Amaros said, laying a hand on his shoulder. "A true adventurer never knows what is around the next corner. I travelled for over fifty years and when I needed food and shelter, people from other planets invited me into their homes. When I required a bath, I stumbled across natural hot springs. And when I was seeking entertainment, I came upon a snake-charmer or a soul-wrangler or a star-flare surfers' convention." He smiled to himself. "Now, *that* was something…"

Arthur feared they might have to listen to all of Amaros's adventures and would have turned into three puddles of slime before he was finished, but then the hero shook his head. "Anyway, that's a story for another day." He checked his notebook. "If I'm not mistaken, in order to get home and free the other heroes, you need only discover which realm Milo Hertz is trapped in."

"Yes, but that's an almost impossible task," Arthur said. "There are hundreds to choose from, and all we know is that it's one Tiburon designed." He felt frustrated that he hadn't had time to take a photo of the realm list earlier, but if he had, he might not have made it out of Milo's head-quarters alive...

Amaros stroked his beard. "There is *someone* who might know where Milo is, another hero."

Arthur frowned. He'd thought heroes didn't have any contact with each other. Tomoe had said they were forbidden to leave their realms.

"I don't know her name," Amaros continued, "or what she is famous for, but I do know it will cost you four hours' hard work to meet her."

Four hours? Arthur glanced uneasily at Ren and Cecily. "I suppose we could spare that if it means getting home. What do we have to do?"

Amaros turned to another section in his notebook. "Some time ago, I noticed that wanderers who had visited Realm Forty-Two were all humming the same tune. Whenever I heard the lyrics I jotted them down and it quickly became apparent that whoever was teaching the song was hiding messages within it."

Of course. Wanderers were the only people who moved freely between realms; it made sense that they would have to carry any communications.

"Disguised as a mimic, I began teaching songs in the taverns here, hoping my lyrics would travel across the Wonderscape and be heard by other heroes. Soon enough I was talking with the hero from Realm Forty-Two." He lifted his chin. "There is a network of us now, all communicating through song. I'll admit I'm not the best composer in the group, especially since Beethoven joined us, but my tunes are effective enough." He crouched at the foot of the Wonderway and tapped *42* into the keypad. "Friend, do you have the realm-key?"

Cecily passed it over and soon the hefty black frame was replaced by a spiralling mass of blue smoke. The door in the centre was made of gnarled tree roots, as if woven by nature itself. Arthur tugged on the straps of his rucksack, preparing himself to face yet another realm. He tried to find solace in what Amaros had said about not knowing what was around the corner. There *could* be a good surprise on the other side of this door.

"Be careful," Amaros warned. "According to your story, this will be the *fourth* Wonderway you have passed through in two days. You need to sleep. I've seen what happens to wanderers who overdo it."

Cecily rested Cloud down and took hold of his lead. As Ren pushed the door open, sunlight poured in from the other realm, making them all squint. "It's morning," she said, shading her eyes with her hand. "I can see a sun rising." She nodded goodbye to Amaros Ba before walking through.

"Thanks for everything," Arthur said, offering Amaros a weary smile as he and Cecily plodded after her. Just as he stepped over the threshold, he realized there was something he'd forgotten to ask. "Wait!"

But as he turned round, the door vanished.

"What's wrong?" Cecily asked. They were standing in the middle of lush green countryside. Birdsong filled the air and the sky glowed gold with the light of dawn.

"I forgot to ask him about the Wonderskill you will have received," Arthur said, remembering that she had collected the realm-key. He shrugged. "I guess you'll learn about it later."

Cecily unfastened Cloud's lead and he scampered off to roam the terrain. Compared to the dry, barren landscape of the desert, the fields around them were abundant with life. Ferns and shrubs carpeted the rich red-brown soil, and insects buzzed in the trees. A set of tyre tracks led downhill towards a wide dirt road, where a rusty old safari bus had stopped. Arthur could see figures milling around outside.

"I don't feel so good," Cecily said, swaying. "I think I need to sit down."

Without warning, Ren collapsed into the long grass like a sack of potatoes.

As Arthur went to help her, his vision blurred like he was having a head rush and before he could steady himself, his legs gave way. Then everything went black.

Cloud's barking was getting quieter. Arthur lifted open his eyelids, feeling groggy. His cheek rested against soft earth and he felt the sun on his skin. In the distance, he spotted a heavyset woman wearing a brightly coloured dress moving towards him. Her hair was tied with a scarf made of the same patterned material and as Cloud ran up to her, she kneeled to greet him.

"Hello again," he heard her say in a rich voice, as the little dog wagged his tail and jumped on her knees.

Arthur pushed himself onto his elbows, watching the two of them together. Despite the fact that his mind felt like cotton wool, something was obvious.

Cloud *knew* this woman, which meant he had been to Realm Forty-Two before.

19

Arthur shook Ren's arm. "Ren, wake up." She was lying on her back with her mouth open, catching flies.

"Huh?" Ren rolled onto her side and got a face full of grass. "What the—?!" she spluttered, batting the blades away. "What happened?"

"We fell asleep," Arthur said, nudging Cecily's shoulder. He glanced back at Cloud, trotting happily towards them. The lady who had been stroking him had disappeared.

"Erg, I feel like I was knocked over the head," Cecily groaned, rubbing her temples.

Arthur thought back to Amaros Ba's warning. It must have been that last Wonderway they'd travelled through; it had sapped all their energy. "Cloud just recognized someone," he told them, getting to his feet. "She was here, in this field. She wasn't wearing a Wondercloak and she didn't have hover-wheels for legs, so she must be the hero of this realm."

"Did you see where she went?" Ren asked.

He squinted into the distance. "No, but that old safari bus is the only place people seem to be hanging around. We should try there."

Cecily brushed soil off her leather jacket as she stood. "How much time have we lost?"

Arthur read his watch. His mind was too fuzzy to make the calculation but he felt Newton's Wonderskill help him out. "Eight hours," he concluded grimly. "Which means we've got just under eighteen hours to get home." He tried not to think about what would happen if they didn't succeed. They'd come so far he had to believe they were getting closer.

Shouldering their bags, they set off towards the bus. Although the mid-afternoon sun beat down on their backs, it was nothing compared to the stifling heat of the desert. They'd only been walking for a few minutes when two puffs of red gas burst in the air, and swirled to form words:

WONDERSCAPE

REALM 42: FOREST OF THE LEOPARD

Loot: Realm-key

Travel with wonder,

HXPERION

The message was promptly followed by a riddle scroll, which landed in the grass. Cecily cleared her throat before reading the contents aloud:

"Once you've travelled the hero's road,
Seen the truth and broken the code,
Consider where your steps should lay;
Look to the trees to show the way.
Nature gives us all we need:
To save the future, plant a seed."

Peering over Cecily's shoulder, Arthur took note of the curly, looped handwriting. "So the realm-challenge involves code-breaking and ... *gardening*?" he questioned. He wondered why there wasn't any DIRT in the loot, and why the realm-challenge didn't sound as life-threatening as the others they'd faced. He couldn't help feeling mistrustful; nothing in the Wonderscape was that straightforward.

As they trudged onto the road, the safari bus came into closer view. It had a tatty canvas roof, windowless sides and six oversized wheels that lifted its chassis high off the ground. Thirty or so wanderers were bunched near the door at the front.

Ren scanned the area, her fingers reaching for her bow. "I don't see any mimics yet. Keep your eyes open."

Edging closer, Arthur fiddled with the shadow patch on his wrist, hoping it would do its job. After Tiburon's threatening message, he was certain that if they were caught, they wouldn't be going home.

Splattered with baked mud, the safari bus was painted with the Hxperion logo and a tagline which read: *Infinity Tours: Never-Ending Fun!* The wanderers chatted excitedly as they queued to get on. Arthur overheard a girl with a chameleon-skin Wondercloak discussing which realm to visit next.

"The next realm-key I win, I'm travelling to Realm Twelve," she said, adjusting her cloak. "I've heard it belongs to Frida Kahlo."

"Really?" Her companion, a boy sporting a wood-grain-textured Wondercloak, chuckled. "I was thinking Realm One Hundred and Forty-Eight would be fun: Harry Houdini."

A tall, thin man in safari uniform was standing with his back to them, ushering everyone on board. "Take your seats to start the challenge," he instructed in a dreary voice. "If you can't fit on this vehicle, there'll be another along in a few minutes."

It wasn't till he turned round that Arthur realized why he sounded so lacklustre. *"T-class!"* he hissed, pointing to the hover-wheels at the end of the man's safari trousers.

Cloud whimpered and ran behind Ren's combat boots. Although her neck stiffened, she lifted her chin. "If Amaros Ba is right about these shadow patches, then we've just got to act natural and everything will be OK." With that, she bundled Cloud under her cloak and strode forwards.

Arthur tried to stay calm as they fell in at the back of the line, but the longer they waited, the sweatier his hands became. He gritted his teeth as the wanderers in front dawdled up the steps. *Come on, come on…* When it was finally his turn, he felt a hand touch him on the shoulder. "Cecily, I—"

But it wasn't Cecily.

The T-class swept an icy gaze over Arthur's face and Wondercloak. For a heart-stopping moment, Arthur thought he had been recognized, but then the mimic pushed him forwards and droned, "Keep it moving. We can't set off until you're all in your seats."

As he glided away, Arthur let out a heavy sigh of relief. The shadow patch had worked. For now.

Inside the safari bus were ten rows of wooden benches with an aisle down the middle. Cloud wriggled out from under Ren's cloak and scampered to the back. When they found him, he was sitting on an empty bench, wagging his tail and gazing up at them expectantly as if to say, *Look! I saved you a spot.*

Cecily gathered him into her lap and slid over so Arthur and Ren could sit down.

The bus rocked and creaked as the other wanderers got settled. Fixed to the back of the bench in front was a steel handrail with a single Hxperion-branded button in the centre. Arthur wondered what it did, but he wasn't about to press it to find out. It was probably lethal.

When everyone had finally taken their seats, the T-class whizzed on and closed the doors. Next, he grabbed a large wooden box and moved along the central aisle. "Take one each," he instructed, offering the contents of the box to the wanderers at the front.

Arthur watched the girl with the chameleon-skin Wondercloak seated three rows ahead of them. She reached into the box, collected a small, curved piece of metal and then hooked it over the top of her ear.

"Remember to pay attention to everything your tour guide tells you," the T-class advised. "And of course, travel with wonder."

"Tour guide?" Ren repeated, collecting three of the mystery devices and passing them along.

As soon as Arthur slid the contraption over his ear, he had to blink. A faint blue-tinted holographic screen now hovered a few centimetres from his face. When he turned his head, the screen moved with him.

"That's so cool," Cecily said, waving her fingers in front of her nose.

She looked cross-eyed, but Arthur didn't have the heart to tell her. He found it curious that he couldn't see *her* screen; they must only be visible to the user.

"Good morning, wanderers!" announced a husky French voice. Arthur started as a familiar half-human, half-lizard in a tailored purple suit materialized on the left of his screen. "Welcome aboard this tour of Realm Forty-Two."

It was the same reptile who had been their driver in the Pipsqueaks-mobile. Arthur wondered if he was some sort of famous entertainment personality in the twenty-fifth century. "This will be a bumpy ride," Lizard-Man warned. "So please hold on to the rail at all times. There is an emergency bell in front of every bench. If at any point you want to get off, give it a press!"

That's what the button does, Arthur realized. He grabbed hold of the handrail as the bus set off along the road, its tyres crackling over the dirt.

They soon turned onto a potholed track with forest on one side and open grassland on the other. A warm breeze blew through the bus, carrying the scent of dry grass and animal dung. Arthur had just retrieved the riddle scroll from his rucksack when Cecily tapped him on the arm. "Look!" she breathed. "They're amazing!"

As he lifted his head and saw what was outside, he almost slipped off the bench.

A herd of zebra stood only a few hundred metres away, flicking their tails as they stopped to graze. With so many stripes packed so tightly together, they almost created an optical illusion. Arthur had only ever seen footage of the creatures in wildlife documentaries; they didn't exactly roam wild around Peacepoint Estate.

Even Ren was stunned. Her jaw hung loose as they drove past several buffalo, grazing at the roadside. "I can't believe all these animals are here. Maybe the hero is someone who worked alongside them?"

The lizard-guide signalled with his scaly, clawed hand. "On the right we are approaching a waterhole where you can view examples of giraffe, flamingo and elephant."

Sure enough, they soon drew alongside a large muddy pool dotted with spindly-legged flamingos, preening their coral-pink feathers in the afternoon sun. At the water's edge, two adult giraffes lowered their heads to drink as a herd of leather-eared elephants lumbered closer behind them. Their combined squawking, grunting and splashing was so loud Arthur felt like it was being played right into his ears.

"I know we're not on Earth any more," Cecily said, "but this place looks a lot like…"

"*Africa*," Arthur finished. It was just as he'd imagined it from movies and TV: sun-baked grassland that stretched to the horizon; vibrant, noisy and thriving with life.

Cecily's hair sparkled like jewels as she leaned over the edge of the bus, resting her chin on her arms. "I've *always* wanted to go there. My dad promised he'd take me to Abuja last summer to show me where his parents grew up." She snorted. "*That* never happened."

Arthur interpreted from her tone that her dad had been too busy to take her. He thought how disheartening it must feel to have promises broken, especially when they came from people you loved. His dad was always true to his word, something he appreciated even more now. "Abuja – that's in Nigeria, right?"

She nodded. "He's Nigerian and my mum's French. That's why their salon brand is called Afrocheveux. I think it's a stupid name but it's popular in focus groups, apparently."

Arthur's French wasn't great. He thought *cheveux* was either "hair" or "horse", and given the circumstances, he plumped for the former.

Cecily sat up straighter. "Hey, I was just thinking – since we've been in this realm, nothing's tried to kill us yet. Maybe that's why Cloud has visited the place before – because it's safe?"

Arthur got a sinking feeling in his stomach. *Nothing* about the Wonderscape was safe. Given that they'd faced hurtling avalanches, swinging boulders and rocket launchers in the last three realms, he decided something wasn't right.

He read the riddle scroll again: *Once you've travelled the hero's road, seen the truth and broken the code...* The *hero's road*, he imagined, could well be the one they were riding along, but he hadn't come across any codes.

Scanning the bus for clues, his attention eventually wandered to the underside of the canvas roof, which was plastered in posters advertising various Hxperion merchandise. They all featured glossy photos, plus various enthusiastic tag lines:

Never forget your Hxperion water bottle, wherever you're wandering!

Everybody wants a head torch from Hxperion!

Pro-wanderers always wear their Hxperion hiking boots!

Only the best will do: take home a Hxperion compass today!

Arthur noticed the first letter of each slogan was written in a different font to the rest. On a hunch he tried stringing them together to see if they formed an acrostic, but the beginning four letters – *N E P O* – didn't make any sense. Then, when he read the letters backwards, the hairs on the back of his neck stiffened. The letters *did* spell something in reverse. Three words.

OPEN

YOUR

EYES

Arthur had to check he wasn't seeing things, so he slid off his over-ear device—

—and the unpleasant truth hit him like a mound of zebra poo to the face.

Everything he'd been looking at was a lie.

Outside, where there had been grassland and endless scrub, a field of blackened tree stumps spread into the distance. The flamingos were in fact small tree-cutting robots, busy sawing what remained of the charred wood. Instead of two giraffes drinking at the waterhole, a pair of heavy-load cranes droned to and fro, lifting logs onto the back of a huge grey lorry. It was one of a fleet, parked right where the elephant herd had been standing.

Arthur went numb. The land had been decimated. There wasn't a single blade of grass left for a zebra to eat; no water for a giraffe to drink; no habitat for any living thing at all. The vibrant, bustling landscape he'd marvelled at only moments before was gone. With a heavy heart, he reached over and slid off Cecily's earpiece.

She blinked, then gasped and covered her chest with her hand. Arthur elbowed Ren and got her to remove her device too.

Her eyes widened as she beheld the scorched earth. "Why?" she asked simply.

"I don't know…" Try as he might, Arthur couldn't find an answer. He skimmed the rest of their surroundings to see what else had changed. To their left, the forest they had been driving alongside was now encircled by a dizzyingly high fence made of thorns and tree roots. The T-class mimic was still sitting in the driver's seat but the rest of the bus felt emptier. Arthur couldn't see the girl with the chameleon-skin Wondercloak, and he was fairly sure half a dozen other wanderers were missing. "Something happened while we were watching the animals," he said. "Other passengers have got off the bus somehow."

Ren gestured to the Hxperion-branded button on the rail in front. "That lizard dude said if we wanted to get off at any point, we just had to press this," she reminded them. "Maybe that's what the others did?"

Just like that, the dots started to connect in Arthur's

mind. *Infinity Tours: Never-Ending Fun.* He didn't even need access to his personal Newtoncyclopaedia to understand what had happened. "I don't think this tour *ever* ends," he realized. "And I think the wanderers who aren't here figured it out sooner than we did. It's all part of the challenge: *Once you've ... seen the truth and broken the code.*"

With an unexpected confidence, he reached out and slammed his hand on the Hxperion button.

The effect was immediate. His seat collapsed from under him and he tumbled into darkness.

20

The darkness didn't last long. Sunlight glared into Arthur's eyes as he thudded onto a rocky floor, sending up a choking cloud of dust. He heard the rumble of the bus's engine and looked up as it drove away.

"What happened?" Cecily asked, coughing.

"I think that button released some kind of hatch underneath us," Arthur explained, realizing the reason the vehicle's chassis was so high was because it needed space to dump its passengers below. "The bench must have folded down and we fell out." He staggered to his feet, brushing dirt off his jeans.

Not far away, several groups of wanderers trekked towards an opening in the forest fence. Arthur couldn't see another safari bus along the road, but judging by the number of people, he figured there had to be an entire fleet driving around. "The next part of the challenge is probably that way. Come on."

Cecily attached Cloud's lead to his collar and, keeping

their heads down, they ventured into the trees. No one – including the wanderers they were following – could move very fast. The forest floor was a giant trip-hazard of sprawling tree roots, slippery mud and tangled vines, so everyone had to hop, scramble and leap to make it through. As their feet disturbed the terracotta earth, the scent of wet soil and damp tree bark lifted into the air.

"We need to be careful," Ren whispered, scanning the shadows. "The realm-challenge was called Forest of the Leopard, remember?"

Arthur's nerves tingled as he scanned the higher branches for golden fur with brown spots. He considered how they might defend themselves against a wild animal. They could use tiger-Cloud, but she would undoubtedly draw too much attention. Arthur briefly wondered whether Tiburon or Valeria might be tracking Cloud, but he decided it was unlikely. After all, Milo Hertz wouldn't have sent Cloud away with the time-key if it was possible he could be traced.

"I was thinking, maybe the hero of this realm is someone who fought against all that destruction we saw?" Cecily commented. Arthur could tell by the furrows in her brow that she was still troubled by what they'd witnessed. He pictured the desolate expanse of charred tree remains – each one like a gravestone – and shuddered. Perhaps she was right. A hero wouldn't harm the environment like that; they would *save* it.

"These other wanderers could already know who she is," Ren pointed out quietly. "They certainly seem to know which direction to go in, and it's not like there are any signposts."

Behind the hum of insects, Arthur could hear the wanderers discussing something as they pointed into the trees. A couple of lines from the riddle surfaced in his mind. *Consider where your steps should lay, look to the trees to show the way...*

He studied the trees closest to him and noted they were all different species. Some had smooth, peeling bark and branches that spread like umbrella spokes; others had gnarly trunks with closely woven boughs. Where one variety had jagged, diamond-shaped leaves, another had narrow, feathery fronds.

Ahead, the wanderers turned left, by a tree sprouting bright blue-purple flowers. Arthur glanced over his shoulder and saw that the same species was dotted along their entire route. "Whoa," he breathed as he realized. "There *are* signposts showing us the way – the trees." Keeping his voice low, he drew the others to one side to explain. "The ones with the blue flowers are leading everyone through the forest. It's like the riddle said." He was about to repeat the rhyme, when Ren shrieked.

"Erg!" She jumped up and down like she'd just trodden on spikes. "Get it off! GET IT OFF!"

Arthur stepped closer. "What is it? What's happened?"

He scanned her for injuries but couldn't see anything. There was a thumb-sized grasshopper-type bug on her shoulder, so he brushed it away. "Are you OK?"

"Has it gone?" she asked, twisting her neck so her ponytail swished in Arthur's face. "Did you get it?"

He batted hair out of his nostrils. "You mean the *bug*? I flicked it into the soil."

She nodded, sighing heavily. "OK, OK, OK…" she repeated, like she was trying to convince herself she was.

"Do you have a fear of insects?" he asked gently. He raised his eyebrows at Cecily, who reflected his confusion by shaking her head. Up until now, they had both had the impression that Ren wasn't scared of anything.

"They freak me out," Ren confessed with a shiver. "They're always scuttling around, hiding down plug holes or in dark corners." Her kohl-lined eyes skimmed the trees. "We've been surrounded by creepy-crawlies since we arrived in this realm. I've been trying not to think about it."

Arthur couldn't believe it: despite her tough persona, Ren was just as vulnerable as he and Cecily were. "Well, you're doing a good job," he remarked, trying to hide his surprise. "I didn't even notice." He felt honoured that Ren had trusted them enough to open up; you didn't share your fears with just anyone.

Ren swept her hands down either side of her Wondercloak, her neck tense. "Come on, let's keep going."

The blue-purple flowering trees guided them out of the

forest, into an area of open countryside. There was an orchard to the left, which banked down to a trickling stream, and to the right, fields were planted with neat rows of fruits, vegetables and baby trees. There were cane pyramids covered in climbing beans, bright-green bananas hanging on tall plants and golden squash bedded with straw. Ahead, the land climbed up to a modest farmhouse on top of a hill.

The fields were full of wanderers. Their various textured cloaks flapped around as they planted seeds, dug out weeds or picked produce. A large wooden sign stood like a scarecrow in the middle of one field. As Arthur, Ren and Cecily cornered a plot of sweet potatoes, they could make out what it said. *"WM's Organic Fruit and Veg Farm,"* Arthur read. *"All profits go to the Intergalactic Green Belt Movement."* The sign was painted with a colourful design of pea pods, yams, figs and bananas.

"Do you think this is what Amaros meant when he said it would cost us four hours' hard work to meet the hero?" Ren said. "Why else would wanderers be doing all this? It must be part of the challenge."

Arthur agreed, but they wouldn't know for sure until they got to the farmhouse. As they approached, he studied it carefully. The wooden building was two storeys high, with white-framed windows and a wide porch that ran all around the ground floor. Wanderers holding small bowls filed up the steps and through the double front doors.

"Over there." Ren nodded to the side of the building,

where a V-class mimic was dispensing bowls to those waiting. Her flame-red tresses were contained in an unflattering hairnet and she was wearing a frilly green apron with the words *Chef's Assistant* sewn onto it.

Arthur kept his voice low as they hurried to the back of the queue. "The shadow patches only mask our identities from mimics. What if a wanderer recognizes us as the Flying Pipsqueaks?"

"We deny it," Ren said, pulling up the hood of her gilet. "Or better still, we don't say anything at all."

As they fell in behind a group of wanderers, Arthur was feeling jumpy. Tiburon Nox could have spies anywhere.

The V-class handed them a bowl each, and after queuing for ten uneasy minutes, they walked through the front doors of the hut to be greeted by the roar of chatter and the mouth-watering smells of home-cooked food. Arthur hadn't eaten since Milo's headquarters, and it made his stomach gurgle. The floor was set out like a huge open-plan canteen, with chairs and tables arranged in rows and a long serving hatch in the back wall, where the queue finished. A Hxperion-branded jug of water, stack of beakers and tray of cutlery was placed in the middle of each table.

"Plantain stew," Ren read from a blackboard suspended above the hatch. She lowered her voice as the wanderers behind them shuffled closer. "Well, I could do with eating, but this doesn't really help us with the challenge..."

Arthur scoured the room, making sure to avoid the

gaze of any other wanderers. The walls were decorated with photos. They showed wanderers working in the tree nursery, painting the farmhouse or cleaning the kitchens. Over at the serving hatch, several V-class mimics shuffled around in the steam, ladling soup into people's bowls. Among them was a familiar-looking woman with black hair tied in a brightly coloured headscarf.

"I think that's *her*," Arthur said, pointing. The sleeves of the woman's dress were rolled past her elbows, revealing strong, muscular arms. "She's the hero. I'm sure of it."

She had a wide smile that made her eyes and nose crinkle, and a defined face with prominent cheekbones. "I don't recognize her," Cecily admitted. "Maybe these photos can tell us who she is?"

As the line moved forward, they studied the walls. The images were arranged by date, reminding Arthur of a school yearbook, because each group commemorated a certain period of time on the farm. When the Wonderscape was still new, Arthur saw how wanderers had built the farmhouse, ploughed the land and harvested the first crops. There were pictures of people sitting around campfires with guitars or singing in the fields as they worked. He guessed they might be learning the songs that Amaros Ba had spoken about.

The plot had changed dramatically over the years, with new orchards planted and extensions built. Towards the front of the queue, animals appeared in the photos as well as wanderers. There was a strutting rooster with green and blue tail feathers, a floppy-eared grey bunny and a sheep with chocolate-brown wool.

Arthur stopped in his tracks when he spotted another animal, one he'd met before: a large greyish-brown pig with a blond beard. "I think these are all Cloud," he whispered, sharing his theory with Ren and Cecily. "These pictures are dated from three years ago; that must have been when he was here."

As the people in front of them moved aside, the trio came to the serving hatch. Arthur searched for the woman in the headscarf, but she had vanished again. He plucked up some courage and said to a V-class mimic with a whisk for an arm, "Excuse me, there was someone else here – a lady wearing bright colours and a headscarf. Can you tell me where she's gone?"

The mimic poured a measure of steaming plantain stew into his bowl. "Your request cannot be processed," she said derisively.

Arthur chewed on his lip as he followed Ren and Cecily over to a table. "Maybe we can't meet her because we haven't completed the challenge yet?" he said, keeping his head low. "Everyone she was serving must have already done their four hours' work on the farm."

He took a seat opposite Ren, hunching over his bowl with his elbows tucked in, so as not to brush arms with another diner and give them an excuse to talk to him. Next to Ren, Cecily reached for a jug of water and three beakers.

"We'll just have to do the work, then," Ren said, sticking her spoon into her stew. "The sooner we get started, the better."

The stew tasted amazing – sweet and sour with just the right amount of seasoning. Arthur mopped his bowl clean with his finger, feeling re-energized. Once they'd cleared away and used the toilets, they went out to find another V-class.

"The fig orchard will be fairly quiet," she advised them stuffily, after they enquired whether they could do four hours' work away from other wanderers. "But it isn't really in the spirit of things to work on your own. The task in this realm is about coming together as a team for the good of the environment."

Arthur couldn't think of a decent enough excuse to explain their request until he saw Cloud chewing on Cecily's bootlaces. "Some people don't like dogs. We *are* thinking of others."

The V-class didn't appear entirely satisfied with their reason, but after collecting a wheelbarrow and several wooden crates, they made their way to the fig orchard on the other side of the farmhouse.

Peacepoint Estate, unsurprisingly, didn't have an orchard, so Arthur had never walked in one before. The sun through the leaves cast dappled light on the ground and the air smelled of blossom and wet earth. Cloud ran around happily, chasing his tail and sniffing at any fallen fruit. The trees were planted in narrow lanes with two muddy ruts between them, where barrows laden with produce had been pushed before. Arthur wheeled their first crate into position and the three of them started picking.

The task was fairly monotonous. They looked for a fig, they grabbed the fig, and then they put the fig in the crate. The ripest fruits were on the outside and lower branches; anything too small or too green they left on the tree. Arthur found it strangely relaxing.

"You know what I miss the most about the twenty-first century other than my family and friends?" Cecily said at one point, inspecting her water bottle. "My wardrobe."

Arthur laughed.

"Come on, aren't you sick of wearing these cloaks and second-hand outfits?" she argued. "Plus, it freaks me out that I'm broadcasting my feelings all the time through these sunflowers."

"I miss understanding how everything around us works," Ren said. A branch cracked as she tugged at a fig. "Here, you watch videos through microscopes and cloaks give you superpowers. I know it's science but it creeps me out." She hesitated as she dropped another fig in the crate. "And my bed, I miss that too."

"What about you, Arthur?" Cecily asked.

He thought carefully. "Other than my dad's enchiladas – which are *the best*, by the way – I suppose the most unsettling thing about where we are is that we don't *know* where we are. I didn't realize it when we were back home, but it's comforting knowing exactly where you are on Earth; it gives you an anchor." He imagined himself from a bird's-eye view. He knew where the orchard was in relation to the forest and the farmhouse, but what was beyond the farm? How big was the planet they were on, and where on its surface were they?

"It's *obvious* where we are," Cecily said, as if Arthur was joking. "The planet Nyiri, in the Clamshell Galaxy." She held her thumb and forefinger up in an L-shape and aimed it at the sky. "Latitude of approximately zero point one five degrees south, I should think. Near the equator."

Arthur blinked and peered into the sky, where Cecily had been gazing. "How can you tell that?"

"Easy," Cecily replied. "It's the angle between the lowest star in the Psi Constellation, and the northern horizon. Nyirian people measure their prime meridian from the city of Doveton in the northern hemi—" She stopped, and frowned. "Wait … how do I *know* all that?"

Ren pointed to the sunflowers on Cecily's Wondercloak, which were now covered in thin red grid lines and annotated with the same strange writing they'd seen on the tent-flap Wonderway to Amaros's realm. "Look! This has to be something to do with your Wonderskill from Amaros Ba. The language is probably Tyrian."

Arthur remembered one of the postcards they'd read on the IGC building. "Of *course*. Amaros was a famously good navigator – you must have inherited his talents." He inspected the lining of his Wondercloak to check whether Cecily was right. Sure enough, orbiting a large green planet was a flashing ring of text that read, *REALM 42: PLANET NYIRI, CLAMSHELL GALAXY.*

"OK, which way is north?" Ren asked excitedly.

Cecily pointed behind them. "There."

Ren's eyes widened. "You're like a human compass!"

Before they could test Cecily's new Wonderskill further, a bell rang over at the farmhouse and the V-class with the hairnet called over, saying they'd completed the challenge. Four hours had passed already. As they hauled everything back to the farmhouse, Arthur estimated, with a little help from Isaac Newton, that they'd picked over a thousand figs each. On the approach to the farmhouse, he noticed a swirling ball of red mist nestled between the figs in their cart. When he touched it, a holographic coupon for fifty per cent off Hxperion merchandise appeared, along with a snow-white realm-key. He left the coupon in the cart and stowed the realm-key in his pocket.

Inside the farmhouse it wasn't plantain stew on the menu, but little sugary doughnuts called *mandazi*. To Arthur's disappointment, there was no trace of the woman in the headscarf – not behind the serving hatch or anywhere in the rest of the canteen.

"What do we do now?" Cecily asked, as they took three places at one of the tables.

Other wanderers piled in around them, munching eagerly. Arthur had to admit the *mandazi* were unbelievably good. So good, in fact, that while he was devouring a bowl of them, he didn't notice a woman sit down right next to him.

"What's your name?" she asked gruffly.

He tensed and kept his eyes on his plate, until Ren kicked him under the table.

"Arthur," he replied, immediately stuffing his mouth full of *mandazi*, so the woman would get the hint he didn't want to talk.

But then Cecily kicked him too and he looked up.

The woman sitting next to him had a smile that made her eyes crinkle and her cheeks glow. "It's nice to meet you, Arthur," she said. "My name's Wangari Maathai and the five of us have work to do."

21

Wangari Maathai? Arthur hadn't heard the hero's name before and by the blank expression on Cecily's face, neither had she. Ren, however, was frowning as if she knew who the lady was but couldn't quite place her.

"You must listen carefully and do as I say." Wangari's voice was tense but her movements relaxed. "Follow me, and make sure none of the mimics see you." She rose swiftly from the table and proceeded across the canteen floor towards the far corner of the room.

Arthur scanned for V-classes and spotted one through a window. She was outside, distributing plates to the remaining wanderers in the queue. The T-classes were all busy serving behind the hatch. "Everyone's distracted," he told Ren and Cecily. "Let's go."

Cecily grabbed Cloud's lead and they weaved through the tables, dodging wanderers who were either leaving their seats or taking their places. Wangari stood close to the wall, tracing her fingers over an area of the photos, as if feeling for something underneath. Her hand paused over one particular picture; she pressed a spot in the middle, there was a subtle *click* and a hidden door opened. "Inside," she hissed, shoving Arthur, Ren and Cecily over the threshold.

As he passed through the door, Arthur marvelled at how well concealed it was. The edges were covered by carefully placed photos, so you would never see it at all.

They emerged into a small room dimly lit by candles. A square wooden table in the centre was scattered with architectural drawings of the farmhouse; there was a noticeboard on one wall pinned with a large map of Kenya and a bookcase crammed with books on biology, zoological science and African history stood against another wall. At the back of the space, framed certificates and photos stood on a sideboard along with a display case of gold medals. A Wondercloak hung from a hook on the wall and Arthur spotted a handful of shadow patches resting on the side.

"Useful, aren't they?" Wangari said, catching Arthur adjusting his own shadow patch. She shut the door soundlessly behind them and locked it with iron bolts at three different places. "With a Wondercloak around my shoulders and a patch on my arm, I can explore this realm unseen by Hxperion."

Just then, Ren gasped and dashed over to the sideboard. "I know what that is," she exclaimed, peering through the glass display case at a shiny gold medal. "We did a whole project on this award at my old school – it's the Nobel Peace Prize!" She gawped at Wangari Maathai. "I *thought* your name sounded familiar – you're *Professor* Wangari Maathai, the first environmentalist to receive this."

"And the first African woman," Wangari added, as they all drew closer. "I was awarded the medal in large part because I founded the Green Belt Movement – an organization that empowers communities to care for their environment by planting trees."

Ren's eyes widened. *"Nature gives us all we need: to save the future, plant a seed,"* she recited from the riddle scroll. "Now it all makes sense."

"When we plant trees, we plant the seeds of peace and hope," Wangari said wisely. "The Green Belt Movement became a voice for change. Together we halted the construction of a sixty-storey tower block in a park in central Nairobi and fought against our government's greedy land-grabbing that caused the loss of precious forest."

Listening to Wangari's accomplishments filled Arthur with confidence. If just one person could achieve so much, maybe the three of them really could save the heroes and make it home in time. He examined the professor's memorabilia. Among several other prestigious-sounding prizes were photos of Wangari holding protest banners and giving speeches alongside powerful world leaders and famous film stars. "So the safari-bus challenge…"

"…was about opening your eyes to the problems around

you," Wangari said. "The bus journey is similar to one I took as a child, across the foothills of Mount Kenya. It was the first time I had seen large-scale deforestation."

"But why was the realm-challenge called Forest of the Leopard?" Ren asked. "I didn't see any big cats stalking around the farm."

Wangari laughed. "*Wangari* means 'she who belongs to the leopard' in my language. It's a nickname of sorts." She unstacked five chairs and slid them around the table. "Enough questions. We only have a little time before one of the mimics notices I'm gone. Sit."

Arthur dropped his rucksack on the floor and took a place opposite Ren. Cecily was between them, with Cloud on his own chair next to Wangari. He looked bright-eyed and alert, as if he'd been preparing for this meeting.

Wangari leaned forward. "The farm is a well-meaning project that helps fund a new intergalactic version of my Green Belt Movement," she began, "but it is a cover for my *real* activities. I am part of a secret activist group of heroes. Between us, we have been gathering intelligence on Hxperion, with the aim of escaping our realms and helping Milo Hertz. It all started when I first met Cloud."

The little dog ruffed proudly, lifting his chin as if to say, *That's right.*

"He arrived through a Wonderway three years ago, not far from where I was working in the forest," Wangari continued. "Thankfully, the V-class with me didn't spot him, but I knew he was special, so I kept him close and tried to puzzle out where he'd come from."

Arthur stared into Cloud's fluffy, white face, wondering what other secrets he might be hiding. "The first time we were alone – right here in this room – he finally explained himself." She lifted her chin at Cloud. "Go on – you're in safe surroundings now – show them what you showed me."

Cloud sniffed the air like he might be checking for the scent of danger. Once satisfied, he turned around and obediently lifted his back-left foot. For a mortifying second, Arthur thought he was about to pee on Wangari Maathai, but the little dog remained perfectly still. There was a snapping sound, like a cog turning, and Cloud's right ear pricked up and a hologram projected out of it.

Unlike the crystal-clear, pixel-sharp holograms they'd seen in the Wonderscape, this one was fuzzy and broken. It showed a flush-faced man with a mop of messy dark hair, dressed in a tattered T-shirt. Despite his ragged appearance, Arthur recognized him. It was Milo Hertz.

"If you're watching this, then you're one of my all-time biggest heroes and it's an honour to be talking to you," he said breathlessly. Daylight highlighted grease marks on his clothes and a sweaty sheen to his skin. "My name is Milo Hertz and I'm one of the founders of Hxperion. Like you, I am trapped in the Wonderscape and I need your help."

Arthur's skin tingled, thinking this was just like in *Star*

Wars: A New Hope, where the droid R2-D2 was found to be carrying a secret message from Princess Leia.

"My older brother Tiburon has trapped me in a closed realm," Milo continued. "He is a master strategist and has ensured there is no way for me to discern which number it is – even the map on my Wondercloak has been disabled. What's more, part of the realm-challenge here can only be completed by a *team* of people, so I'm unable to win a realm-key and leave." His hands moved closer to whatever device he was using to make the recording and he slowly swung it 360 degrees.

He was surrounded by an empty fairground, twinkling with white lights. There was a towering big wheel, a colourful carousel and a corkscrew roller coaster called the Black Maria in the distance. The stony land was reddish-brown and so flat you could see all the way to the horizon in every direction.

"Soon after I arrived here, I connected to a *Wondernews* feed and learned what Tiburon had done to all of you in my absence." As his face returned to the frame, he lowered his head. "I am ashamed to say that the technology he is using to travel through time is something *I* designed, something I should have destroyed long before Tiburon was able to steal it.

"Using scavenged parts from this realm, I was able to transmit this recording to Cloud in the hope that he would share it with each of you. Tiburon has eyes everywhere, so Cloud is programmed to do so only when safe, and to only trust those he's sure are from a foreign time. Please, if you're watching this now, you *have* to find me. With your help, I can escape and stop my brother once and for all."

With that, the hologram vanished and Cloud's ear went floppy again.

"So Cloud's on a mission," Cecily said, smiling proudly across the table at him. "Ever since he received Milo's recording, he's been travelling around the Wonderscape, finding heroes to play it to. That must be why he was on the *Principia* – to locate Isaac Newton and show it to him."

With the first officer lurking around, Arthur figured Cloud had never got the chance. He wondered how many other heroes Cloud had managed to share the recording with over the years. "Perhaps the time-key also allows you to move between realms, like a realm-key does?" Arthur guessed. "Newton said it could be used more than once, so that would explain how Cloud has been able to move through the Wonderscape. But we still don't know why Cloud opened a Wonderway to *our* time, or what caused that massive explosion at Number Twenty-Seven." He suspected something else had transpired, something neither Cloud nor Milo Hertz had ever intended.

Ren reached over and tickled Cloud under the chin. "At least we know why the Fuzzball's been helping us – we're from a foreign time, just like the heroes. He thinks we're one of them."

If Professor Maathai was surprised by the fact that they were from another time, she didn't show it. Instead, she gathered up the architectural drawings that were scattered across the table. "After Tiburon Nox's broadcast this morning, I had a hunch something might have happened to Cloud, so I sent a covert message to the activist ring to prepare themselves. We communicate through song. The idea was inspired by something I learned fighting the Kenyan government: the more voices you have, the louder the noise you make."

"Well, your tactics still work," Cecily said, describing what had happened during their hot-air balloon encounter with Amaros Ba. Wangari added Amaros's name, which she hadn't yet learned, to a list of others she had pinned to her noticeboard, along with their respective realm numbers.

"I've shared an escape plan with the others," Wangari revealed. "They've been told to acquire a shadow patch and a Wondercloak, and to steal a realm-key off a wanderer. When the time comes, they'll travel to Milo's realm and free him. The trouble is, I don't know which number it is." She hurried to the bookcase and fetched a large leather-bound volume with green writing on the spine. As she opened it on the table, Arthur read the title: *Trees of the Known Universe*. "I've watched Milo's recording several times, and the only clue I've spotted in the background is this." She pointed to an illustration of a thorny-barked tree with silvery leaves. "The Taran'yu tree, found only in the Jingsell Galaxy."

With a thought, Arthur removed his Wondercloak and spread it reverse-side up on the table. The stars on the Wonderscape map glittered like diamonds. "Maybe we can figure out which realm he's in using a process of elimination. We can start by identifying any realms located in the Jingsell Galaxy."

Wangari traced her finger over the map, like she'd done this before. "There's one here," she said, pointing to a small purple-blue sphere with a cratered surface. The text around the edge wasn't flashing, but it was still easy to read the word *Jingsell*. "And another here."

"And here," Ren added.

Seconds later, Arthur found two more. "Here too."

Altogether, there were six. Arthur tried to stay positive, but his spirits plummeted. His watch showed they had just over nine hours to go, so there wasn't time to try them all.

"Cloud, can you show me Milo's recording again?" Cecily asked, frowning. "The bit where he moves the camera around the landscape." With a twitch of his ear, Cloud helpfully obliged. "OK, I need you to pause it right … *there*," she commanded.

The video froze on an image of the horizon. The misty shadows of mountains loomed in the distance and the prickly figures of Taran'yu trees dotted the rocky earth.

"If this realm is somewhere in the Jingsell Galaxy, then those stars must be part of the Eighth Constellation," Cecily said, gesturing to a cluster of pale dots in the dim sky. Out of the corner of his eye, Arthur noticed Tyrian symbols glinting on the petals of her sunflowers and figured Amaros Ba was helping her out. "It's only visible on planets with a thin nitrogenous atmosphere. So with that criterion in mind – " she assessed the map on Arthur's Wondercloak and pointed to three of the planets they'd identified – "it must be one of these three."

Wangari hastily pulled the cloak towards her. "Realm Sixty-Eight, Realm Ninety-Four and Realm One Hundred and Fifty-Two," she read. With a glance at her noticeboard, she smiled. "Well, it can't be Realm Sixty-Eight – one of the heroes in my activist group resides there."

Arthur examined the geography of the planets on which the two remaining realms were situated. Annoyingly, they both had barren, rocky landscapes with reddish earth. "That narrows it down to one of these two – but which one?"

Wangari shook her head. "There's no way of knowing." Standing, she pointed to Realm One Hundred and Fifty-Two, labelled: *PLANET NAERES, JINGSELL GALAXY.* "You three journey to this one. I'll send a command to my activist group to travel to the other."

Arthur shared a nervous glance with Ren and Cecily. It was a decent plan, but it had risks. Big slimy ones. "The thing is, Milo's the only person who can help us get back to our own home," he explained, "and we have a seriously tight deadline. Will you tell your activist group that if they meet Milo first, they're to explain our plight?"

"Of course," Wangari said, slamming *Trees of the Known Universe* closed. "There's a Wonderway behind the farmhouse. You'd better hurry – my instincts tell me we've lingered here too long."

Minutes later, Arthur, Ren, Cecily and Cloud found themselves gathered on a shady patch of grass at the rear of the farmhouse, beside a swirling vortex of petrol-blue mist. A wooden door in the centre was bordered by dazzling light bulbs. Wangari put her hand on each of their shoulders. "Good luck. Those of us who know the truth must not tire or give up," she said firmly. "We must persist."

Arthur's mind flooded with worries. Time was tight, and if this realm was the *wrong* one, they'd have to complete another realm-challenge just in order to leave. He guiltily wondered if trying to save the heroes was going to mean he would never make it back home to his dad …

… but then he considered how threatened and alone the heroes must be feeling after all the terrible things Tiburon had done to them. He *had* to help them; it's what his dad would want too. He glanced over at Ren and Cecily. "Let's go."

Together, they stepped into the unknown.

22

The rainbow-coloured lights of a huge fairground twinkled in the distance. Shielding his eyes from the whirling dust motes in the air, Arthur spotted the same Ferris wheel they'd seen in Milo's recording. "Over there, look!" he exclaimed. "We must be in the right place!" His legs wobbled, giddy with elation. Ren and Cecily were beaming at him. Finally, they were close to going home. It felt like they'd been climbing a mountain and had just seen the summit for the first time.

As they set off, he took in the details of their surroundings – the wind whistling eerily over the plain, the cracked red earth, the grey sky looming overhead – and shivered. "What a miserable place to be stranded," he commented, imagining how Milo Hertz had survived alone in a place like this.

Cecily wrapped her arms around her. "I know. Four *years* he's been here, and all after his own brother double-crossed him." Cloud sniffed the ground and barked joyously as if to say, *Yay, we found the right realm!* Then, he went running off to explore.

They entered the fairground under a torn *TRAVEL WITH WONDER!* banner, which was surrounded by the red, blue and white stars and stripes of the American flag. A wide path stretched ahead of them, flanked by various souvenir stands, a water-pistol shooting gallery and a hook-the-duck stall. The stuffed toy prizes included unicorns, bears and a lizard-headed man that reminded Arthur uneasily of their safari-bus-tour-guide-cum-driver-of-the-Pipsqueaks-mobile. In the distance, the sideshows and amusements gave way to beautiful white architecture, domed greenhouses and a vast blue lagoon moored with old-fashioned sailing ships.

"Look alert," Ren blurted, quickly withdrawing her bow and nocking an arrow. She swivelled left and right, covering all angles. At first Arthur wasn't sure what had spooked her, but then he spied the body of a T-class mimic lying up ahead.

"He must have been assigned to work here when the realm was originally due to open," Arthur realized. "Before Tiburon made the last-minute decision to use it as a prison for Milo." He reminded himself that thanks to Ren, the realm *was* now open and would be working normally. The mimic was dressed in a red and yellow striped suit with the word *STAFF* embroidered onto the jacket pocket. Judging by the dents in his chest and his broken hover-wheels, he'd been in a fight. Narrow tyre prints circled the ground around him, as if he'd had an altercation with someone riding a bicycle.

"The tracks lead that way," Ren said, pointing with her arrow.

They followed the tyre marks deeper into the fairground, passing more defunct T-class mimics along the way. Every time a breeze blew, one of the attractions would creak, making the three of them jump. Arthur's senses were on high alert. This place had been closed for four years; who knew what they were going to find?

Soon, they came to a crossroads between a ghost train, a stall selling science-fiction novels, a towering helter-skelter and a fortune-teller's tent. Arthur peered along each path and sighted another T-class body on a track heading north.

"Have you noticed the mimics are all leading us in the same direction?" Cecily said. "They must have all been moving towards the same target when they were attacked. Do you think it has something to do with Milo?"

Arthur's skin went cold as he realized something. "The recording Cloud showed us of Milo is from years ago. What if Tiburon ordered the T-class units to attack Milo and he's been injured – or worse?"

Cecily gasped. "Then we'd be stuck here and turn to slime!" She grabbed Cloud's lead and they all sped up. Following the tyre trail, they hurried across the dodgems and past a waltzer, where they almost tripped over the headless remains of another robot. This one wasn't a mimic. It had basketballs for fists, a unicycle for legs and the torso of a carousel horse.

"Creepy," Ren remarked, kicking one of the basketballs. "Maybe Milo built it to defend himself?" Further along, they found another robot cobbled together from fairground junk; this model had a stuffed-toy panda for a head.

Finally, they turned a corner and came to a portico trimmed with white lights. Beyond it was a long concrete platform with a glossy black train pulled alongside. Even though it had wood-framed windows and old-fashioned doors, Arthur saw no steam engine at the front. Painted in fancy gold lettering on the side was the name *Menlo Express*. Something about it felt familiar to Arthur, but he wasn't sure why.

The grisly remnants of a dozen T-class mimics lay scattered around a door to the rear carriage. "Come on," Ren said. "Hopefully Milo's this way." She swung her bow round to her back and began clambering over the mimic remains to get onto the train. As Arthur followed, he glanced towards the driver's cab at the front, and saw that the train tracks led out of the fairground and across Naeres' barren landscape.

The *Menlo Express* was easily the most luxurious train Arthur had ever been inside. The carriage was finished in polished mahogany and decorated with velvet curtains and sinkable armchairs. Delicate glass ceiling lamps hung overhead and a plush wine-red carpet covered the floor, feeling spongy underfoot. The dry air smelled of furniture polish and popcorn, like in an upmarket cinema.

Cloud had just leaped onto a chair and started bouncing, when two puffs of red gas shot across the carriage like a pair of arrows and wrote a message in the dim light:

WONDERSCAPE

REALM 152: WORLD OF THE WIZARD

Loot: 1500 DIRT and realm-key

Travel with wonder,

HXPERION

"World of the Wizard – do you think there really could be a wizard here?" Cecily asked excitedly. "You never know, they might exist somewhere in the Known Universe and the hero could be like Amaros Ba – someone from our future?"

Arthur shook his head, the *Menlo Express* still tugging at his memory. If the hero was from their future, he wouldn't find it familiar. "Wizard might just be another nickname – like leopard was for Professor Maathai."

"Wait for it," Ren said, holding her hand out expectantly for another riddle scroll to drop out of thin air. But it didn't come. Instead, Arthur spotted two tea-stained sheets of parchment pinned to the wall at the far end of the carriage. One of them had a riddle written on it in small, precise handwriting:

> *All aboard the* Menlo Express,
> *On a journey heading west.*
> *Use your logic to decide*
> *How to progress through this ride.*
> *Only dreams and innovation*
> *Will bring the train into the station.*

Ren folded her arms, thinking. "*How to progress through this ride* – that sounds like you have to make your way through the train. In the recording, Milo mentioned that he couldn't complete the realm-challenge on his own. Maybe he only got halfway?"

"We can easily test that idea," Cecily said, reaching for the door handle to the second carriage.

But before she had a chance to open it, Arthur cried, "No, leave it closed!" He ran his finger over the text on the second sheet of brown parchment pinned to the wall. "These look like instructions for the realm-challenge – and it says we can only open that door once."

The others gathered next to him to read the list.

WHICH SWITCH?

1. All the doors on the *Menlo Express* are currently locked.

2. There is a standard light bulb hanging in the next carriage along. The light bulb is operated by one of three switches – A, B or C – located in this carriage. It is your task to find the correct switch. When you do, all the doors aboard the *Menlo Express* will unlock.

3. You may open the door to the next carriage once, but the light switches can only be activated when it is closed.

Travel with wonder,

HXPERION

Arthur's mind was reeling as he puzzled through the instructions. "All right, so there should be three light switches in this carriage. Can anyone see them?"

After only a minute's search, Cecily found them in the very corner of the carriage, half hidden behind a velvet curtain. They were similar in design to the Hxperion-branded button Arthur had pressed to evacuate himself from the safari bus, except they were labelled *A*, *B* and *C*.

"I don't understand – why don't we just open the door

so we can see the light bulb, flick all the switches and see which one works?" Cecily posed.

"I wish we could," Arthur said, rubbing his temples. "But the instructions say the switches can only be activated when the door is *closed*. That's the difficult bit about the challenge – how can we tell which switch works when we can't see the light bulb?"

Ren kneeled by the door. "There's some sort of rubberized seal around this. I don't think we'd see any light escaping."

"Yeah, and the next carriage has no windows either," Cecily called, hanging her head outside.

They each flopped into an armchair to mull it over. Arthur reached for his Wonderskill, hoping Newton might have some answers, but all that hovered at the edge of his mind were facts about the properties of light – speed, refraction, polarization and dispersion – nothing that would help in this instance.

"You'd think we'd be good at puzzles by now," Ren groaned. "We could turn on switch A, open the door and check to see if the light bulb is working. But if it isn't, it means one of the other two switches is the correct one and we'd have to shut the door again to try each of those."

Cecily chewed on her lip. "That's exactly the problem. The riddle scroll said, *Use your logic to decide* – so there must be a reasonable way to determine whether the light bulb is working without actually seeing it."

Arthur stared at the sealed door, picturing the light bulb switched on behind it. He imagined shadows being cast around the room and the bulb's warm glow radiating out from it. *Hang on...* His breath caught in his throat. "I've got it!" he spluttered. "Bulbs don't just emit light. They release heat too – that's how you can tell if a light bulb is working without being able to see it. You *feel* it." He stood up and hurried to the switches, running through the various options in his head. "OK, how about we turn A and B on at the same time and leave them for, like, ten minutes? Then, we turn A off and open the door."

Ren's forehead knotted, but she nodded slowly. "If the light bulb is *on*, the correct switch is B. And if it's off but still *warm*, then the correct switch is A."

"But if it's off and cold, then the correct switch must be C!" Cecily's eyes widened. "Arthur, you're a genius!"

Arthur felt his cheeks flush and his chest swell with pride. He hadn't even needed Newton's help.

They followed the plan step by step. When they opened the door into the next carriage, they found a long dark space – furnished the same as before – with a podium in the middle. Screwed on top was a large light bulb, switched *off*. Arthur stepped closer and, covering his fingers with the end of his sleeve, touched the glass. "It's warm," he told the others, the heat making his fingertips tingle. "So the correct switch must be A."

As soon as he'd spoken, the floor started creaking like

the train was laughing at his answer. Then, in quick succession, there followed a series of loud bangs.

Cecily ran to the next door and tried the handle. "I think we did it," she exclaimed, almost tripping backwards as it opened. "That sound must be the doors unbolting!"

"Come on," Arthur said, peering through into the shadows of the next carriage. "Milo's got to be in here somewhere."

They raced along the central aisle of the next three carriages, passing several flashing neon vending machines on the way. As Cecily opened the door to the fourth, Cloud tore himself from her grip and went running ahead. Everyone else stepped over the threshold cautiously.

They emerged into another windowless carriage with the same polished mahogany trim and thick burgundy carpet. It had a cosier feel than the rest of the train because it smelled overwhelmingly of candyfloss and was furnished with items collected from all over the fairground. There was a table fashioned from an upturned ghost-train wagon; a popcorn trolley converted into a bookcase; and a bed constructed from two halves of a giant teacup, with a straw-filled mattress between. A small desk in one corner was scattered with scavenged tools – a hammer from a high striker, brass pipes from a carousel organ that had been altered into spanners, and screwdrivers made from huge metal bolts.

"Cloud!" A broad-shouldered man dropped to his knees

in the middle of the floor. He was wearing a pair of magnifying goggles – which made his grey eyes look the size of planets – and dressed in a baggy T-shirt with trousers stitched from the same striped material as the T-classes' fairground-staff uniform. Over his shoulders hung a long mantle of dry autumn leaves.

Arthur's lungs emptied with relief as Cloud shot over like a rocket, jumped into the man's lap and started madly licking his face. Arthur recognized the man instantly, and there was only one person Cloud would be that happy to see: Milo Hertz.

"I've missed you too!" Milo laughed, tickling Cloud's tummy. He appeared unmistakably older and wearier than he had done in the recording; his cheeks were hollow and his neck gaunt.

Arthur edged forwards. "Milo Hertz? I'm Arthur and these are my friends, Ren and Cecily." He realized as he said "friends" that he'd never actually called them that before, but after everything they'd been through and all they'd shared, it just felt right. Cecily glanced over and flashed him a smile.

Milo got to his feet, pulled off his goggles and squinted at them as if they weren't real. "You're … *wanderers*?"

"Not exactly," Ren replied. "We're from the twenty-first century. That's where we met Cloud."

Milo offered them a seat on his teacup-bed while they delivered their story, explaining they had only hours left to get home. When Ren told him about Valeria planting a bomb in his headquarters and Tiburon threatening to delete them, he lowered his head. "I know you must think my brother and sister are monsters, but I remember a time when they weren't so obsessed with DIRT or making Hxperion powerful. When we first founded the company, they were just like me: excited about the possibility of creating a truly great I-RAG. I have to believe there's still good in them."

Ren folded her arms, as if she'd be less forgiving.

"But now you're *here*," Milo whispered, like he still couldn't quite believe it, "which means I can escape and make things right. When I was first stranded here, I destroyed all the T-classes so Tiburon couldn't spy on me, then I focused my efforts on transmitting a message to Cloud. After that, I had years to formulate my plans." He drew his eyebrows together in a determined scowl. "First things first, I'll send the three of you home, then I'll destroy the time crystal Tiburon stole and free the heroes trapped in the Wonderscape."

Hope bloomed in Arthur's chest. "Can you repair Cloud's time crystal?" he asked, remembering that was the name Milo had also used in M-73's recording. "Isaac Newton calls it a time-key."

Milo's face brightened. "Newton's been studying *my* inventions?" He shook his head in disbelief and took a seat at his desk. "Let's take a look." He whistled once and Cloud came scurrying over. Milo pulled down his magnifying goggles, unclipped the time-key from Cloud's collar and held it up to the light. "The damage appears to be consistent with exposure to infrared radiation," he concluded quickly. "No surprises there. This key, like the one Tiburon stole, was a prototype. They both react strongly to infrared. In tests, the radiation caused them to discharge varying waves of energy."

"That must have been what the explosion at Number Twenty-Seven was," Arthur said, thinking carefully. He cast his mind back to when he, Ren and Cecily first walked onto the *Principia*. "Newton had some experiments set up in his cabin. Perhaps one of those was emitting infrared?"

Milo shrugged. "All we know for sure is that the Wonderway Cloud used to get to Newton's realm must have still been open when the time-key was exposed. The energy it discharged must have disrupted the open Wonderway in such a way that it shifted its centre of space–time and opened a portal to the twenty-first century."

So it was all just bad luck, Arthur thought. If the time-key hadn't been exposed to this radiation, they would never have been cast into the future.

"With the right tools I *could* repair this," Milo said, rubbing his chin, "but it would take days, not hours." He held his hands up before they could all panic. "Don't worry. Inventors always build several prototypes before they make the final product. I made another time-key, one without the weakness of the first two. In order to return you home we just need to retrieve it." He went over to the popcorn-cart-cum-bookcase and began tossing books out. "I hid it in another realm, somewhere I thought Tiburon would never, ever think to look." He came across the volume he was hunting for and chucked it over.

Arthur held it between them so they could all see the title: *Frankenstein; or, the Modern Prometheus.*

The cover showed a tall humanoid monster with yellow-green skin, holding his arms out like a zombie. Arthur hadn't read the book, although his dad kept a copy on the shelf in their hallway, but he had watched an old movie adaptation. The story was about a scientist, Victor Frankenstein, who created a monster out of old body parts.

None of the characters in the story were based on real people, so Arthur knew they couldn't be the heroes of a realm. "Is it Mary Shelley's realm?" he suggested, reading the name of the author.

"One of my absolute heroes," Milo told them. "Tiburon was obsessed with *Frankenstein* when we were growing up. That's why he built his headquarters in Mary Shelley's realm, and that's why it's the last place he'd expect to find the third time-key – because it's right under his nose."

"You hid it where Tiburon's headquarters are?" Ren repeated, incredulous. "That's…"

"Ingenious," Arthur finished, eyeing her to calm down. There was no way to change it now.

Milo smiled. "It's Realm Eighteen – the same age Mary

Shelley was when she wrote the book."

"Eighteen?" Cecily said. "That's not too much older than us."

"Impressive, isn't it?" Milo said, grabbing a couple of bags of candyfloss. "First, though, we need to complete the final part of the realm-challenge here, in order to win a realm-key and escape. The hero is one of the greatest inventors of all time, and he was one of the first to apply teamwork to the process of invention – that's why the task is impossible to complete on your own." He raced towards the front of the train and pulled open a door into the next carriage. "Come on, we need to start the engine."

Arthur's mind whirred as he and the others chased after Milo. *A great inventor.* He considered the light-bulb puzzle and the American flag they'd seen hanging at the entrance to the fairground, and abruptly remembered where he'd heard the name "Menlo" before.

Menlo Park had been home to one of the most famous American men in history.

Thomas Edison.

23

The small driver's cab of the *Menlo Express* was unusual in that it contained no actual driving controls. As Arthur and the others huddled inside, he started to feel increasingly twitchy, wondering what lay in store in the next part of the realm-challenge.

"The *Menlo Express* travels in one direction," Milo said, lowering a window in a door on the left and pointing ahead of them. "Forwards."

A breeze blew in from outside, carrying the candyfloss scent of the fairground. On the opposite side of the cab was a door with another window, and at the front, a Hxperion-branded motorbike helmet hung from a hook on the wall. Other than that, the tiny space was empty. "The gears, acceleration and brakes are configured automatically," Milo continued. "All we can do is start the engine."

"And how do we do that?" Ren asked, scanning the room. "There's nothing here."

Arthur had already seen from the outside that the *Menlo*

Express wasn't a steam train. Knowing the locomotive was themed around Thomas Edison, he recalled what he knew of the inventor's history. As luck would have it, they'd done a whole project on him in physics last term. Edison had been an important figure in the War of the Currents – a technological battle to see who could introduce electric power to America first. "The train could run on electricity," he speculated. "Perhaps there's another set of switches somewhere?"

"Ah, she uses far more environmentally friendly fuel than that," Milo said excitedly. He unhooked the motorcycle helmet from the wall. Its black shell was slightly transparent and Arthur could see lights glowing under the surface. "The *Menlo Express* is powered by *ideas*."

As Milo pulled on the helmet, Arthur found himself smiling at how apt that was. He remembered his physics teacher saying Edison had believed that ideas moved us forward. It made perfect sense, then, that a train named the *Menlo Express* would be powered by them.

There was a low rumble as the floor vibrated and the train jerked. Arthur steadied himself against the wall as they started rolling forward. "That will only get us so far," Milo said, pulling off the helmet and offering it to Arthur. "You try. The more original the idea, the more power it gives the train."

Arthur hesitated, realizing what must have just happened – the train's engine had sparked to life because Milo had fed it an idea *through* the helmet, somehow. "Err…" He wiped his sweaty hands on the back of his jeans, before accepting the helmet from Milo. "Can it be any idea at all?"

Milo nodded. "One from each of you should give us enough power to take us where we need to go."

Arthur glanced uncertainly at Ren and Cecily before wiggling the helmet over his head.

Tiny lights flashed inside. The mix of colours – purple, yellow, green, red and blue – gave him the disorientating feeling of being inside a disco ball. He furrowed his brow and tried to think of something brilliant.

Unfortunately, the first thing that popped into his mind was an idea for a garden gnome burglar defence system. As he considered how it might work (the gnomes would have cameras in their eyes and invisible laser beams shooting from the ends of their fishing rods), he felt the floor wobble and had to steady his legs as the train sped up.

Ren slapped him on the back as he took the helmet off. "Good one," she said. "What did you think of?" When he told her, she laughed. "I've got my idea already," she said. "Spaghetti Bolognese toasties – best invention I've ever come up with."

Cecily crinkled her nose. "Yuck, they sound gross."

"Sound gross and look gross," Ren agreed proudly. "But taste *delicious*."

The train sped up once Ren had the helmet on, and accelerated again when it was Cecily's turn. "It's difficult to think of something under pressure," Cecily admitted, pulling the helmet off. "I thought about those awful make-up-themed weapons the V-classes use and imagined a shield to defend against them. You wear it as a necklace, and when you're attacked it turns really big to save you. Oh, and it matches whatever outfit you're wearing."

Arthur laughed and stuck his head out of the window as they left the fairground behind and ventured across the dusty, red land. Wind roared in his ears. "Where are we going?"

"Can you see the mountains in the distance?" Milo asked.

Arthur squinted. An outcrop of jagged orange rocks crowded the horizon.

"There's a train station on the other side. In order to get there, we have to switch to another set of tracks while the train is still in motion – *that's* the challenge. If we don't move onto the new tracks, these ones take the train all the way back to the fairground."

Arthur remembered the riddle scroll hanging in the first carriage. *Only dreams and innovation will bring the train into the station.* The clues had been there all along.

Milo's finger squeaked as he drew a traffic light in the condensation on the opposite, closed window. "The points are controlled by a mechanical lever that looks like this. It has three numbered paddles on it. We have to hit the correct one as we go past. Trouble is, the correct one changes every time."

"So how do we know which one to hit?" Ren asked. "Is it just down to luck?"

Arthur could hear the worry in her voice. With all that was at stake, they couldn't afford to rely on chance.

"Right before the switch, the train passes through a tunnel," Milo explained, cleaning a large circle in the condensation with his sleeve. "Three numbers appear on the walls of the tunnel at the exact same moment. Added together, they give you the number of the paddle we need to hit."

Arthur puzzled it through logically. "So one of us should remain here at the front of the train, ready to hit the paddle. The other three will need to be positioned along the train at different points in order to see the numbers."

"Then we just need to find a way to communicate the numbers to the person at the front," Cecily said, following.

Milo smiled at them. "Exactly."

"Ren, you should be at the head of the train," Arthur decided. "You've got the best chance of hitting the correct paddle with an arrow."

Milo glanced at the huge bow slung over Ren's shoulders. "What other Wonderskills have you three collected?"

"Arthur has an encyclopaedia in his head and I'm a human compass," Cecily answered. "If I remember correctly, I don't think there was a Wonderskill mentioned in the loot for Wangari Maathai's realm-challenge."

"Wangari Maathai?" Milo's face brightened. "No, I

designed that realm. Instead of a Wonderskill, every time a wanderer completes the challenge Hxperion donates DIRT to the Intergalactic Green Belt Movement." He added with a huff, "Tiburon only allowed it because Valeria said it would be good for PR."

Arthur liked the idea. Wangari Maathai would certainly approve.

The cab swayed as they ran over an uneven section of track, and the carriage behind rattled. "How are we going to communicate with Ren? It's too noisy for us to shout out of the window at her," Arthur noted.

"I've had years to design a solution to that," Milo said. "Come back inside, I'll show you."

Arthur was expecting something high-tech, maybe involving holograms or nano-particles. What he got was rubber ducks.

"As soon as you see your number appear on the tunnel wall, you write it on a duck," Milo explained, standing next to an inflatable pond full of the yellow plastic birds. He'd obviously gathered them from the hook-a-duck stand in the fairground. "Then you attach it to this," he continued, signalling to a rope strung outside. "It's connected to a system of pulleys and runs the entire length of the *Menlo Express*."

Arthur hadn't noticed the rope before – perhaps because it was fixed to the opposite side of the train from where they'd boarded. "Pulling on the rope will carry your duck all the way to Ren," Milo continued. "Then she just needs to add all three numbers together and shoot at the correct target."

Ren smiled nervously. Arthur figured this would probably be the most important calculation she ever did.

With fifteen minutes to go before they reached the tunnel, they got into position. Milo handed them each a bag of candyfloss – the only food he had an unlimited supply of – and as Arthur waited alone, he devoured the entire portion. The instant sugar rush was just what he needed to keep focused.

His nerves bubbled as he gripped his rubber duck in one trembling hand and a lidless marker pen in the other. Through the open window in front of him, the landscape of Naeres flashed past in an orange-red blur. Arthur hadn't faced a Wonderscape challenge without Ren and Cecily by his side before, and he could feel the difference. His legs were more jelly-like, his belly somersaulting as if it were doing an Olympic display routine. When the three of them were together, he felt stronger. That was the power of friends. "See the number, write the number on the duck, send the duck to Ren," he drilled to himself. He hoped the others were managing to keep their anxiety in check better than he was.

Outside, it abruptly fell dark. Arthur tensed, knowing they must have entered the tunnel. He could hear the hiss and rattle of the train wheels echoing inside.

Breathing deeply, he concentrated on the rocky wall, determined not to mess up.

Seconds passed that felt like minutes.

Then a number flashed in red light on the stone. *16*.

Arthur's fingers shook as he wrote it as clearly as he could on the duck's breast. Dropping the marker on the floor, he secured the duck to the rope and began to pull. With every stroke of his arms, he was reminded of the ticking hands on his watch. If they messed up this challenge, they'd find themselves back where they started with little chance of returning home before the universe went into auto-correct...

His heart leaped as another duck slid by on the rope. It had to be Cecily's – she was stationed a couple of carriages down from him.

Light returned through the window as the train rocketed clear of the tunnel. Still tugging on the rope, Arthur stuck his head outside and got a face full of wind. His pulse quickened as he watched the *Menlo Express* race towards a junction in the tracks. *Come on, Ren. You've got this.* Up ahead, the strange signal box that Milo had drawn was planted in the dry land, several metres from the side of the track. Three paddles numbered *18*, *34* and *72* protruded from its right-hand side.

Arthur had no idea which was the correct one. He tensed as an arrow streaked through the air and hit the number seventy-two squarely in the middle. The paddle spun around like a wind turbine ...

... and, with a loud creak, the tracks shifted. Arthur

felt the floor jerk as the train switched over. "Yes, Ren!" he cheered, releasing his grip on the rope and running towards the front of the train.

His whole body felt lighter as he dashed through each carriage. When he got to the driver's cab, Milo and Cloud were already there, celebrating. Ren's cheeks were flushed. "Thanks," she mumbled, when Arthur congratulated her. "I don't think I've ever felt more pressure in my whole life."

Cecily arrived to further cheers and delirious barking from Cloud. Arthur felt so proud of them all. They'd started off barely able to work together as a team, and now look at them...

The train rumbled on for a few minutes before it started to slow. A station appeared in the distance, drawing closer. It was similar in design to the one they'd left behind at the fairground, with bright lights outlining its structure like a vanity mirror.

As the *Menlo Express* came to a stop alongside the platform, a ball of red mist materialized in the driver's cab and a realm-key fell into Milo Hertz's waiting hands. Staring down at it, he swallowed. Arthur could see emotion shining in his pale grey eyes. "I've dreamed about this moment for four years," he said slowly. "Thanks to you three, it's really happening. I'm finally getting out of here."

As they stepped onto the platform, Ren drew her bow. "Since you've never made it this far, there might still be active T-class units here," she said, turning left and right.

Arthur scanned the place warily. Save for a jukebox vending machine flashing wildly at the opposite end, it was eerily deserted. He and the others wandered under a portico and into a large wood-panelled hall with a high white ceiling. Shelves lined the walls, filled with an odd assortment of machine parts – giant plastic tubes, camera lenses, metal cylinders, wooden cogs, intricate glass dials and reels of wire – Arthur even spied a rubber car horn. In the centre of the room were two devices he recognized from his project on Edison. Used for recording and playing sound, a shiny brass phonograph sat on a table beside a large wooden cabinet with a peephole viewer at the top – a kinetoscope, an early device that allowed people to view motion pictures. Sunlight fell through a bay window that opened onto a terrace at the back.

Cloud pushed his nose against the floor and gave it a sniff.

"Where are we?" Cecily asked, venturing outside.

Following at her shoulder, Arthur passed a well-worn leather armchair beside a coffee table. Upon it was a scale model of the entire railway, featuring a miniature version of the fairground, the mountain tunnel, the track junction and the *Menlo Express*. Small sections of the model lay scattered across the table's surface like board game pieces. It was almost as if someone had been sitting there, redesigning it.

When Arthur stepped into the sunlight, he gasped. The

terrace overlooked a busy street corner where old-fashioned motorcars rumbled along the roads and mimics in wide-brimmed hats and long raincoats swished past. A few blocks away, behind a multi-storey apartment building, the top half of the Empire State Building rose into the sky.

This wasn't any old city, it was *New York*.

"Those are definitely T-classes," Ren said, staring down the shaft of an arrow. "We need to find a Wonderway and get out of here."

Behind them, footsteps thumped against the floorboards. "Who are *you*?" an American voice asked sternly. "How did you get here?"

Arthur spun around to see an older gentleman in a dark suit and burgundy bow tie rushing towards them. He had bushy brows, neatly parted wispy white hair and intelligent blue-green eyes.

"Mr Edison?" Arthur exclaimed.

The man stopped a few metres short of them. "That's correct." He squinted. "Wait... Are you the Flying Pipsqueaks I've been seeing on the *Wondernews*?"

Arthur cringed. It was embarrassing enough being called a Pipsqueak in the *Wondernews*, let alone having a legend from human history address you that way.

"Sir, it's an honour to meet you," Milo Hertz said, extending his hand.

"I know *you* too," Edison muttered angrily. "You're one of the founders of Hxperion, just like Tiburon Nox!"

"But Milo's one of the good guys!" Cecily blurted. "Please, we're on a mission to stop Tiburon and get home before we turn into slime. Can you lead us to a Wonderway? We don't have much time."

Edison skimmed their faces. "How can I trust that you're not working with Tiburon? He has agents everywhere. This could all be a trap. For four years I've been here on my own and that train has never pulled into the station…"

Arthur could hear the frustration in Edison's voice. After everything the inventor had likely been through in the Wonderscape, Arthur suspected it would take more than words to convince him of their sincerity. "What if we could show you that we're telling the truth?" Arthur said, remembering he still had M-73's neuro-processor in his rucksack. He unshouldered his bag, loosened the top and tipped the contents onto the floor. Amid the crumpled exercise books, pencils and crisp wrappers, M-73's neuro-processor glowed like a magic jewel. "This belonged to an M-class mimic – you won't have met any, but they look like Milo. It contains recordings that prove he and Tiburon aren't on the same side."

Edison took the neuro-processor suspiciously and shut his eyelids. A split second later, they flicked open. "How many other people have seen these recordings?" he blustered.

Arthur deduced from his reaction that mimics were able to view the memories at a faster speed than humans.

"Nobody yet, but that doesn't mean we're on our own. All the heroes we've met so far have been fighting Hxperion in their own way."

Cecily glanced at her feet. "One of them even sacrificed herself so we could get this far," she admitted sadly. "And Wangari Maathai – the last hero we met – she's the leader of an activist group that was set up to help Milo escape."

Arthur briefly remembered that Wangari's team – if they'd successfully managed to leave their own realms – would have found themselves in the wrong realm to save Milo. That meant it was up to him, Ren and Cecily to get Milo safely out of there and give him the best possible chance of vanquishing his brother once he'd sent them home.

"I'd hoped other heroes were trying to fight back," Edison murmured, "but I wasn't sure. Everything I know about the Wonderscape I've learned from reading the *Wondernews* or through my own private study." His brows drew together. "Follow me."

He returned M-73's neuro-processor to Milo and led them through a set of double doors into another hall. Standing in the middle of the floor was a gloomy black Wonderway frame surrounded by a mass of tangled wires, small copper pipes and metal coils, all connected to some sort of wooden switchboard, set up on a nearby table. "You'll have to excuse the mess," Edison said, stepping carefully over a length of insulated cable. "I've been experimenting."

Milo scrutinized the equipment. "This looks like some sort of … communications device."

Mr Edison nodded. "I've been developing a machine that will transmit Morse code through a Wonderway, in order to communicate with other heroes."

"Does it work?" Arthur questioned, marvelling at Edison's resourcefulness and ingenuity. If it did, he had an idea how it might help them.

"Theoretically, yes," the inventor replied. "But I won't know for sure until after you've left. When you insert your realm-key into the Wonderway, it *should* be like turning the ignition in a motor car – my device will harness the power of the Wonderway's 'engine' in order to fuel itself."

"Remarkable," Milo commented, poring over the switchboard. "And you've used a non-conductive buffer to counter the electromagnetic pulse – such a neat solution." He explained to the others, "Wonderways emit bursts of electromagnetic energy when you pass through them that can disrupt electronic equipment."

Ren touched her trouser pocket. "*That's* why our phones haven't been working, isn't it? Every time we travelled through a Wonderway, they got zapped."

Arthur wanted to understand more, but he could sense time slipping away. "Mr Edison, if your machine *does* work, would you be able to send a message to Wangari Maathai for us, and tell her what's happened?"

"And the other heroes we've met," Cecily added hastily.

She grabbed a pen and sheet of paper off a table and scribbled the necessary names and realm numbers.

Edison assessed them thoughtfully. "I will do my best. Which realm are you off to now?"

"Eighteen," Milo said, tapping it into the Wonderway keypad. The inventor made a note on the same sheet, and Milo inserted the realm-key.

Assembled before the Wonderway, they all took a step back as fingers of blue smoke curled around the frame and grew into a twisting mass. A grey stone door appeared in the middle.

"I really hope that's not blood," Cecily said, signalling towards a suspicious red stain at the foot of the door.

Arthur swallowed as he got ready to walk through. He glanced at his watch. Their window was closing.

24

Rain pattered against the grey stone cobbles. Arthur pulled up the hood of his Wondercloak and peered out at the narrow street ahead. Tightly packed buildings with sharp roofs rose several storeys high on either side. Behind their ground-floor windows, displays of Hxperion-branded souvenirs sat in the dark.

Cloud growled and dipped his paw into a puddle, distorting the reflection of the foggy sky above. "I don't think the Fuzzball likes this place," Ren commented, crouching to give him a reassuring stroke.

Cecily tucked her plait inside her hood. The sunflowers on her cloak were already dripping. "Where is everyone? I expected this realm to be full of wanderers."

Arthur surveyed their surroundings. The place was as deserted as Naeres, which gave him a bad feeling. Given Tiburon's headquarters were located there, Arthur had thought the realm would be busy. He wondered if the lack of people suggested that Tiburon might be expecting them...

"This is the first time I've felt rain in four years," Milo shared unexpectedly. He was holding his face up to the clouds, letting the raindrops run over his cheeks and trickle down his neck. "It's only ever dry on Naeres." A smile spread across his face as he enjoyed the downpour for a moment longer, before fixing his attention on the road. "Tiburon designed this realm to resemble Ingolstadt," he told them as they walked. "It's a medieval town in Germany where Victor Frankenstein goes to university."

Arthur didn't know anything about medieval architecture, but the zigzagging wooden beams and looming bell towers definitely gave off a fairy-tale vibe. Tiburon's plus-sign cross was everywhere – patterned into the cobbles and inlaid on the building sides, a creepy reminder that they were heading straight into the lion's den.

"I don't know what changes my brother's made to this realm since I last visited," Milo admitted. "I assume Mary Shelley is here now, somewhere…" His brows drew together, like he was conflicted about the prospect of possibly meeting her.

At the end of the path they turned into a cobbled square lined with more shops and restaurants. A three-tiered fountain decorated with terracotta tiles bubbled away in the centre. There were a few T-class mimics dressed in fur-trimmed tunics scuttling around, collecting rubbish, but they didn't appear to pay Arthur and the others any attention. Arthur unconsciously touched the back of his wrist, where his shadow patch was stuck. It had to still be working. As the rain fell harder, the group retreated under a café awning for shelter.

"So where's the third time-key?" Arthur asked Milo. "Is it close?"

Before Milo could answer, Cecily threw her arm out, pointing to a nearby shop window. "Over there, look!" A ghoulish message hovered behind the glass in letters made of red gas. The words were slightly blurred by the rain, but Arthur could easily read what they said:

WONDERSC⊕PE

REALM 18: CASTLE OF THE DOCTOR

Loot: 1500 DIRT and realm-key

Travel with wonder,

HXPERION

Moments later, a riddle scroll fell with a splash into a puddle by their feet. Arthur wiped it dry on his Wondercloak before unfurling it so the others could read the neat, elegant handwriting:

Hidden in this stormy city
Is a creature you should pity.
Seek the centre of the maze
Through the deadly mist and haze.
There is nowhere you can hide
From the monster deep inside.

"So, there's some sort of *Frankenstein*-themed maze here?" Ren noted in a gloomy tone. "Sounds lovely."

Milo cringed. "About that…"

"Please don't tell us the time-key is in the maze," Arthur begged. With time running out, it was the worst possible challenge he could think of.

"It isn't *in* the maze, exactly," Milo replied awkwardly. "The time-key is in Frankenstein's lab, in the university. But the university is surrounded by the maze. You three will have to get to the centre of it in order to retrieve the time-key and go home."

"What do you mean, us three?" Ren asked. "Aren't you entering the maze with us? If you've done the challenge before, you'll know how to succeed."

Water dripped from Milo's hair as he shook his head. "That's just it – because I've completed the task before, I *can't* do it again. It's one of the Wonderscape's rules: realm-challenges become 'locked' once you've finished them. The maze won't let me enter. I have to access Frankenstein's lab a different way."

Cecily bit her lip. "I don't suppose you can just fetch the time-key for us and meet us back here?"

"Afraid not," Milo replied, offering her a sympathetic smile. "The closest Wonderway is also in Frankenstein's lab, so you'll *have* to make it through the maze anyway in order to get home." Shadows flickered in his grey eyes, like he was recalling an unpleasant memory. "You must be careful. Mary Shelley's novel is all about loneliness, so the only way to beat the maze is to navigate it individually. It's designed to test your greatest fear."

Our greatest fears. Arthur shivered, trying to decide what his might be. Right now, he could think of lots of fears – being hit by a swinging boulder, having exploding perfume bottles thrown at him, being shot at by a rocket launcher – the list went on. Probably the greatest among them was being turned to slime and never seeing his dad again.

Milo positioned himself a healthy distance away, then beckoned Cloud over and got to his knees to fiddle with Cloud's collar. "Cloud and I will fly in, over the top. I'll meet you in Victor Frankenstein's lab. It's north of here."

And just like that, he was lifted into the air on the back of a huge green dragon. Cloud's scales glittered like emeralds. Her wings gave a loud thud as she stretched them out, filling them with air. "And hurry," Milo called down. "There's no time to lose!"

Arthur, Ren and Cecily shrank back as Cloud beat her

wings, spraying them with water. Arthur had been riding her the last time she'd taken off, so he had no idea how impressive it was to see a dragon take flight. Cloud did a running jump, her claws striking the flagstones, and then, with one pull of her wings, launched into the sky.

"There's no time to lose," Ren repeated grumpily, watching Cloud fade into the mist. "Like we don't know that already."

Cecily nodded to the other side of the square. "Well, north is that way, but I don't think we need my Wonderskill to help direct us to the university." She gazed into the distance. "I'm guessing *that's* it."

Rising over the rooftops of the town, several pointed black spires pierced the fog. Arthur could just see the grey stone walls of a castle looming in the mist. With its narrow stained-glass windows and round turrets, it looked more like a fortress than a place to go to school, but Arthur drew his hands into fists, feeling a surge of determination. "Let's go."

They hurried through the damp, deserted town until they came to the banks of a stagnant moat. It was crossed by a bridge decorated with winged statues. On the other side, an imposing barbican with an arched gothic roof and a black portcullis led into the university. Arthur searched the battlements for Milo and Cloud, but couldn't spot them. He hoped they'd made it safely.

As they approached the bridge, it became clear that the

winged statues were gargoyles. Most of them had fangs for teeth, gnarled skin and bony bodies. "I don't remember these from the film," Arthur said, as the eyes of a particularly gruesome creature seemed to follow him. "Tiburon Nox must have added them in."

After passing through the barbican, the labyrinth came into sight. Its imposing black stone walls looked at least five metres tall and they were covered in moss too slippery to climb. The entrance was marked by two more gargoyles, who sat facing each other, their teeth bared. Beyond, a cobbled path was clouded with fog so thick, you couldn't see further than a few paces inside.

"Seek the centre of the maze through the deadly mist and haze," Ren recalled. "I'm presuming something horrible is going to happen when we breathe that stuff in."

Cecily rubbed her shoulders. "And Milo said we have to navigate the maze *alone*, so we won't be able to help each other."

Arthur was still ruminating over Milo's warning that the maze would test their greatest fears. His palms sweated, wondering what he might soon be facing. "I'll go first," he said, wanting to get it over with. They were so close to going home they couldn't fail now. He stepped between the gargoyles and hesitated, looking back over his shoulder.

Beneath their hoods, Ren and Cecily's faces were in shadow. "I'm sure I read somewhere that there's a method for solving mazes," Cecily said. "You have to keep touching the left-hand wall. That way you won't get lost."

Ren's Wondercloak showed designs for a suit of armour. "We'll see you in the centre," she said firmly. "Whatever happens, don't give up."

With their advice ringing in his ears, Arthur set his jaw and walked into the smog.

At first, all that happened was a lot of coughing. The gas tasted of strong chemicals, which cloyed at the back of Arthur's throat like hairspray. Unable to see beyond the end of his nose, he kept his fingers against the wall on his left as Cecily had suggested, and staggered forwards, zombie-like, with his other arm held out in front of him, hoping he might be able to feel his way to the centre.

Eerie noises filled the air. Doors creaked; wolves howled; voices shrieked. It was as if someone had edited together all the jumpy sounds from a horror movie and was playing them back over a loud speaker. He tensed as something brushed past his leg, but when he glanced at the floor he couldn't see anything.

His mind churned, imagining what might be lurking in the mist around him. When he was little, he'd been scared of the monsters in *Doctor Who* and had hidden behind the sofa whenever his dad watched the show on TV. If the maze was tailored to his own fears, Arthur wondered whether some of them might be about to pop up now.

He curled the toes of his trainers around the cobbles,

hoping to keep his feet gripped to the floor – and himself gripped to reality. *It's a game,* he reminded himself. *Whatever happens, this is all just a game.*

Following the wall to his left, Arthur made several turns, venturing deeper into the maze. Slowly, the fog began to subside; the ground became spongy underfoot and hulking shapes appeared around him. His knee hit something hard and when he looked down, he saw a wonky tombstone sprouting from a patch of grass. Another couple of steps, and he came across several more. The maze must have a graveyard, but he couldn't remember *that* being in the *Frankenstein* movie either. He swallowed, wishing Ren and Cecily were there beside him. He understood why it was more difficult to explore the maze alone: because then you weren't just fighting whatever obstacles it threw at you, you were fighting the fear and worry that came with loneliness.

"Arthur?" called a familiar voice.

Arthur froze. It was unmistakable. *"Dad?"* His fingernails scratched the wall as he ran forwards and bumped into another gravestone. "Dad, is that you?"

"Arthur! I'm over here!"

Arthur wanted to believe the voice was a trick of the maze, but could he really take that risk? It was possible, he knew, that Tiburon had travelled back in time, captured Arthur's dad and brought him to the Wonderscape in order to punish Arthur.

"Arthur, please!"

His dad sounded panicked. Fear bubbled in Arthur's throat and before he knew it, he'd let go of the wall and was weaving through the tombstones, heading in the direction of his dad's voice. "It's all right, Dad, I'm coming!" He stumbled over the uneven earth, splashing cold mud onto the back of his jeans.

The mist was disorientating and after following his dad's voice for a while, Arthur started to wonder if he was going in circles. Every time he thought he was getting closer, a shout came again which sounded further away.

Eventually, Arthur came to a thinning patch of mist where two gravestones stood next to each other. "Dad, where are you?" he called again.

"Over here," replied the voice. Only this time it sounded muffled, like it was coming from behind a thick wall. As Arthur picked up his foot to continue, he tripped and fell into the earth. "Erg," he grunted, lifting his head. "Don't worry, I'm—"

Then his body went rigid.

The pair of gravestones displayed names he recognized. The first he'd kneeled beside many times before – *Mary Louisa Gillespie* – his mum. But the second stone was newer and freshly chiselled with a different name: *Simon Gillespie*. Arthur's dad.

His throat tightened as his hands started shaking. This was it, wasn't it? His greatest fear was losing the one parent he had left and ending up alone. Tears prickled at the corners of his eyes as he imagined life without his dad. He already missed him so much. "Dad?" he whispered.

A warm, chuckling voice sounded in the corner of Arthur's memory. *There's nothing to be frightened of, Arthur,* his dad said as Arthur crawled out from behind their sofa. *It's just TV. It can't hurt you. It's not real.*

It can't hurt me, Arthur repeated, sniffing. *It's not real.*

As he wiped his nose on the back of his hand, he noticed that his skin felt slimy. When he touched his jeans, they were slippery too. The mist must have condensed on the surface of his clothes. He wondered what it was made of and why it was there. Perhaps it was affecting him somehow, distorting his sense of reality?

He shook his head and tried to straighten his thoughts. He was trapped in a maze that was designed to test his greatest fear. If he wanted to escape, he would have to face it head-on.

To bolster his confidence, he thought of Ren and Cecily and everything they'd overcome together. With friends like that, he didn't think he'd ever feel alone. He took a deep breath and looked back at the gravestone…

His dad's name was gone. Arthur ran his fingers over the surface of the stone, but it was smooth. He wondered if the letters had ever been there, or if they – *and* his dad's voice – had all been in his head.

Slowly, he pushed himself to his feet and gritted his

teeth, the memory of his dad making him more determined than ever to get home.

Scrambling on, he reached out on both sides for the maze wall and rejoined it after a few metres. As it guided him around a corner, he started to feel taller. He was walking with purpose now, each step taking him closer to home, to his dad. It was strange – the stronger he felt, the more the fog seemed to disperse. Soon the air cleared completely, and he found himself in a square courtyard enclosed by tall castle walls.

Several stone doors, similar to the one that had appeared in the Wonderway, were positioned around the edge. They all had words etched into their surfaces. He wasn't sure if he was in another section of the maze, or if he had, in fact, reached the centre …

… until Cecily ran out of the fog behind him.

"Arthur!" She looked ragged and wide-eyed. The sunflowers on her cloak were trembling.

"What happened? Are you OK?" he asked, wondering if she'd had to survive another swinging-boulder run or something else that triggered her vertigo.

She rubbed the sides of her face. "It was a nightmare. My parents… They didn't even know who I was. It was like they'd forgotten I exist."

Arthur figured she'd endured a similar experience to him. He was still shaken up about seeing his dad's gravestone, but he tried to push his feelings aside. "It wasn't real," he told her assuredly. "You know that, right? Your parents would never forget about you. Ever."

As she nodded, Ren burst out of the mist, panting. She was sheet-white and her quiver was empty, except for one arrow which rattled around as she trembled. "Spiders," she hissed. "Really. Big. Spiders."

Cecily pulled her in for a hug. "Well done. Mine was horrible too."

While they shared horror stories, a churning ball of red gas appeared in the centre of the courtyard. Arthur raced over and collected the realm-key, then hurried around the edge of the courtyard. *"Botanical Science, Astronomy, Theology,"* he read on the doors. "These must lead to the different departments of the university."

"So where would Victor Frankenstein's lab be?" Cecily posed.

Ren kicked the bottom of a door with a suspicious blood-red stain on it. "It's got to be this one."

Arthur read *"Anatomy"* on the front, and shuddered. "Yeah, sounds about right."

Through the door, they crept along a corridor lit by flaming torches and up some winding stairs. The rain beat loudly against the castle walls and soon the rumble of thunder joined the roar of the storm outside. At the top of the steps, they found themselves in a shadowy entrance hall with a grand, curving staircase that led to a balcony above. The floor was covered in thick, red carpet and a flickering chandelier hung from the ceiling.

"Hxperion has told wanderers to leave this realm," a voice called.

Arthur hesitated. The voice sounded like it had come from behind the stairs, but everything echoed so much, it was hard to tell.

"We're undergoing a security drill," the speaker continued, in a polite English accent. "It isn't safe for you to remain."

Arthur briefly considered what the voice was saying. Tiburon Nox must have wanted the place cleared of wanderers. Arthur wondered why…

"The person talking has to be Mary Shelley," Cecily hissed over Arthur's shoulder. "There's no one else here."

Arthur straightened his Wondercloak – the only part of his outfit that was somehow completely dry – and ventured into the middle of the hall. "Err … good evening," he said, immediately realizing he actually had no idea what time of day it was in that realm. "Mrs Shelley?"

"As I said, you need to leave," the speaker repeated.

"We can't," Ren replied, dripping onto the carpet as she stomped forwards. "We're from the twenty-first century and we've got to get to Frankenstein's laboratory in the next two hours, or else we're going to turn into slime."

There was silence for a moment.

"I see." The speaker sighed impatiently. "In that case, will you do me the kindness of not staring?"

A hulking, seven-foot figure plodded out from the shadows. As it came into the light, Arthur's legs turned to jelly.

Mary Shelley was a monster. Specifically, she was a version of the creature from her novel, with yellowish skin and milky eyes. She had a lumpy, balding scalp, a black slash of a mouth and criss-cross scars over her cheeks where she'd been stitched together. Her outfit, in contrast, was stunning. She wore an off-the-shoulder crimson velvet dress with large puffy sleeves and a full skirt. Dainty white lace gloves covered her large hands and a jewelled necklace with a huge ruby hung around her neck.

Cecily whacked Arthur on the arm. "You're staring."

He shook his head. "Err, Mrs Shelley, my name's Arthur and this is Ren and Cecily," he spluttered. "We need your help."

25

Mary Shelley curled her mouth into a smile which was both friendly and terrifying. "You're soaking wet," she observed. "Follow me."

She guided them into a much smaller room with a crackling fireplace flanked by more stone gargoyles and pulled up some armchairs. Feeling guilty about his reaction to her appearance, Arthur decided to sit right next to Mary Shelley. Despite her grotesque features, she had intense hazel eyes and patches of fine red-gold hair. He could imagine her as a human woman; elegant and beautiful. Given how Tiburon admired Mary Shelley's writing, Arthur wondered why he'd chosen to create her mimic in such a cruel way. Maybe Tiburon feared her more than the other heroes and wanted to exert his control...

Beside Mary's extra-large chair, a china teapot, jug of milk and stack of cups sat on a trolley. "Drink this," she said. "It'll warm you up."

"Err ... we don't really have time." Arthur didn't want

to seem impolite, but they were in a rush. "We know what Tiburon Nox did to the heroes in the Wonderscape," he said gingerly. "But we weren't aware they'd put you into *this* mimic."

Mary Shelley sipped some tea. Arthur could see the stitches in her shoulder stretching. "Women have lived through worse," she said defiantly. "I'm not expected to wear a corset here, which is something at least." She returned her teacup to its saucer and surveyed their faces. "I would be eager to learn what the twenty-first century is like. I only have books to tell me."

Arthur scanned the room. It was a palace of learning. The walls were lined with bookshelves and in the light of a candelabra, someone – Mary Shelley, he assumed – had been writing at a desk.

Ren cleared her throat. "Mrs Shelley, not wishing to be rude, but if Tiburon Nox realizes we're here, we won't ever get home. It's important that we hurry."

"Nox." Mary Shelley squeezed the armrests so hard Arthur heard the wood crack. "That man is a villain."

"The reason we need to get to Frankenstein's laboratory is because we're meeting Milo Hertz there," Arthur explained, racing through an account of the situation they found themselves in. "He wants to stop Tiburon and free you and all of the other heroes."

"Then you're right, there's no time for tea," she decided, standing from her chair. Her heavy dress shuffled over the floor as she headed for the door. "Come, let's discuss plans with your friend, Mr Hertz. Oh, and please excuse the ghosts. They have the *worst* manners."

They followed Mary Shelley down several flights of twisting stairs. "I don't get it," Arthur said as they descended. "There are no ghosts in the movie version of *Frankenstein*. Do they only appear in the book?"

"Absolutely not," Mary Shelley said. "The ghosts were added to this building after wanderers complained that this realm was too frightening. Their programming malfunctioned several years back and now they operate outside of Tiburon's control."

Arthur exchanged confused expressions with Ren and Cecily, unable to understand how ghosts would make anything *less* scary. Were they cute and cuddly?

"After the ghosts went rogue, they developed an obsession with stealing things from wanderers – trinkets, gemstones – anything shiny." Mary Shelley touched the ruby hanging around her neck. "They've had their eyes on this for years."

At the bottom of the steps, she opened a heavy wooden door labelled *Anatomy Theatre* and a long groan echoed in the space beyond. Lifting her skirt above her lumpy yellow ankles, she clomped over the threshold, leaving everyone else to follow.

The anatomy theatre really did look like a theatre. It was a large, circular hall with steep, tiered seating built around the edge. Rain drummed against a round glass roof which peered up at the stormy sky. Frankenstein's laboratory was arranged in the centre, although it appeared more like a luxury hamster gym than a place to carry out scientific experiments. There were transparent tubes running everywhere, in all directions. One came down from the roof, spiralled around a long coffin-shaped box, and then connected to some metal apparatus standing on the floor. Another tube ran along the edge of a table topped with flasks of different coloured liquids. Arthur's heart soared when he spotted doggy-Cloud curled up in a soggy lump under a chair.

Kneeling at the foot of a Wonderway frame, Milo lifted his head and smiled as they entered. "You made it!"

His face immediately dropped when he saw Mary Shelley.

"Sorry to give you a shock," she said. "You were expecting these three, I believe." She signalled to Arthur, Ren and Cecily as they hurried out from behind her.

Milo rushed to greet them. "Are you OK?"

"We're fine," Arthur whispered. "But Mary Shelley..."

His voice was grave. "I can see."

The seating creaked as Mary Shelley lumbered down after them. Milo took her fingers in his hand and tipped his head, like a Victorian gentleman. "Mrs Shelley, it's a pleasure to meet you. I'm so unimaginably sorry."

Mary Shelley regarded him curiously. "From what I understand, you've been through quite an ordeal yourself," she said frankly. "Tell me, how are you planning to stop your brother?"

As Milo started to explain, Arthur was distracted by a rattling noise coming from under a table. Crouching down to investigate, he discovered a trembling cupboard door and tugged on the handle experimentally.

"No, wait!" Milo cried.

But it was too late.

A flurry of pineapple-sized ghosts erupted out of the cupboard like confetti from a party cannon. They were dressed in clownish onesies with pom-pom buttons, and apart from their size and transparent green skin, they looked fairly human. Hanging from their earlobes, necks and wrists was an assortment of glittering jewellery, as if they'd raided Tutankhamun's tomb. One blew a raspberry in Arthur's face before flying up to the glass ceiling to laugh and dance with the others.

"Well done, numbskull!" one of them called down. "You found us!"

"What a dodo-head!" another squealed.

Arthur groaned as he wiped ghost spittle off his cheeks. The ghosts weren't just holographic projections; if their spittle was real, then they must be too. He wondered if they were perhaps another type of mimic. "I see what you mean about their manners." *And about them making this place less frightening.* It was difficult to be terrified by anyone throwing Victorian playground insults.

"I'd convinced them to play hide-and-seek," Milo explained with a sigh. "It's the only way to keep them contained. They're built using nano-particles, so they can normally pass through whichever walls they like." He shook his head and tapped a few numbers on the keypad at the bottom of the Wonderway. Arthur recognized the time and date – it was the same morning, three days ago, that he, Ren and Cecily had left the twenty-first century and arrived on the *Principia*. "As I was saying, once you three have been sent home, I'll share M-73's recordings with every news association in the Known Universe. With Tiburon's true actions revealed, he'll be forced to answer for his crimes." He glanced at the time-key on Cloud's collar. "Then I'll liberate the heroes and destroy all three time-keys once and for all."

He turned to the coffin-shaped box wrapped in hamster tubes. Arthur noticed a tiny stream of silver particles flowing through them. As Milo lifted his hand over the centre of the box, a holographic dial appeared beneath it. He moved his fingers a quarter-turn anti-clockwise and then a half-turn clockwise. The dial spun and tiny red lasers scanned his fingertips. Then, with a hiss, a small window opened in the top. "Right where I left it," he muttered cheerily, reaching in and pulling out an ornate metallic casket, the size of an egg box.

Arthur's skin tingled with anticipation as he shared a weary smile with Ren and Cecily. After everything they'd been through, their journey was almost at an end. In a few minutes, the Wonderway would open and they'd step back into Number Twenty-Seven. He got butterflies at the thought of seeing his dad again, although that wouldn't be till later. First he'd have to leave Peacepoint, get to school and try to explain to his form tutor why he was late. He couldn't believe how desperate he was to have everything back, even the ordinary things that he usually moaned about.

Sliding aside a beaker of yellow liquid, Milo set the casket on the table and lifted open the hinged lid. His face drained of colour. "But ... that's impossible!"

Arthur craned his neck to see over the top, and felt his stomach crunch.

The casket was empty.

"What's happened?" he said, going cold. "Where's the time-key?"

Milo frantically felt around inside the casket, but it was no use. "I don't know. I'm the only person with access to this box and no one – not even Cloud – knew it was here."

Arthur gritted his teeth. Milo obviously wasn't as clever as he thought he was, hiding the time-key there. A strange expression passed over Mary Shelley's monster features, but with all the lumps, scars and stitches Arthur found it difficult to read. He wondered if she knew something more.

"What do we do *now*?" Ren asked. "We can't have much time left."

As Arthur went to check his watch, a rattle echoed around the theatre and the floor rumbled. Suddenly, a torrent of armed T-class mimics blasted through the upper door and came thundering towards them, their long black robes billowing like storm clouds. Arthur's heart crawled into his throat as, one by one, more units appeared until they must have numbered over a hundred. Their long faces and ice-blue glares fixed on him and the others as they swiftly circled the room.

At the very end of the line strode Tiburon Nox himself; his chin held high, his oily black Wondercloak sweeping the floor by his ankles. "Congratulations, brother," he spat as he descended the steps. "You've surprised me. I didn't think you'd ever solve my Menlo puzzle. You really shouldn't have ridden a dragon here, though. Even with the storm, you were easy to spot."

Arthur felt a crawling sensation across the back of his neck as the ring of T-class mimics drew closer, smoke rising from their blades. He spotted Ren and Cecily edging in front of the chair covering Cloud, but Mary Shelley was nowhere to be seen...

Milo snatched a beaker of bubbling pink jelly off the closest table and lurched forwards. "I won't let you hurt anyone else, Tiburon. Hand over the time-key."

Two T-class units zoomed towards him and restrained his arms behind his back. Despite his considerable size, after a moment's struggle, Milo's jaw stiffened and he went still.

"Leave him alone!" Ren roared, reaching for her bow. Before she'd notched her final arrow, another T-class sped over, wrenched the weapon out of her hands and restrained her.

Arthur saw red and charged. Cecily rushed forwards too. Arthur had only made it a few paces when cold fingers dug into his shoulder and his arm was yanked back. "Argh!" he yelled, pain shooting down his spine. He kicked his foot backwards as hard as he could, but it only passed harmlessly through a hover-wheel. Too late. The strong arms of a T-class unit wrapped around his body.

Cecily was easily overpowered by another T-class, who lifted her off the ground while she screamed. As the three of them squirmed, their shadow patches were ripped from their wrists and their Wondercloaks removed.

With a gleeful smile, Tiburon lifted a dark time-key out from under his collar. It was fixed to a chain around his neck. It looked just like the time-key on Cloud's collar and Arthur guessed it must be the other prototype that Tiburon had stolen from Milo years ago. But if Tiburon didn't have the time-key that Milo had hidden in the lab, then who did?

"The trouble with you and your friends, Milo, is that you lack vision," Tiburon said. "You would rather destroy this than use it. And then where would Hxperion be?" He shook his head and skulked towards the Wonderway. "I really wish there was another way, but you give me no choice. I can't let you interfere again." Crouching, he tampered with the keypad at the bottom.

"What are you doing?" Milo barked, struggling against the T-class.

Tiburon locked eyes with his brother. "I expect you've never tried inputting a *fractional* realm number into a Wonderway, have you? The thing is, it's impossible to transport an object to two different places simultaneously. Not in *one piece*, anyway."

"Tiburon, no!" Milo squirmed as the two T-classes hauled him towards the Wonderway.

"It was uncharacteristically short-sighted of me to dump you in a closed realm," Tiburon added, fetching a realm-key from his pocket. "This is a much tidier long-term solution."

Arthur's pulse hammered in his ears. *Not in one piece?* That meant ... Tiburon was going to kill Milo! Arthur knew he had to do something; he just wasn't sure what. Never mind that without Milo, they had no chance of getting home. He had to save him.

Across the floor, the T-classes squeezed Ren and Cecily tighter as they struggled. Ren's teeth were gritted and Cecily's eyes shone with pain. Cloud, Arthur noticed, had retreated into the shadows under a table, trembling with fear. Arthur balled his fists and tried to remain calm. He couldn't come up with an escape plan if he wasn't thinking clearly...

Just then, the click of heels sounded in the stairwell outside and everyone, including Tiburon, looked towards the door. Arthur had a horrible sense of déjà vu as a mob of stylish security V-class units strutted through the door-way like models on a runway, followed at the rear by their fashion designer, Valeria Mal'fey. The mimics were dressed head to hover-wheel in green camouflage and equipped with the same make-up-themed weapons Arthur had seen them wielding at Tomoe Gozen's house. "It's true, then," Valeria sneered, glaring at Milo. Her mirrored Wondercloak looked like armour as she marched into the centre of the theatre. "I always suspected you'd come sniffing back when business took an upward turn."

"Valeria!" Tiburon's expression faltered. "How did you—?"

"I have my spies too, brother," she said smugly. She signalled to Arthur, Ren and Cecily. "I've been following these brats for two days. They're working for Milo."

It dawned on Arthur that Tiburon had not anticipated his sister's arrival. He wondered if there was a way to use that to their advantage.

"Valeria, help me," Milo wheezed, struggling to fill his lungs under the T-class's bear-hug grip.

She folded her arms. "Why should I? I understand exactly why Tiburon's angry with you – you abandoned us when the company was in trouble." She thrust a glittery nail at her older brother. "If it hadn't been for his new line of mimics and my PR genius, Hxperion wouldn't exist now." She turned her nose up at Milo's filthy fairground outfit. "Where have you been, anyway? You look awful."

Arthur realized Valeria had no clue Tiburon had been responsible for Milo going missing. He suspected that she didn't know that Tiburon had been using one of Milo's time-keys either, or she would have mentioned it. He saw Tiburon's lips draw into a snarl as he whispered something to a nearby T-class. Realizing he might not get another opportunity, Arthur took a chance and yelled, "Tiburon trapped Milo in a closed realm! He's been lying to you!"

"Silence!" Tiburon boomed, making the smoke on the T-classes' weapons flicker.

Before Arthur could utter another word, cold fingers covered his mouth. "Mmm!" he mumbled.

"Tiburon stole Milo's techno—" Cecily managed, before she too was gagged. Ren hadn't yet taken a breath when the T-class holding her clamped a hand over her face.

But it didn't matter. Arthur could tell by Valeria's expression that they'd said enough to plant a seed of doubt in her mind.

Valeria's gaze slid across to her older brother. "Tiburon, what are they talking about? Do you know where Milo's been?"

"Stay out of this," Tiburon said curtly, signalling to the two T-class units holding Milo. "I did what was necessary. I don't have to explain myself to you."

As the T-classes dragged Milo towards the Wonderway, Arthur made as much noise as he could, wriggling and kicking with all his strength.

Valeria's green suede gloves curled into fists. "You mean ... this is *true*? All this time you've been lying to me?"

"I have everything under control," Tiburon growled. "Trust me."

"*Trust* you?" Valeria's cheeks flushed. "You're the most devious person I know – I wouldn't trust you if my life depended on it." She signalled to her V-class units, who all reached for the hair-clip throwing stars on their weapons belts.

Tiburon's jaw tightened. He motioned to his T-class army. "Valeria, I'm warning you..."

One by one, the T-class units raised their smoking swords. Peeking above the fingers of the T-class holding him, Arthur stared at Ren and Cecily. This might be their only chance to get away.

"You're wrong, Tiburon," Valeria said, lifting her chin. "You *do* have to explain yourself to me." And with that, all hell broke loose.

The mob of V-class mimics surged towards the T-classes, launching their glittery throwing stars. Some stars were deflected by the T-classes' blades; others made target, striking the Tiburon-lookalikes with such force they were thrown backwards. The T-classes slashed precisely, their smoking swords melting their opponents' skin with a loud sizzle wherever they struck. The crack of splintering wood echoed around the room as mimics on both sides crashed into the theatre benches.

Two V-classes unpinned a couple of perfume grenades and rolled them onto the floor, where they burst into smoke. The theatre filled with fog, reminding Arthur spookily of his time in the maze. In all the commotion, he thrashed wildly, trying to break free.

Out of the mist a V-class came looming towards him, a barbed blow-dry brush in her slim hand. Arthur's captor stiffened and tried to lift his sword but, still holding Arthur, he wasn't able to. The V-class grinned and swung. Arthur sank his head into his neck and squeezed his eyes closed, anticipating the blow...

Instead, he felt his stomach shoot into his mouth as he slipped out from under the T-class's arms, and landed with a jolt on the floor. Opening his eyes, he saw the T-class who had been restraining him zip past at his shoulder and spring into combat.

His heart rattling, Arthur scrambled under a nearby table and leaped to his feet on the other side. "Ren! Cecily!" Shadows whipped through the smoke, but he couldn't tell if any of them were his friends.

Then he heard a breathless voice. "Arthur! Down here!" Ren.

Down here? Arthur wondered what she meant. He scanned the floor and noticed wet paw prints leading towards the rear of the room. Shaking with nerves, he hurried through the mist after them.

He clambered over the remains of a couple of defunct

V-class mimics and dodged the reach of a lame T-class who crawled out of the smoke, dragging his defunct hover-wheels behind him. The shattering snap of furniture, clash of weapons and angry shouts of mimics resounded all around.

The paw prints stopped at the edge of a circular hole. A rusty iron manhole cover sat on the concrete next to it. Arthur peered over the edge and saw Ren, Cecily and Cloud standing in a puddle of dark water, a few metres below. The rungs of a ladder glinted in the dim light.

Cloud wagged his tail and barked.

"Hurry!" Cecily called up.

Fast as he could, Arthur swung his legs into the opening and found the ladder with his foot. As he lowered himself down, he saw a figure creep out of the gloom in the anatomy theatre ahead.

Tiburon Nox's long face was sweaty and streaked with blood, his upper lip curled into a snarl. "You and your friends have caused me a lot of trouble," he said menacingly. "I don't want you using the time-key around that dog's neck to cause any more. Now you *will* give it to me."

26

The splash of Cecily's footsteps echoed as she ran. "Eurgh!" She tugged her T-shirt over her nose. "The air is one hundred per cent fart down here."

Arthur coughed, trying to remove the foul stench from the back of his throat. They were hurrying along a wide, brick-built tunnel with openings on either side. Shafts of moonlight filtered through grates in the curved ceiling, illuminating the flooded floor below. "This must be a sewer under the city," he said, recognizing the outline of a building overhead.

A clatter echoed behind and the rumble of a hundred hover-wheels filled the tunnel, sending ripples through the murky water at their feet.

"FIND THEM!" Tiburon Nox shouted.

"This way!" Cecily called, darting into a connecting passageway.

They sprinted – and, in some tunnels, waded – until their thighs burned and their shoes were soaked through. No matter how fast they went, the roar of Tiburon and his

T-classes never sounded far off. Eventually, they came to a dry circular chamber with six tunnels leading off in different directions. "Which way now?" Cecily queried.

Cloud plodded around the edge of the room, sniffing the air in each passageway.

"I don't think it matters," Arthur said, panting. Their pursuers were close; he could hear it. "Tiburon designed this realm, so he probably knows the sewers inside out. We can't outrun him."

"We can't outfight him either," Ren said, feeling across her shoulder for where her bow and quiver used to rest. "We've lost all our Wonderskills."

Now he had a moment to think about it, Arthur felt cold and empty. When he reached to the corners of his mind, Newton's fountain of knowledge wasn't there any more. He hadn't realized how much he'd liked having it. He drew back the sleeve of his raincoat and almost stumbled over. "We've only got twenty-seven minutes left!"

Ren's legs shuddered and Cecily covered her mouth like she might be sick.

There was no point asking what they were going to do next, because Arthur already knew the answer: there was nothing they *could* do. Cloud's prototype time-key was broken (not that Tiburon knew that); Milo's finished time-key was missing and the only other one they could possibly use to get home was hanging around the neck of a maniac with a robot army.

"Does that mean—?" Ren's eyebrows knotted together as she struggled to say what they were all thinking.

"We've run out of time," Cecily said gravely. With her shoulders against the wall, she slid to the floor and rested her head back on the bricks. Tears shone in her eyes. "This is it. We've come to the end."

Cloud whimpered and butted his head against her knees, so she pulled him into her lap. Ren slumped beside them both.

Arthur swallowed down an ice cube of dread. "I don't know what to say," he admitted, joining them on the floor. He brought his knees up to his chest and hugged them tightly. After everything they'd overcome, they were going to die anyway. It seemed so unfair. Tiburon had won. He would keep stealing heroes from history and forcing them to work for him. He would continue to have the power to mess with time, however he liked.

They sat in silence for a short while. Arthur's thoughts drifted to his dad, which made the back of his throat swell and his bottom lip wobble. He imagined the patchy lawn in his back garden; the shed with the window he'd broken playing football last summer; the blanket his mum had embroidered that lay on the couch in the front room. More than anything, he wished he could be there now and not in a dank sewer, four hundred years away.

"I can't turn into slime," Ren said, scowling. "I haven't *done* anything in my life. Nothing important, at least."

Arthur reflected on the things he'd achieved in his thirteen years on Earth. At the beginning he'd learned how to walk and talk – that was pretty momentous – but since then he'd just been … growing up.

He wanted to do so much more. He *could* do so much more. He considered the list of heroes' names he'd seen in Milo's headquarters. Each one of them had been his age once, and look what they'd gone on to accomplish. Arthur had the potential to be an inventor, a scientist, a campaigner, an explorer – the possibilities were endless.

Except, now he wouldn't get the chance to find out.

As he dropped his chin into his knees, he spied lights flickering in one of the tunnels opposite, and stiffened. "Can you two see that?"

He pushed himself up just as Ren got to her feet beside him. "Tiburon must have found us," she said bleakly.

"Well, I'm not going down without a fight," Cecily decided, wiping her nose as she stood. "If we're going to turn into snot, I hope we splatter all over those T-class units and mess up their circuits." Shaking his coat dry, Cloud barked in agreement.

One last act of defiance, Arthur thought. Wangari Maathai would approve.

Nerves fizzed in his stomach as they crept towards the tunnel entrance. Several shadowy figures were drawing closer...

Arthur swung round his rucksack, planning to thump the first T-class with his maths textbook. After searching through her pockets, Ren brought out her key ring multi-tool and flicked open the corkscrew attachment. Cecily crouched to adjust Cloud's collar. "Dragon or tiger?" she whispered.

Squinting, Arthur tried to estimate how many mimics they were facing. Then he spotted something. "Wait a moment," he said, resting a hand on Cecily's shoulder. "Maybe I'm seeing things, but I think one of those T-class units is wearing…"

Ren's eyes widened. "Unicorn slippers!"

Arthur felt like he'd just been lifted into the air as Professor Isaac Newton came hurrying out of the tunnel, dressed in his captain's finery, with his glittery unicorn slippers – now soaking wet – hanging off his feet. "I abandoned ship as soon as I could; there wasn't time to change," he explained, moving aside as Wangari Maathai barrelled out behind him.

"Arthur! Ren! Cecily!" She hugged each of them in turn, getting her blouse damp and muddy in the process.

Next to emerge was Amaros Ba, holding a long curved blade in his hand. He lifted it to the sky and announced something in a language Arthur presumed was Tyrian, but without his Wondercloak to translate, he didn't understand. "English?" he pleaded, feeling like an embarrassed tourist.

Amaros made the switch quickly. "I told you before: a true adventurer never knows what is around the next corner!"

"Unless he has a map," Thomas Edison corrected, appearing over Amaros's shoulder. His downy white hair was ruffled and his bow tie set off-kilter. "There were problems with my communications device," he recounted. "I had to recalibrate it twice, but the message got through eventually. I told everyone to get to Realm Eighteen as fast as they could."

Silent as a shadow, one last figure strode out behind them all. Dressed in battered but colourful armour, with several new scratches across her face, Tomoe Gozen smiled.

Arthur's heart soared. "You're OK!"

Cecily bolted forwards and threw her arms around the legendary warrior, who muttered something in Japanese.

"She said: it's good to see you too," Ren told Arthur.

Newton fetched his gold pocket watch from his waistcoat. "I hate to be a – what's the expression? – *party pooper*, but we have twenty minutes before these three turn into protoplasm."

Seeing Tomoe Gozen and the other heroes had made Arthur want to crumble with relief, but the urgency in Newton's voice quickly focused his mind. "It's no use," he said, shaking his head. "The only time-key left is the one Tiburon Nox is wearing around his neck."

"He's somewhere in the sewers," Cecily added seriously.

"But he has a group of T-class mimics with him."

Wangari Maathai put her hands on her hips. "So, what, you're just going to *give up*?" She shook her head. "No, no, no. There are opportunities even in the most difficult moments. You only need to seize them."

Hearing her words, Arthur felt a seed of hope sprout inside him. "Well, Tiburon's that way," he offered, pointing in the direction they'd come.

"Then we shall plan on the move!" Amaros declared, taking the lead.

As they set off, Arthur decided that running through a stinking sewer towards certain doom was infinitely better when you had five of humanity's greatest heroes running alongside you.

"With the right materials, I'm sure I could invent something to help," Edison muttered, arguing the merits of various solutions with Isaac Newton. Tomoe Gozen raced along at Amaros Ba's side, discussing battle tactics. Arthur didn't know what they were saying, but it sounded intense.

Ahead, Wangari Maathai raised her fist, signalling for them all to stop. She crept to the edge of an archway and peered through into an adjoining chamber. As the splash of her footsteps subsided, Arthur heard noises reverberating inside. "It's Tiburon," she whispered. "And he's not alone."

Quietly as they could, Arthur and the others flattened themselves against the adjacent wall. Tomoe notched an arrow. Amaros Ba drew his sword. Newton flapped open one side of his navy brocade coat to reveal an assortment of small brown bottles with chemical labels. "I grabbed as many as I could before I left," he whispered conspiratorially. "If I mix them correctly, I've got smoke bombs *and* stink bombs."

Edison patted him on the shoulder. "Well *done*, sir."

Cecily gathered Cloud into her arms and began to fiddle with his collar. Ren brought out her key ring multi-tool. "Ready."

With a rolled-up maths textbook in his hand, Arthur swallowed and peeked round the corner.

Wangari Maathai had said Tiburon wasn't alone, but she'd failed to mention how many mimics were with him. Arthur's stomach dropped as he counted the long-faced T-class units holding smoking swords. *Ten, twenty, thirty, forty...* They were hovering in perfect formation throughout the chamber and connecting passageways, as if the whole place had been covered in mirrors and was reflecting their image everywhere.

Tiburon Nox stood in the middle of the crowd, looking smug. As he moved under a grate, the time-key hanging around his neck glinted. "I know you're in here, Pipsqueaks!" he called. There was an amused tone to his voice. He had the upper hand and he knew it. "I only want the time-key that the dog is wearing. Hand it over and you can go free."

Arthur's jaw stiffened. He couldn't let Tiburon win, but

the odds were impossible – even *with* the heroes fighting at their side. He wished there was another option.

As he turned back against the wall he caught sight of Ren's key ring multi-tool and remembered something Milo had told them. "Does the laser pointer on that work?" he hissed.

Ren pressed a small button at one end and a green dot of light projected onto the floor. Arthur tensed. He had an idea, but he wasn't sure he could go through with it. "I think there's a way we can use it," he whispered nervously. "Milo said that Tiburon's time-key is a prototype that reacts to infrared radiation – and that's what the laser emits. If you shine it at the time-key it should trigger a blast of energy like we felt at Number Twenty-Seven."

Newton shuffled closer. "That makes sense. I was working on an experiment involving infrared radiation aboard the *Principia* – Cloud's time-key must have been exposed to it in the captain's cabin." He frowned. "But if you damage Tiburon's time-key, you won't be able to use it to get home."

Arthur offered Ren and Cecily an apologetic glance. Part of him wanted to forget the idea entirely, but another part of him knew it was the right thing to do. He thought of all the struggles and sacrifices the heroes had undertaken during their lifetimes in order to achieve everything they had. One of the things he'd learned from their stories was that the right thing was always worth doing, no matter how hard it might be. "What Newton says is true," he told Ren and

Cecily, feeling a renewed sense of purpose. "But if Tiburon keeps that time-key, think of all the damage he could do – not just to people in the twenty-fifth century, but in our time too. No one should have the power to meddle with history." He swallowed and added bleakly, "Also, the chances of us beating all those mimics in the time we have left are zero."

Cecily and Ren risked a peep around the corner and quickly returned with their cheeks flushed. "So if we do this," Cecily whispered slowly, "Tiburon won't be able to threaten the heroes any more. They would be free to live out their second lives however they wanted."

"And we'd have done something with *our* lives before we turn into protoplasm," Ren pointed out. "Something that counts."

Arthur nodded and, without thinking, held his hand out between them all. Cecily placed hers on top and Ren smiled as she did the same. "All right," she said firmly. "Let's do this."

Her fingers tightened around her multi-tool and before any of the heroes could stop her, she stepped into the open, activated the laser and aimed it at Tiburon.

27

The rotten stench of sewage filled Arthur's nostrils as he came to, blinking in the dim light. Everything hurt. Pain throbbed in his chest; his ears were ringing and he could taste blood at the back of his tongue. A thick layer of brick-red dust coated his skin and clothes, making him feel like a chicken drumstick dipped in paprika.

Slowly, he pushed himself to his knees. "Cecily, are you all right?" he asked, jogging her shoulder. She and Cloud were soaking wet.

"Erg," she groaned, rubbing her jaw. "What happened?"

A metre away, Ren was propped against the dripping wet sewer wall, her face streaked with blood. "Arthur's idea worked," she croaked.

Remembering they were about to turn into slime, he checked his watch. They had twelve minutes to go.

Behind him, the heroes stirred. Newton coughed loudly as he rose to his feet; Edison was already up, brushing his suit clean. Although their clothes were damp and filthy, they both seemed unharmed. Arthur supposed their mimic bodies had withstood the blast better than his human one.

"Shhh," Wangari hissed, as she was helped to her feet by Tomoe Gozen. "Can you hear that?"

Amaros straightened his mud-splattered turban and collected his sword from a puddle. "What is it?"

"Nothing," Wangari replied. "Silence."

As the group staggered into the main chamber, Arthur drew his breath. Tiburon Nox was sprawled in a pool of steaming water, the time-key resting on his chest, still attached to the chain around his neck. His army of T-class mimics were frozen in strange positions around the floor, as if they'd been playing musical statues during a yoga class. Arthur noticed the translucent haze which usually circled their hover-wheels had evaporated.

"The blast must have disabled their engines," Edison concluded.

Scanning the scene, Newton rubbed his chin. "What do you say to the theory that the walls reflected a certain amount of force back inside this chamber?" he asked Edison. "Surface evidence would suggest it was felt much more intensely in here than where we were."

Edison nodded and glanced at Arthur. "Ingenious, my boy. Truly."

Arthur smiled gingerly, accepting the compliment even though he had no idea what the two were talking about.

Wangari leaned over Tiburon's body and, with two fingers against his neck, took his pulse. "He's alive," she said. "Just knocked out." She carefully unhooked the time-key from the chain around his neck.

Amaros Ba strode out among the mimics, nudging them with his sword to check none were still functioning. Arthur felt a hand on his shoulder and turned to find Tomoe Gozen had gathered him, Ren and Cecily together. Light flashed in her dark eyes as she uttered something in Japanese.

"What did she say?" Cecily whispered out of the corner of her mouth.

Ren was blushing. "She said: *Thank you. You're my heroes.*"

Cloud gave a triumphant bark that echoed off the sewer walls, like he might be saying: *I've known they were heroes all along!*

Arthur felt a lump in his throat. Everything was so overwhelming he didn't know how to respond. His plan to stop Tiburon had been successful, but now their fates were sealed: they were going to die there.

"Come," Wangari Maathai said solemnly. "You three have saved our lives in the past and the present; I won't allow you to spend the last few moments of yours in this dingy sewer."

As they plodded towards the entrance of the sewer, Arthur felt numb. He wondered what it was going to be like, turning to protoplasm. Would it be painful? Would he even know it was happening, or would everything just switch off like a light in his head?

Back in the anatomy theatre, everything was wet and dusted with shards of glass. The roof had shattered. Rain dripped through the empty ceiling onto the laboratory floor, which was covered in black scorch marks, as if the ghosts had played rodeo with a set of Bunsen burners. Valeria and her V-classes were nowhere to be seen, but Milo Hertz was sitting on the edge of an empty bench.

When he saw them, his eyes widened. "You're alive!" He jumped up and ran towards them. From the number of burns on his arms and face, Arthur guessed he'd been fighting T-classes while they were in the sewers.

"What happened? Where's Tiburon?" Milo scanned their faces, searching for injuries.

"We've only got a few minutes," Ren mumbled miserably.

"Right," Milo said excitedly. "Of course." He rushed to the closed Wonderway and began tapping numbers into the keypad at the bottom.

Arthur wondered what had got into him, until he saw Mary Shelley stomping across the room towards them. Her sickly yellow skin was flushed red and the huge ruby necklace around her neck was missing. Arthur remembered she'd abandoned them just as Tiburon had arrived, but he didn't have the energy to be annoyed.

"It was the ghosts," Mary Shelley said breathlessly, reaching into a pocket on her dress. "They had it all along.

I only realized when Milo mentioned that no one else could have possibly gained access – but you see, the ghosts can pass through walls."

Arthur blinked as she pulled out an obsidian time-key and passed it to Milo. Confused, Arthur glanced at Cloud, who still had his time-key dangling from his collar. The other prototype Arthur had just seen Wangari Maathai remove from Tiburon Nox's neck, which could only mean one thing...

"Is that the third time-key?" he exclaimed. His tongue went leaden. "How did—?"

Mary Shelley gestured to her empty décolletage, and Arthur realized what had happened: she'd given the ghosts her necklace in exchange.

28

"Using data from Cloud, I've programmed this to send you back to the exact moment you left," Milo said hurriedly, standing beside the Wonderway. "You've only got a few minutes to say your goodbyes."

Arthur stared into the churning vortex of sapphire smoke, moments away from going home. A dizzying mix of emotions swept over him – relief that their quest was over, but also uncertainty over what would happen next. Only minutes ago, he'd been preparing to die...

The portal hummed with energy, making the hairs on his arms stand on end. It felt just like the first Wonderway they'd walked through at Number Twenty-Seven. He couldn't believe that had only been three days ago. It felt like so much longer.

Wangari Maathai gathered Arthur, Ren and Cecily together in a four-way hug. She smelled like her forest, of damp earth and honeysuckle. "Promise me you'll take care of each other."

"Promib," Arthur agreed in a muffled voice.

Edison and Newton shook Arthur, Ren and Cecily's hands, and wished them luck. Tomoe bowed and repeated something in Japanese. "My friend wishes she had more time with you," Amaros Ba translated, with an easy smile. "As do I. We could have some great adventures together."

"Here," Milo said, scooping doggy-Cloud off the floor and handing him to Cecily. Arthur cringed when he saw Cloud's matted wet fur and sandy paws. The little guy needed a serious bath.

Cloud wagged his tail as Cecily held him close and rubbed her nose into the fur on his head. "I'll miss you, Cloud."

"Me too, Fuzzball," Ren said, patting him on the head. Her upper lip went stiff, like she was trying hard not to cry. Arthur felt the corners of his mouth tugging down. He'd grown fond of Cloud too.

"Actually, you're not saying goodbye." Milo reached over and rubbed Cloud under the chin. "I am."

Cecily's face brightened. "Cloud's coming with us?"

Milo nodded. "Everything that has happened to the three of you cannot be repeated to another soul. There may be times in your life when it is difficult to keep that secret, when it is hard to live in the present, knowing what you do about the future. But Cloud will help you. He will be there for you, always."

Cloud gave a firm bark as if to say, *That's right!*

Amaros Ba winked at them. "Also, we'll have a canine sleeper agent in the past. You know – just in case the future needs saving again."

"What will happen to you and the other heroes in the Wonderscape?" Arthur asked.

"They'll be given a choice," Milo said solemnly. "They can remain here as mimics in the twenty-fifth century, free to explore the Known Universe, or I'll go back in time and undo what Tiburon did to create them, so they'll never know they were ever here."

Arthur wondered what everyone would choose. He hoped the heroes they'd met would decide to stick around in 2473. The universe always needed people like them.

"And your brother and sister?" Ren asked. "Where will they go?"

"I'll use evidence stored on M-73's neuro-processor to explain to the authorities what they did," Milo said. "Tiburon will have to answer for his crimes. As for Valeria, I don't know. Perhaps the authorities will question her too – if they can find her."

Arthur assessed the remains of Frankenstein's laboratory. Mist rose from the surfaces of several chemical spillages; there was smashed glass and broken apparatus everywhere, and the hamster tubes had all been destroyed during the fighting. In some bizarre way, he was going to miss this marvellous mess. Yes, the Wonderscape had almost killed him; but it had also given him experiences he'd remember for the rest of his life, as well as two extra-ordinary friends – all of which he was grateful for.

Milo took a deep breath. "It's time."

Blue mist clouded Arthur's vision as he stepped through the Wonderway and emerged on the upstairs landing of Number Twenty-Seven. As his brain freeze faded, he surveyed the garish 1970s decor and felt a swell of emotion. He might have only seen the place once before, but it was still Peacepoint Estate in the twenty-first century. It was *home*.

Ren beamed. "We're here. We're really here!"

Cloud trotted through the Wonderway next, followed by Cecily. As she pressed the toe of her shoe into the shaggy avocado-green carpet, tears streamed down her cheeks. "I never thought I'd be so happy to see this again," she said giddily.

Arthur laughed and steadied himself against the railings. The mix of joy and relief coursing through his body was delirious. He glimpsed the pale-yellow morning sky through a broken window and remembered it had looked that colour just before the gnome-explosion. It was as if no time had passed at all.

"Come on," Cecily said, wiping her face on the sleeve of her leather jacket. "We've still got to get to school. We can't have anyone asking questions."

Arthur wanted to see his dad more than anything, but he knew Cecily was right. They had to act as if their trip to the future hadn't happened; at least around other people.

When school was over he'd run home and give his dad the biggest hug ever. Until then, he had to be patient.

"Like *this*?" Ren spread her arms, presenting her damp second-hand outfit. "I haven't showered in three days, and I've been using the end of my finger to brush my teeth. People are going to notice. And what about our uniforms?"

Arthur sniffed his armpits and recoiled. "Ren's right; if we turn up like this we'll raise suspicions. We have to go home to wash and change into fresh clothes. I don't have a spare blazer so I'll have to make up a story about losing my old one."

Hurrying out onto the street, they could hear police sirens. "I would have only called them a few minutes ago," Cecily realized, biting her lip. "We can't still be here when they arrive. I'll have to convince them that I was so shaken up by the explosion I went back to my aunt's."

"All right, but who's taking Cloud?" Ren asked. "My mum's allergic to dogs. I won't be allowed to keep him."

Cecily gathered him up and smiled as he licked her face. "I've already thought about that. I'm going to tell my parents that if they have to go away so often on business, then I *need* him. And that's the end of it."

She said it with such assurance, Arthur didn't doubt it would be.

"We're going to be late," Ren noted as they rushed along the road. "I guess I'll see you two in detention?" She waved as she turned off towards her house.

Arthur and Cecily continued in the same direction. "The one good thing about staying at my aunt's is that I don't now have to go to the other side of town to get a shower," she commented.

Arthur lifted an eyebrow. "The *one* good thing? Aren't you forgetting that Ren and I also live here?" He imagined how things would change now. If he needed help, if he wanted someone to talk to, he could call on Ren and Cecily. They didn't care how much money he had or where he came from; they were *real* friends – they liked him for him.

Hiding a smile, Cecily pretended to shrug. "I suppose I will be able to see you more. Hey, maybe we could watch *Frankenstein* together this weekend?"

Arthur thought of the copy on his dad's bookshelf. "Sure, but I'm gonna read the book first. Actually, I'm gonna read about all the heroes we met."

"Me too," she agreed. "Except Amaros Ba, of course." Before they parted, she looked pensive. "It's strange to think that even though we've travelled to the future, we still have no idea what will happen in our own lives."

"Our futures are full of possibility," Arthur said, feeling light. "They always have been."

Acknowledgements

The heroes depicted in *Wonderscape* are fictitious versions of incredible real people. I consulted a range of books, articles, paintings, podcasts, films, TV programmes and websites when writing them. Readers who are interested in learning more could visit their local library or bookshop and ask for advice from a librarian or bookseller.

Wonderscape has been a challenge to write and I wouldn't have come close to completing it without the generous support of others. I'd like to thank my editors, Denise Johnstone-Burt and Megan Middleton, for giving me advice on how to refine the story; and copy-editors Jenny Glencross and Clare Baalham for helping me polish the text.

My gratitude goes to illustrator Paddy Donnelly, designer Ben Norland and typesetter Anna Robinette for making the inside and outside of the book look amazing. Huge thanks also to Kirsten Cozens, Jo Humphreys-Davies and everyone at Walker Books who has been behind *Wonderscape* every step of the way.

Polly Nolan, thank you for guiding me along the sometimes-prickly path of professional writing. You are the best agent in the world and I am so proud and grateful to be represented by you and your agency, Papercuts.

A very special thank you to Sarah Bryars for offering the best advice and Alice Lickens for her good humour and endless patience. Tara Kemsley, thank you for listening to me, laughing with me and being the greatest brainstorm partner ever. I am beyond grateful to count you among my friends.

Peter, I love you for always believing in my writing. Thanks for the endless encouragement, and for the jokes and hugs. They were important.

Mum, thank you for being my hero and for knowing that even though I'm a grown up, I still need you to hold my hand sometimes.

Finally, I want to say a massive thank you to my sister, Beth, who inspires me every day. You are a wonder.

Londoner **JENNIFER BELL** worked as a children's bookseller at a world-famous bookshop before becoming an author. Her debut novel, *The Uncommoners: The Crooked Sixpence*, was an international bestseller. She is also the author of Agents of the Wild, an adventure series for younger readers. *Wonderscape* is inspired by some of her favourite heroes from history (there were too many to fit in the story) and her love of gaming. Find out more about Jennifer at www.jennifer-bell-author.com or say hello on Twitter at @jenrosebell and Instagram @jenbellauthor.

Enjoyed **WONDERSCAPE**?
We'd love to hear your thoughts.

#Wonderscape

@WalkerBooksUK
@jenrosebell

@WalkerBooksUK
@jenbellauthor